T0082751

DREAM ON

DREAM ON

Persistent Themes in My Dreams

JAY THOMAS WILLIS

DREAM ON
PERSISTENT THEMES IN MY DREAMS

This is a work of fiction. All of the characters, names, incidents, organizations, and dialogue in this novel are either the products of the author's imagination or are used fictitiously.

iUniverse books may be ordered through booksellers or by contacting:

iUniverse
1663 Liberty Drive
Bloomington, IN 47403
www.iuniverse.com
844-349-9409

Because of the dynamic nature of the Internet, any web addresses or links contained in this book may have changed since publication and may no longer be valid. The views expressed in this work are solely those of the author and do not necessarily reflect the views of the publisher, and the publisher hereby disclaims any responsibility for them.

Any people depicted in stock imagery provided by Getty Images are models, and such images are being used for illustrative purposes only. Certain stock imagery © Getty Images.

ISBN: 978-1-6632-0411-0 (sc)
ISBN: 978-1-6632-0412-7 (e)

Library of Congress Control Number: 2020913361

Print information available on the last page.

iUniverse rev. date: 07/27/2020

DEDICATION

To Clara.

CONTENTS

ACKNOWLEDGMENT

Thanks to every anonymous individual who has helped me along the way without my being aware of it.

ALSO BY JAY THOMAS WILLIS

Nonfiction

A Penny for Your Thoughts: Insights, Perceptions, and Reflections on the African American Condition

Implications for Effective Psychotherapy with African Americans

Freeing the African-American's Mind

God or Barbarian: The Myth of a Messiah Who Will Return to Liberate Us

Finding Your Own African-Centered Rhythm

When the Village Idiot Get Started

Nowhere to Run or Hide

Why Blacks Behave as They Do: The Conditioning Process from Generation to Generation

God, or Balance in the Universe

Over the Celestial Wireless

Paranoid but not Stupid

Educated Misunderstanding

Longing for Home and Other Short Stories

Poetry

Reflections on My Life: You're Gonna Carry That Weight a Long Time

It's a Good Day to Die

1

TOO MANY CHOICES

Clara lived in Fieldtown, Texas. Her parents owned a white-brick Georgia Colonial mansion on the outskirts of the city just beyond the city limits. Her father was an attorney, and her mother was a college professor at Bridgestone College, a local college. They were pillars of the community and active in community affairs. Her parents drove a new Cadillac Coupe De Ville and a Mercedes. Clara had everything she wanted, and never had to toil a day in her life. She was known for getting lavish gifts without there being a special occasion. Clara's father drove her to school and picked her up every day. Clara could have gone to a prep school on the East Coast but preferred to attend the local high school. She was promised a car when she was old enough to drive. She had one sister who was in college and drove a red 1964 GTO Pontiac. The sister went to college at Vanderbilt University in Nashville, Tennessee; and did take advantage of a prep school in Boston, Massachusetts.

Clara was five-five and weighed 115 lbs. She was smooth and lean. Nice-smooth legs, pretty face, proportionate hips, erect breast, and hourglass figure

1

(32-22-32). She could easily have been a model of some kind. She had all this at only fifteen years of age.

Gill was a country boy from Newton, a small town ten miles north of Fieldtown. He lived in the middle of nowhere in a tin-roof shack. His folks were isolated on a small farm. His family didn't have a telephone or indoor plumbing. His parents weren't active in the community. In first grade they finally built a road to his house, before that there was only a pig trail, and there was no electricity. Gill spent most of his time doing farm chores. His brother did give him his car for his birthday in October 1963. His brother felt sorry for him being isolated with no means of transportation. He would have traded it in but figured he couldn't get much for it. It was a 1960 Bel-Aire Chevrolet, a nice-looking car. It was black with white racing stripes down the side, and red and white seat covers encased in bubble plastic. The interior was also red and white. It had moon hubcaps that you could see your picture in. The car purred like a kitten when his brother gave it to him.

Gill was five-seven and 130 lbs. He was handsome to look at but not much muscle mass. He could have had his choice of girlfriends if he only had the nerve to approach them. He suffered from lack of self-esteem and self-confidence. Several years later a number of girls told him how they were interested in him and wanted to date him in high school. In school Gill participated in no extra-curricula activities. Newton High was so small that there was only band or sports.

Jesse lived five miles west of Newton while Gill lived 20 miles south of Newton. Jesse lived in a two-story-brick home situated on 200 acres of land. He lived with his grandmother and grandfather. They were rich and retired. His folks were pillars of the community and active in community affairs. His grandmother was especially active in the PTA. Jesse, though he had much more material things than Gill, was envious of his car. Jesse had most of what he wanted, but he didn't have a car of his own.

Jesse was about Gill's size. He was about five-seven and 125 lbs. Gill had a little stronger body build than Jesse. Jesse was a strikingly handsome young man and was also very intelligent. Jesse was in the band, ran track, played basketball, and baseball.

Gill had known Jesse since Jesse came to Newton Elementary School in second grade. Jesse's parents died in an Amtrak train wreck in Los Angeles. That's when Jesse and his brother came to live with his grandparents. His brother was in college. Jesse always said Gill was *one brick shy of a load*. In spite of this, they were fairly close friends. Jesse had been introduced to Clara by mutual friends; these friends first went to Newton High and then transferred to Washington High when they moved closer to Fieldtown. They gave Jesse Clara's number and told him to call her. Gill first met Clara on a bright, cool, Saturday morning in December 1964 during the Christmas season. They both were out to buy Christmas gifts. Gill saw Clara coming out of Bell's department store in Fieldtown. He took a long look at her. She was exquisite, charming, and graceful. She had the refinement of an East Coast prep school graduate. She apparently imitated her sister in some ways. But Gill was at a loss to figure out where she obtained such training. He knew there was no training for charm and sophistication in Fieldtown. Gill was just a country boy; he didn't know anything about class and staying within one's social structure. He decided to speak to her.

"Hello there, how's it going?" Gill asked.

"Its fine, how's it going with you?" she replied.

"I hadn't seen you before. Where've you been keeping yourself?"

"I've been around all the time. We probably travel in different circles."

Gill knew that if she traveled at all it was in different circles.

"Where do you go to school?"

Realizing there's only one Black high school in town, and the schools were not integrated. There's only one school she could have attended, unless she went to school out of town, which was a distinct possibility.

"I attend Washington High School," she said.

Gill knew Washington High was the only Black high school in Fieldtown.

"I attend Newton High," Gill said.

"I've heard of it. What grade are you in?"

"I am in eleventh grade."

"I'm only a freshman," she said

"You've got to start somewhere."

"Nice to meet you."

"I'd like to get to know you."

Even though he said it, he kept thinking he might be in over his head.

"That's entirely possible."

"Could I come by to visit you on Sunday?"

Gill speeded up the process knowing his folks were always in a hurry to get back to the country, and when they got ready to go, they didn't want to be held up. He had gotten into trouble any number of times by getting out-of-pocket. He did all the driving for his family. Neither his mother nor his father could drive. This came from being isolated for so long with nothing but a trail to their house.

"Sure, you can if you have transportation."

She was making it easy for him, even though he had some doubts about attempting a relationship with her.

"I have a car of my own."

"You're riding high then. I'll see you Sunday."

She seemed impressed with the fact that he had his own car.

"OK."

He got her address and telephone number.

"Looking forward to seeing you," she said.

"Be good."

He came by to see her on Sunday at five o'clock. He had no idea Jesse was seeing her as well. Jesse had been seeing her since the beginning of the school year. He sat down for a few minutes and who walked in but Jesse.

"What are you doing sneaking around to see my girl?"

Jesse was outdone. He always liked to be demonstrative and put on a big show.

"I didn't know Clara was your girl."

"I'm not going steady, I'm nobody's girl. My parents say I'm too young to have only one steady friend," Clara said.

"But I thought it was you and me, baby," Jesse said.

"Gill is a free man, and he can go and come whenever he likes," Clara said.

Gill knew Jesse could get angry very quickly, so he left without saying anything else. He said, "Good-bye Clara."

"You don't have to go," she said.

"It's probably best that I go."

"If you think you should leave, but don't let Jesse run you away."

Gill walked out the door.

One day they were sitting in American History class at Newton High. The teacher was out; all the girls were in a special meeting.

Again, he wanted to know, "What're you doing seeing my girl behind my back?"

Again, I said, "I didn't know you had exclusive rights to her."

"You don't even know when you're outclassed. This girl is too rich for your blood. You're just a farmer. She is high society."

Gill had no idea what Jesse was talking about. All he knew was that she was a girl and he was a boy. The rest didn't matter. Before he could clarify, he approached Gill and swung at him wildly, it was unexpected. Gill counterpunched with a barrage of constant flurries straight to the gut. Gill's punches were powerful for a guy his size and build. One of Jesse's wild swings cut him on the forehead over his right eye, but Gill had Jesse penned against the blackboard. A guy who had dropped out and returned to school, he was older and stronger than the rest of them, stepped in and got between Jesse and Gill. Gill was clearly getting the best of Jesse, except for the fingernail cut on the forehead.

It took Gill a long time to get over that experience with Clara and Jesse. Gill had to stay out of school for a week and had an intense relationship for six months with a therapist. The therapist encouraged him to find someone else and forget Clara. But Gill didn't want anyone else and certainly not to forget Clara. For a while it was difficult for Gill to concentrate on his schoolwork.

Nothing more was said about the incident until during Gill's freshman year in college. Clara was a junior in high school. Gill decided to go by and see her over the Christmas holidays. His friend from nearby where he lived went with him.

Her father came in the living room and spoke to Gill, "Hi Gill, how're things going in college."

"They're going pretty good, sir."

"I've heard so much about you from Clara."

It was the first time Gill had seen her father. He seemed to know all about Gill.

"Good, sir."

"You don't have to call me sir, call me Frank."

He was friendly and considerate, and never mentioned Jesse.

"OK."

"What's your major?"

"Business and economics."

"Those are good majors. How long will it take you to graduate?"

"This is my first year, I have three more years."

"Is this your friend? Does he attend school with you?"

"Yes, he does."

"My name is Frank," he spoke to Jimmy.

"Jimmy," my friend said.

"I wish you guys much success. Good talking with you Gill. See you again soon."

Frank walked out of the room. We sat there for a while talking, and before long Jesse walked in.

"What am I going to have to do to convince you that this is my girl," Jesse asked, "you're a stubborn guy who won't seem to give up even though you're out of your league."

"I apologize, man," Gill said.

"You don't have to apologize, just be more careful."

Again, Gill knew Jesse was fed up with him, so he walked out. Gill's therapist had told him what Jesse meant by being outclassed. He said good-bye to Clara. He didn't see her again until he graduated college in 1970. Gill wrote her a letter but didn't have her exact address in college. All he could do was write it to her in care of the school. To this day, he didn't know if she ever got the letter. In the letter he asked her to marry him. Since she didn't respond, he thought it was a clear sign that she was rejecting him, but she probably never got the letter. Gill never quite got over his relationship with Clara. A freshman attending the same university Gill attended was going by to see his friends at Lone Star State. The freshman had gone to school with Clara. He had a nice car. Gill wanted to show off his degree, so he went with him after graduation on a cool December night. He had no intentions of seeing Clara.

They got to the campus and found somewhere to sleep for the night. The next day Jesse saw him coming down the walkway. He approached him.

"What're you doing out of school during examination time?"

"I graduated last night."

"I thought it took at least four years to graduate from college."

"All it takes is the required credit hours.

He looked surprised.

"I can't seem to convince you that Clara is my girl. You come all the way down here looking for her. You must care for her a great deal. Maybe I underestimated you and how much you two care for each other."

"I'm convinced. I come to see you brother, not Clara. I have just about gotten over Clara. I wanted you to see what I could do." I pulled out my tassel with the year 1970 hanging from it.

"Let's go and have a drink. Something like this is better discussed over a drink."

"OK."

We went to a café called the Cat's Cradle and finished our conversation.

"I've decided to make you a proposition."

"What proposition?"

"What would you think of sharing in a relationship with Clara?"

Jesse always was bold, shocking, direct, and quick to get to the point. He was also known for being radical, unorthodox, progressive, and different.

"What're you saying? Isn't that illegal in this country?"

"It's illegal to marry more than one person, but not to live together and share expenses."

All Gill had ever thought about was the traditional way of doing things.

"Where did you get this idea from?"

"Clara and I talked about it and decided to give it a try. We can get a house, share the rent, and the utilities. That is of course, if you don't have plans of your own. Everything could be divided into thirds. Clara was the one to decide that might be a good idea."

"I'm willing to try it," Gill cared enough about Clara to try almost anything. Gill hadn't had a girlfriend since he met her coming out of Bell's department store.

"Clara will be glad."

Clara had already discussed this arrangement with her parents. Clara's parents apparently wanted whatever their "baby-girl" wanted. They were open minded enough to be accepting of this arrangement.

Gill got a job working for the State of Texas. When Jesse and Clara graduated, they bought a house in Houston. In the meantime, Gill visited both Clara and Jesse at Lone Star State. The house was a three-bedroom house, and each of them had a room. Clara would alternate sleeping with one for a while then the other. They usually went out together unless one or the other wasn't feeling well. They never brought children into the picture. They thought that might complicate the situation. They were happy in their non-traditional situation. They shared the bills on everything and lived together until they all passed away.

2

KISSING COUSINS

I got up early that Saturday morning did my chores, had some grits, fatback, scrambled eggs, and fresh-cows milk. We lived in a rural-farm area of East Texas in a town called Hallsville. We engaged in light farming for our livelihood. My brothers ran the farm, while my father had a public job on the Gulf Coast, three-hundred miles away. We didn't have butane, telephone, or indoor plumbing. We weren't able to get these things until many years later. There was only a red-dirt road to our house and that had only recently been constructed. My fourteen-year old sister and I were on our way to visit a neighbor. I was eight-years old. It was 1955, and *Brown vs. Board of Education of Topeka* had just outlawed the "separate but equal doctrine." The same year Emmett Till would be killed for saying baby to a white woman. His murderers would go unpunished.

It was July and so hot you could fry an egg in the sand. The wind was blowing, and sand was swirling in the air. We walked down the hot-dusty-red-dirt road for about a mile and went down a hill to my neighbor's house. After meeting two twins I started to play with them. I adapted readily to most situations at that age.

Their names were Danita and Juanita. At that age I was also open to any and all relationships and willing to engage, I didn't have any hang ups about interpersonal relations at that time; it took further learning or lack of it to become dysfunctional. There wasn't much time for play; my time had to be spent doing whatever chores my mother would assign to me. We started to play, and we were roughhousing for a while. They didn't seem to be enjoying it, just going along because of me. Before I knew it, my penis became erect. I didn't know what was going on. It was the first time I remember getting an erect penis. I kept trying to kiss them after my penis became erect.

My sister and their sister looked at me strangely. I don't know if they noticed my penis sticking out against my pants. At that age I didn't have any shame or guilt. They were one year younger than I; at least they were one year behind me in school. I was a year behind in school myself. This meant they were probably two years younger than I. I didn't start school until I was seven. Their sister was about my sister's age. I heard later that this sister had gotten pregnant and later got married. They came from a big family, not big as mine, but at least six or seven children. There were ten children in my family.

Their great-uncle was my mother's uncle. Their great-uncle and his wife lived in the house. They never had any children. He was the twins father's uncle. My mother seemed to have some kind of paranoid fixation against their great-uncle. She thought he and his wife were trying to find a way to poison our wells, cut our fences, burn our barn, burn down our house, make our crops less productive, turn their livestock into our fields, or put some kind of voodoo fix on our family. She thought he didn't want our family on the land. The land had been handed down through our common ancestors. I finally figured out that it was mostly all in my mother's mind. I couldn't see any damage they were doing. The twin's great-uncle and my mom's mother were sisters and brothers. My mother wasn't on speaking terms with the great-uncle and his wife. Of course, my mother rarely left the house. My mother continued this fixation until she died in 1989.

I remember not seeing the twins for a long time after that initial meeting. I did know that their father visited his uncle frequently, because his car was visible from the road. I guess I just never saw them when they came around. The girls never came to our house. The great-uncle lived about 100 feet off the road. Their brother did come by to visit us once when he was in the military. He tried college but didn't like it. He seemed to like the military. Of course, we had no way of knowing when they visited their great-uncle. We lived at the end of the road and didn't mind anyone else's affairs. The brother came by walking up that dirt road in his spit-shinned shoes and clean-green uniform—brass buttons all over it. He looked impressive. He came by on many such occasions during his father's visits.

I don't remember the circumstances under which I next saw the twins. But it was now 1963, and either I had seen them at their great-uncles house by accident, or I saw them at their house in Longview when I drove my father for a visit. My uncle owned a café right across from their house. It's possible I could have seen them at the café. My father would visit the café to see his sister and bring my mother some of my uncle's East Texas famous barbeque ribs.

I remembered there was the funeral of a relative to both our families. My father went by their home in Longview before the funeral. Their father convinced my father to ride with him, while Juanita rode with me. We left for the funeral. The sand had settled in the cab of the truck while riding down the dirt road to our house. The truck must have been in an accident before we bought it. It's the only explanation for the sand coming up through the floor. I felt sorry for her. I'm sure she wasn't used to traveling in such low-class style. She was used to some of the finer things of life. Her father drove a 1963 Cadillac, Coupe De Ville and lived in an expensive-brick home. The ride was rough in a standard-shift truck, and the sand was swirling in the truck. I'm sure she thought I needed some lessons in driving. It was a justifiable conclusion. The sand was getting all over her black skirt, white blouse, her nicely done hair, and satin-smooth stockings. She was easy to look at. I kept noticing how smooth her long legs were in that short skirt. She also had a nice body and a pretty face. I almost lost my composure and didn't know how to act.

After the funeral was over, she suggested we get a bite to eat, in spite of the transportation situation. We went to a local restaurant. We were sitting there, and I didn't know what to say. I hadn't had much experience at making conversation; I had been isolated for a long time, had gotten no help for my speech impediment, and spent most of my time laboring on the farm. I decided to make some conversation just to clear the air.

"I've always liked you Juanita but haven't had much of an opportunity to get to know you."

At that time, I wasn't smart enough to understand the fact that there was a class structure to which people adhered in most circles. I was socially invincible and didn't realize I was outclassed. All I knew was that I was attracted to her, and she was a girl and I was a boy.

We lived close to each other, but the distance between us seemed like many miles apart. My mother's feelings about her great-uncle didn't improve our chances for a relationship. I always thought it would be impossible for us to develop a relationship, in view of my mother's feelings. When you are a child you believe whatever your parents say. I think I resented their father because of my mother's paranoid fixations on their great-uncle, and

I knew her father was close to her great-uncle. I hated to consider it, but the twins were probably considered more middle class, whereas we were more working class. This could have posed some obstacles to our having a relationship other than also being cousins. Also, again, she was used to some of the finer things of life. The difference between the way she was raised and the way I was raised would present insurmountable obstacles to a relationship between us. Her parents also knew my family's history, which was not too favorable for someone looking for a person to establish a relationship with.

"I like you also, Jimmy. But we're too closely related for a more personal type of relationship. On second thought let me talk to my parents about it. I don't do anything that serious without talking to my parents."

"I thought as long as we didn't bring children into the relationship it didn't matter."

"In a situation like that no matter how hard you try, children are going to creep into the relationship. Most people will try to have children at some point in their marriage regardless of the circumstances."

"You could be right."

"I'll write to you and let you know where to meet me for my answer. Give me your address."

We still had no telephone.

I gave it to her, and she wrote and told me to meet her on a Friday night in November at my uncle's café.

We met on a cool Friday night in November at my uncle's restaurant across from their house.

"I can't stay long, Jimmy. My family is going out to dinner. I tried everything I could to convince them, but both my parents feel that we are too close cousins for more than a platonic relationship. I even told them we would not have children."

"OK, baby. I understand."

"I have to run," Juanita said, "I'll talk to you later."

She seemed relieved and in a hurry.

"See you later."

All I could do was drop my head. I figured it would be some disappointing news.

Before she went out the door, she said, "We'll be better off just being cousin-type friends. You really don't know me well."

I graduated high school and went to college in 1966. She and her sister graduated in 1967. Their father told my mother they had gone to Long Star State University, and I went to Washington State University, increasing the distance between us. I thought I would never see Juanita again. But chance or happenstance brought us together again. I really thought such a relationship was out of the question but was willing to dig in the ashes once again to see if I could bank and stoke the embers.

I spent three years on Washington State University campus without a car. Finally, my father broke down and purchased me the best car he could for the money he had in 1968. I was thinking about Juanita on one cool fall night in October and decided to give her a call at Lone Star State. I was lucky enough to get through to her in the dorm. I was lucky to get in touch with her, because they had no phones in their rooms, but there was one in the hallway. One of her friends answered the phone and immediately found her and brought her to the phone.

"Hello, this is Jimmy from Hallsville."

Right away she knew who I was.

"How are you doing stranger? How did you find me?"

"It's not hard to find someone if you want to find them bad enough. Just kidding it was easy."

I was a junior and she was a sophomore.

"What've you been doing for yourself?"

"Not too much, just hanging out."

"Do you have a car?"

"Yes, I do. I recently purchased one."

"Barry White is putting on a concert in Houston on the weekend of the nineteenth. Why don't you pick me up for the weekend and we can spend the weekend in Houston and attend the concert on Saturday night. Barry is my favorite artist. He sends chills through me. Pick me up on Friday at three o'clock. My last class is at one o'clock. I'll be packed and ready. You know where the campus is?"

"Yes, I know where the campus is. I've been there a half dozen times."

"We can't have sex but I offer you my companionship."

"That sounds good. I didn't expect any sex. We're just close cousins remember."

I was more than satisfied with the prospect of being with her and wasn't concerned about sex in the slightest.

I drove to Lone Star State University without any problems on Friday evening, picked her up, and drove to Houston. We found a hotel near the Astrodome where the concert was held. We started sightseeing that Friday night. We went to Herman Park, Herman Park Zoo, went to the movies, AstroWorld, and attended the concert that Saturday night. She really seemed to enjoy herself. I was enjoying myself just seeing her enjoy herself. We hadn't said a great deal, I was not much of a conversationalist either, and that hadn't changed. We did strike up a conversation about our past.

We caught up on both our families, and finally she said, "My parents don't realize what they could have had in you as a son-in-law."

"Do you mean that?"

"Yes, I do. I can't imagine when I've had such a good time."

"I'm glad to see that you're enjoying yourself."

"You understand why we can't have sex."

"Yeah I understand."

"It's no fun doing it with a condom, and I can't take the chance without a condom. I'm caught between a rock and a hard place."

We had two beds, but lie there in the same bed, we kissed and held each other all night, just thinking about our relationship, and hating the fact that it couldn't work out for us.

Sunday morning, we drove back to her campus, and I drove back to Washington State. We didn't say much on the way, thinking it had already been said, and that we were the victims of a cruel hoax. We had discussed our backgrounds, and she realized why I was not much of a conversationalist. I tried but was never able to get in contact with her until many years later.

I saw her at my mother's funeral in 1989. We both had long since graduated college and were working in the private sector.

I thought about her for a long time. She still frequently crosses my mind. I kept wondering how it would have been if we had been able to develop a real relationship.

At my mother's funeral Juanita told me they were both living in Dallas, and she worked as a personnel assistant. She gave me her number and suggested that I call sometimes. I have yet to try and make contact.

3

TRYING A DIFFERENT WAY

I first met Charlotte in fourth grade. She was in third grade. I had seen her across the campus any number of times, but never said a single word to her. At that age I didn't go to school events, I was lucky to be able to attend school at all. The only reason I was able to attend school was because the bus picked me up at my front door. She was a cute caramel colored girl. When I saw her in fourth grade, she weighed about 80 lbs, about four-feet tall, and kept herself neat and immaculate. We went to a little all-Black school in Newton, Texas. It wasn't much advanced over the one-room schoolhouse commonly depicted in the historical literature; certainly, many of its practices were similar. The only difference was we had a separate classroom for each grade, but we still existed on a bare minimum of resources.

She saw me as our paths crossed in front of the classrooms, all of a sudden, she blurted out from out of left field, "You're not so smart," she said.

I didn't think anyone thought I was smart, certainly I didn't. If so, that was the first time I had heard of it.

"What do you mean?" I asked.

I really hadn't given that much thought to her—except that she was a cute girl. At that point I thought she was kind of mean. Of course, at that age some girls let boys know they like them by being mean to them. At the time I was not aware of this. I didn't know she had any impression of me. In any case, I was on an errand and had to get back to the classroom. We were both in a hurry. The teacher frequently sent us on errands and would use different people at different times.

Charlotte's mother opened a little restaurant on Saturdays in Fieldtown. Her sister Anita would be the waitress. I would buy a hamburger just to get a look at Anita on Saturdays. I would grow to like Anita as much as I would come to like Charlotte.

I saw Charlotte between fourth and eleventh grades but never had any sustained contact with her. And she never said another word to me about anything. I thought both of the girls were beautiful. Anita was a little darker and a little shorter than Charlotte, but both of them were well-bred and smooth. They went to a different school when I was in the eleventh grade. At the time I didn't know anything about the details just knew they moved.

After they moved, I heard nothing from either of them until one day on my way back to Jefferson State University, I saw Charlotte and Anita at the bus station in Fieldtown, Texas. It was September 1968. Charlotte was sitting there reading out of a Zoology textbook while waiting on their bus. Anita was reading a General Business textbook. They both had graduated high school at Washington High School in Fieldtown and were presently attending Texas Wesleyan University in Fort Worth. I was surprised to see them. I knew they would both probably attend college because they were both highly intelligent. They ranked high on the honor roll in each of their classes.

I didn't quite know how to approach them. I pretended to be coy, first playing a record on the juke box, and then walking over and sitting down by Charlotte. The juke box was blaring "Soul Man" by Sam and Dave. It seemed appropriate. Anita had someone sitting on either side of her.

"Hi Charlotte," I said, "been a long time since I've seen you. Where've you been keeping yourself?"

"Hi Fred," she seemed excited about seeing me. "I've been around. I've been at Texas Wesleyan University for the past year."

"It's good to see you."

"Good to see you too," she said.

"I didn't know what happened to you guys."

"Why didn't you ask your classmate Bill? He knew where I was."

"I didn't want him to know I was interested. I'm careful about who I tell my business."

"I understand."

"Where are you headed?"

"I'm headed back to college at Texas Wesleyan University in Fort Worth."

"So that's where you guys went. I wondered where you went to school. Imagine running into you guys at the bus station. It must be some kind of auspicious sign."

"I didn't know you thought about me one way or the other."

"I thought you knew I liked you."

"We didn't have many opportunities for you to tell me. We never really associated in high school."

"On the contrary, I thought about you all the time after you left Wheatley, and while you were there. But I never had any idea you were leaving Wheatley."

"Excuse me! I didn't know."

Her bus pulled up. The only reason I was talking with Charlotte rather than Anita was because Anita was sitting next to someone on both sides. I still liked them both equally as well.

As they got up and Anita came in my direction she asked, "How're you doing Fred? Too bad we don't have time to talk. At first, I didn't recognize who you were until the bus pulled up, then it was too late to engage with you."

"Yeah, I'd have enjoyed having more time."

They both got on the bus headed for Wesleyan. Before she left Charlotte gave me her number and asked me to call her sometimes. They lived together in an apartment near the campus. I said I would definitely be in touch. She also gave me her address. I had been to Fort Worth to visit relatives on several occasions and knew where the campus was located.

Several days later I called her at her apartment about eleven o'clock on a Thursday night.

"Hello," Charlotte said.

"Hello, Charlotte," this is Fred.

"Oh, hi Fred, how're you doing?"

"I'm just hanging around studying for a quiz," I said, "You know how it is, when you start out behind the eight ball you have to spend a lot of time catching up. You know those schools didn't prepare us for the realities of the world."

"Believe me I understand."

"What're you doing?"

"I'm studying also, but it's good to hear from you. I'd invite you up for a weekend, but I need all my weekends for study. I'll give you some time during the Christmas break—if you want it."

"Good then, I'll plan to that effect."

"Take it easy and I'll see you over the Christmas break. I hate for us to wait that long, but it's the best I can do. My parents wouldn't want me to waste too much time not applying myself. However, you can call anytime, the best time being on weekends."

"I'm glad to hear that you and Anita could get an apartment together. The dorms can be bad news. I live in a dorm."

"Yeah, we're roommates. She's right here on the couch."

"How's she doing?"

"She's doing fine. Did you want to speak with her? She's studying also."

"Yeah, let me say hello."

"Hi Fred, this is Anita. I'm just sitting here on the couch studying Business Statistics, my major is business."

"It's good to know that everything is OK with you."

"You know how it is. You do the best you can. Yeah, things are fine."

"When're you guys coming home again?"

"We can't afford to academically or financially to come home before Christmas."

"I told Charlotte that I hoped to get together with you guys over the Christmas vacation."

It was selfish of me to think I could have both of them, but I was hoping to do just that.

"We should be able to do that."

"Good. I'll see you then."

"Did you want to talk back to Charlotte?"

"Yeah, let me say good-bye to her."

"Yeah, Fred, I'm back on the line."

"I have to go Charlotte. I can't afford to talk forever. You know going to school is expensive for a poor kid from the other side of the tracks."

"Before you go tell me which one you like, Anita or me?"

She was deliberately teasing me.

"I like both of you. But you've always been the one I like best of all."

"You know what I mean, which one do you want to date?"

"You are putting me on the spot."

"You can see both if you want until you decide which one you like best."

I thought she was just playing with my mind, but there seems to have never been a question about the fact that they came in a package deal.

"Is that OK with Anita?"

"We're way ahead of you. We've already talked about it, and we both are fine with it. It is illegal to marry two people, but not to be close friends with them. Sharing wouldn't be anything new to Anita and I; we've been sharing things all our lives as sisters."

"That sounds good. I will see you at Christmas if possible."

I never thought I would actually get a two-for-one deal, but I couldn't say I hadn't thought about it. I kept thinking that this was a new concept for me and would be difficult to manage, but three open-minded people should be able to handle it. I felt good about both of them and thought we could make it together if we worked at it.

"By Fred," Charlotte said, she sounded so sweet, not like the girl I remembered from Wheatley.

"I'll call and let you know when I get in for Christmas."

I gave her my number in Newton and told her to call me anytime after the eighteenth of December. That's when my Christmas vacation started.

Charlotte called me on the 22nd of December and told me she and Anita were home, and for me to come by on Saturday if I could. I told her I would be there for sure but took her number just in case I couldn't make it. I called back Saturday morning and told her I would be there at five o'clock on Saturday. She gave me directions to her house.

I arrived at a modest white bungalow on the outskirts of Fieldtown. We kissed for the first time. I kissed both of them very passionately. I guess they planned to follow through with what Charlotte had discussed with Anita. Her brother Howard was there with his family. He caught me kissing both of them and wondered what was going on. He wanted to know what my intentions were. I told him we were just three old friends getting together. Howard had never seemed to like me. He and his nephew would pick on me when I was stuttering around the campus at Wheatley as a seven-year old in school. They were seventeen and I was seven.

We were silent for a while, finally Anita said, "I planned a movie for us today."

I hadn't had much experience at entertaining two women at the same time. I was cautious.

"That's fine with me," I said.

We went to a movie and saw "Divorce American Style." It was a decent movie.

After the movie Charlotte said, "Let's get a room."

It was only eight o'clock. I was taken by surprise. I didn't know they were ready for that level.

"Is that OK with you Anita?" I asked.

"It was my suggestion," Anita said.

"Oh, I didn't know."

Charlotte was definitely more talkative than Anita. She did most of the talking.

"I didn't ask you if you could afford a room. It's expensive going to college and it can exhaust most of your funds," Charlotte said.

"That's OK Charlotte, I can afford a room."

Anita decided to speak up when it really counted.

"Let's go to the Holiday Inn."

We got a room at the Holiday Inn in Fieldtown and enjoyed ourselves. After we enjoyed ourselves, we stopped at the lounge for a drink. The lounge was crowded. It was two o'clock, so I took them home.

"Call us tomorrow," Charlotte said.

I noticed it was no longer me but us.

"I will," I said.

I thought about both of them all night long until the next day. I called them about 2 p.m. the next day.

"What's up Charlotte?"

I recognized her voice.

"Let's get together next weekend."

"Is that OK with Anita?

She asked Anita.

"I'm fine with it," Anita said.

"I'll pick you up Saturday at five o'clock."

"We'll see you then"

So, we got together for a concert in Burksville. We saw Tina Turner and the "Ike and Tina Review." Tina was demonstrating her prowess, and Ike was playing his bass guitar. They put on an excellent show. We enjoyed ourselves and went to the Motor Lodge after the show. This time they picked up the tab. We got together many times before we went back to school on January 8. We had developed an incredible bond between the three of us.

When they went back to school, I called them every weekend. On some holidays I would take a bus trip and spend a few days at their apartment. I guess Charlotte changed her mind about visiting only on special holidays. The next year Anita graduated and moved to Memphis. I visited her in Memphis, and Charlotte in Fort Worth. Anita took a job with the Department of Human Services as a business manager, she had majored in business. The next year I took a job with the Department of Family Services in Memphis as a social worker, my major was sociology. The following year Charlotte came to Memphis and took a job in the same department as Anita—her major was business.

At first, we all lived together in a nice apartment. The apartment was a two-bedroom apartment. I would spend time with Anita on some nights and time with Charlotte on others. We usually went out together to most events, unless one of them didn't feel well. We didn't need an automobile because buses and taxicabs were always handy. Our jobs were right around the corner in the State of Tennessee building. If we needed to travel out of town, we would rent a car. We were happy and prepared to live this way the rest of our lives. We didn't feel a piece of paper was necessary to give structure to our relationships.

Later we bought a house in Hickory Hill, East Memphis, but decided that children would not be right for this particular situation. We also purchased a 1980 Chevrolet Malibu just to have some form of transportation, after we purchased a house and moved to the suburban area of Memphis. Charlotte and Anita's relatives never knew the nature of our relationships and were thus somewhat unsatisfied with the situation. When we visited, I was careful not to show any affection toward either of them, pretending to simply be roommates. Their brother Howard still didn't like the relationships, I could tell by his expression when we came to town, but he finally gave up on questioning us.

4

LET SLEEPING DOGS LIE

It was a cool-rainy-windy Friday night. I had come home to Templeton for spring break. My car had backfired a few times on the way, and I thought it wouldn't make it, but it kept on going. I knew it wouldn't last much longer. Everyone was still talking about Apollo 9 returning to Earth, and James Earl Ray pleading guilty to the murder of Dr. Martin Luther King Jr. My father had purchased me a navy blue 1965 Chevy Malibu at the beginning of my junior year. It was not in good condition. It reminded one of a car that had been run in the ground and then totalled. The gears in the five-speed transmission would stick, water poured in around the windshield when it encountered the slightest bit of water, and it smoked— indicating something was badly wrong with the motor. These things were not apparent when we purchased the car. I'm not sure how my brother and I missed it. I was just so happy to be getting a car until I would have purchased anything. When we purchased the car, my oldest brother was there to help my father and I pick out a decent car for the money. My brother assured me it was a good car, consequently we didn't test drive it—that was a mistake. The car didn't last long. The transmission got worse, and the motor soon gave out. I hadn't asked for the car, my father simply decided that I needed one. I did need a car to get around.

I went to a wedding between two-old classmates and friends: Louise Johnson and Lewis Thomas. The wedding was elaborate and took place in one of the biggest Baptist churches in the area. It was a nice wedding. I saw a neighbor at the wedding that I hadn't seen in three years—the day we graduated from high school. In high school she was frail and underdeveloped, with crooked teeth, but in the interim she had matured a great deal. Her breast stood out pointedly, teeth were perfectly aligned, her waist was thin and well-proportioned with the rest of her body, her legs were smooth—long and scissor like, she had a weave in her hair that made it look natural, and her face was smooth and beautiful where I had noticed only pimples when growing up. She was five-five, about 120 lbs, with coco-brown skin. That red dress showed every curve of her curvaceous body, as if someone had melted and poured her into it. She had come home for a week from Compton, California where she was living. I spoke to her briefly but didn't talk for long. She did say she had been in Compton since graduating high school. I hadn't given any more thought to her since I saw her at graduation. Part of the reason for my lack of time and attention to her was because I was immature; I couldn't believe she was that fine, and that we hadn't gotten together in the early days.

She said she came in Wednesday and would be here for a week of vacation. She had a flight out of Dallas/ Ft. Worth the following Saturday at one o'clock p.m. I told her I would be here for a week also, that I would be leaving the following Sunday morning early. We both enjoyed the wedding and said that we would see each other around. I knew at the time that I had to get back with her. I couldn't let her get away without making a play.

We lived about three miles apart, on the same red-dirt road. We both had lived there all of our lives. Yet, we never spoke more than a sentence to one another. Another of my brothers bought me a car in tenth grade, but I never offered her a ride to school events, and she never asked for one. At that time, I simply wasn't interested. I thought she just didn't like going to school activities. I didn't think about the possibility that she could have been waiting for me to offer her a ride. I guess in those days I did lack a certain amount of insight.

I had talked to my youngest sister, and she told me that we were cousins. My sister said her grandmother and my father were two sister's children. So that made us fairly close cousins. That may be why we never got together romantically, but there could have been other reasons we didn't get together. Until my sister told me I had no idea we were cousins. My parents never bothered to tell me who was a relative or who wasn't. My parents had more pressing survival issues to talk about rather than sit around and discuss who was a relative. If it hadn't been for Social Security benefits, there's no way I could have ever made it through high school or the university, but I was determined to make it. We went to school for twelve years with very little communication between us. She had a sister and two brothers close to our ages, yet we never got together to play any games. From what I could figure out most activities took place intra-family rather than inter-family in those days.

Nevertheless, she was a pretty girl, and I felt compelled to get together with her for a movie or a drink of some kind. Prior to this I had never felt the slightest attraction to her. Of course, they say *familiarity breeds contempt.* I guess I had seen too much of her for my own good. I didn't say any more that night, but that Saturday evening I called her about a movie and a drink. I couldn't seem to get her off my mind. My parents had recently gotten a telephone and added indoor plumbing. The telephone made communications easier, and the indoor plumbing made things more convenient. Prior to them getting indoor plumbing I rarely came home from school. It was also difficult to get from the bus station to where we lived in the country, before I got the car. Before my seventh birthday there was no road to our house, only a three-mile trail off the main highway. Only a wagon or a horse could negotiate this trail. Consequently, we had no electricity or any other kind of utilities.

I kept thinking about Cherry late that Friday night. I got to bed late that Friday night after the wedding, when I did get to sleep, I began to drift away. It was about 2 o'clock a.m. All of a sudden, we were back in high school, were out on a date, and were kissing each other madly and passionately for about thirty minutes.

"Don't," she said, grabbing my hand, "Let's go to a motel. I want my first time to be special, not in the back seat of a car."

I wanted her but was somehow surprised at her reaction.

"You sure that's what you want."

"Yes, I'm sure," she seemed to have it already planned.

We had been dating for several years. Neither her parents nor mine were aware of it. We always met in the neighborhood and hooked up from there. We went to a local motel and got a room.

"Whatever you want."

After we got inside the room she said, "Let's take a shower first, I want it to be right."

"OK, baby."

We both took a shower and got under the cover and locked in a warm embrace.

"Oh! Do you have a condom? We can't have sex without a condom. The last thing I need is to get pregnant."

"I think I have a condom in my wallet."

Ever since the first girl I dated wanted to know if I had a condom, I always kept several condoms in my wallet.

"Good," she said.

"OK, baby."

I tried to take my time and please her since she wanted it to be special. The condom also made me slow in obtaining my orgasm, but it worked out for her.

We had sex several times, and she said, "That's the first time I ever experienced an orgasm."

"Did you enjoy it?"

"Yes, I did."

"I'm glad."

"The other reason I wanted you to use a condom is because you know we are related. Cousins should never bring children into the world."

"Yes, I've heard that."

I woke up feeling guilty but lying there alone in bed. My body was aching for Cherry. I thought if I could go out with her that night, we could partially recapture the past. I called her the next day on a sunny-warm spring Saturday morning.

"Hello, may I speak with Cherry," an older woman answered the phone; I assumed it was her mother.

"Sure, Cherry is right here"

Cherry picked up the phone.

"Hello Cherry, how're you doing?"

"I'm fine, who is this?"

"This is Charles."

"Hello Charles, I never expected you to call."

"I didn't think you'd expect me to call."

"That was a nice wedding," she said.

"Yes, it was really special," I replied.

"I never expected Louise and Lewis to get married."

Both of them had lived in the community only a few miles apart, for most of their lives, all of a sudden, they were in love and getting married.

"I didn't either."

"I guess you never know."

"I'm calling to invite you out for a movie tonight and maybe a drink afterward. You hadn't gotten married, have you?"

"No, I'm not married or even going steady for that matter. Sure, we can go out for a while. It's the best offer I've had since being here. In fact, it's the only offer."

I didn't quite know what to say to her about our past. Why I never invited her out while in high school, or never asked her to come along to school activities, when I knew her brothers had left home and that she didn't know how to drive. All I could say for myself was that I was selfish, and that's just the way things were at the time. Our folks did seem to get along well. They always came to one another's aide when they needed something from each other. In the early years before I learned to drive, my family especially had no transportation, and was dependant on neighbors.

We went to the movies and saw "Sweet Charity." We both enjoyed the movie. We decided to go by the Do-Drop-Inn in Lovelace and have a drink. We didn't say much during the movie. In fact, she kept looking at me smiling during the movie, but didn't say much until we got to the Do-Drop-Inn and had a few drinks. I started the conversation.

"I heard your father passed several months ago; let me extend a belated condolence."

"Yeah, it was hard on my mother at first, but she seems to be getting over it."

"How do you like Compton?"

"It's a different world than Templeton. The adjustment was hard for a while, but I soon got over it. Where are you going to school? When I told my mother, I saw you at the wedding, she said you were attending school somewhere nearby."

"Yeah, I go to Washington University. It's about 150 miles south of here. It's in a small town, but people in the university community are from all over the United States, so you don't have that small-town atmosphere on the campus."

"That sounds good."

"When I graduate, I'm going to further my education at Howard University in Washington, D.C."

"How much more education does one person need?"

"A lot more I'm afraid. I want to get a Ph.D. in sociology and teach at a Black college. That has always been my dream."

"You have some big dreams."

"Lots of people have come to the same conclusion."

She decided to change the subject.

"I would often wonder, in the old days, why we never got together for a movie or a burger."

I couldn't explain those details and felt uncomfortable exploring them. I quickly tried to divert the conversation altogether. Knowing I was deliberately changing the subject, she allowed me to do so. I took the same prerogative I had just given her.

"Do you ever see any of our old friends and classmates from high school?"

"I caught the first train going to Compton, and never looked back. That's where Clara my sister went when she left high school. Clara and I live together. Compton is a nice city. I got a decent job working for the city's Department of Human resources. Those typing classes I thought I would never use came in handy. That algebra and geometry also came in handy—not to mention the constant drills in English. I've been there for the past three years. I like my job."

We had several drinks and was laughing and talking about old times. There weren't much old times to talk about, at least not between us, but mostly about experiences in high school. She told me that once before while she was home, she had gotten together with Lenny. At that point I felt envious of Lenny. She kissed me and squeezed my hand; acting as if she wanted to get intimate, but *too much water had run under the bridge.* I admired the changes she had made to herself, but I still wasn't ready for her. We decided that the past was best left in the past, and that you could not recapture it. We drove back to Templeton without much to say except that we had both had a good time. We both realized then that some things are better left unsaid, and some romances left unfulfilled. I dropped her off and continued on home. My car was running poorly, with dark smoke coming out the tailpipe, and the gears sticking when I tried to change them. It was clear to me that my brother had done me a disservice.

I didn't try to contact her again during that week, and subsequently never saw her again. I went back to school, but soon had to get rid of the car. It did get me back to school, but at school a mechanic told me the motor was ruined, and the transmission was shot to hell. The mechanic gave me $200.00 for the car as it was, just to do me a favor. I often thought about Cherry on some cool-rainy nights in the dormitory. The question kept coming up in my mind about why such a beautiful girl and I couldn't have gotten together earlier in our lives. We were cousins, but I don't think that had much to do with it. But again, I didn't really want to think about it.

I got on with my life. I still sometimes think about her when my mind drifts back to those early years. I finally figured out it was better to let the past stay in the past, or as they say, "Let sleeping dogs lie."

5

BETWEEN THE DEVIL AND MR. AND MRS. JONES

It was a hot day, it was hot as the Sahara desert in July, and you could see steam rising from the blacktop. Crystal Lewis received her degree in May of 1974, and Elliott Jones was discharged from the Army in May of 1974. He got out of the Army about the same time that Crystal received her Masters' degree in accounting. Crystal and Elliott had both just gotten new jobs: Crystal was to start in two weeks, and Elliott was to start in August. They went to a party in Saginaw, Michigan, where they were both from, and met at the party. They were both looking for a relationship to get involved in, that's why they came to the party. Both of them started not to come to the party, but decided it was time to get out and explore some new situations. Crystal was exhausted from her studies, and felt she needed something other than academic stimulation. She thought she would never get through her last few months of school, but she did make it. Crystal was still living at home, but her parents had relaxed on the sexual mores, since she was out of college and had begun her career. Elliott was tired of hooking up with strange women in foreign ports. They both felt the urge to merge in a more permanent way. They met at the bar where the party was held.

Crystal was raised in a middle-class family. In her family sex was evil and dirty. Her mother and father cautioned her to stay away from sex until she got married. Crystal was an only child, and her parents demanded she go to college. She had every possible thing she could want in terms of emotional, spiritual, and financial support. She finished high school, attended college, and attended graduate school in accounting. She was five-five, 125 lbs, with long-smooth legs, and a beautiful face. Most men would be attracted to her. Crystal's parents had insisted that she keep the primal urges under control, and though she had many creature comforts, she still had a lot of repressed desires. Her mother was a college teacher, and her father was a real-estate salesman.

Once her parents came home and caught her in her room with a male friend. She said they were just doing homework, but her parents made her promise never to do it again. They gave her the worst tongue lashing of her life. She was a virgin almost until she graduated college. She lived in fear of her parents catching her in a compromising sexual situation. Crystal had engaged in sex a few times at college with a close friend but nothing consistent or serious.

Elliott Jones was raised in a very poor family but was able to attend college on scholarships and grants, studied physics, and received a commission in the Army as an officer. Elliott's parents couldn't afford to send him to college; he had six brothers and sisters. Growing up he barely had enough to eat. Even with scholarships and grants he just made it through college. He was six-feet tall, dark, athletic, and handsome. He went to a special high school that didn't have competitive sports programs, and therefore couldn't get a sport scholarship. Most women would be attracted to Elliott. He was a few years ahead of Crystal in school. Elliott had repressed most of his primal urges for many years, so he could be successful in his chosen career. His mother had taught him about the benefits of the ability to postpone gratification. She also taught him that he must take advantage of every opportunity, because there were limited opportunities for people like him. His father was a maintenance man at a local factory, and his mother was a maid for a chain of hotels. Both of them frequently changed jobs, causing them to remain at the bottom of the economic scale, making little more than the minimum wage.

Until he graduated college most of his sexual experiences had been with prostitutes. He did have sex a few times in college at parties. He was afraid of a steady relationship, fearing it would lead to something that he knew he couldn't afford—marriage. He had never had a loving and meaningful relationship until he met Crystal. Elliott had been involved mostly with prostitutes at various ports.

Elliott saw Crystal and swore *Heaven must be missing an angel,* since there was one walking around on earth. She had on a long-black dress with a split almost to her inner thigh, a pair of six-inch-black pumps, a gold watch, and an assortment of gold chains on her arms and neck. Her hair was done in an immaculate style, and her legs were long and smooth—without imperfections. On top of all that she was wearing a low-cut dress showing lots of cleavage. She was wearing Chanel perfume.

He observed her for a while and decided to approach her, "My name is Elliott, what's yours."

He hadn't had much experience at talking to regular women, only the kind you meet in the streets. He decided to say what came to mind. He at first thought she was just another street woman until he began to talk to her.

"Crystal."

"Where're you from?" looking her up and down, like some brothers do on the street, that was his previous *modus operandi*, but he couldn't help himself.

"Saginaw."

Crystal was deliberately coy and short with him. She didn't want to appear forward. She was adhering to her parent's early conditioning. She was trying to avoid getting in a sexual situation.

"I hadn't seen you around before."

"Where've you been hiding yourself? I've been right here in town."

"I deserved that one. I've been in the Army for six years, and rarely got back to Saginaw."

"I can see where you might be a little out of touch."

Elliott didn't like the situation his parents lived in and tried to stay away from home as much as possible. He finally figured out that their situation wasn't so bad. Out of necessity he moved in with them after the Army and had no second thoughts about it. Their economic situation was a bit more stable in their latter years.

"Sure, you're right."

"There's another reason why you probably haven't seen me. I've also been away at school for a while."

She somehow decided not to tease him and tell him the truth about her situation.

Crystal went to Wayne State for her undergraduate degree and went to Michigan State for her graduate degree. Elliott had gotten his undergraduate degree at Kalamazoo State University.

"That's why we haven't seen each other."

He seemed relieved that there was more than one explanation for why he hadn't seen her.

"I guess so."

Elliot was no slouch. He was clean shaven with his mustache trimmed to the max. His hair had been freshly cut. He was wearing Aramis cologne. He had on a Blue European cut Dior suit that fit his slender frame perfectly; a power-blue, form-fitted dress shirt; with a red and blue tie; and some blue alligator shoes. He also spoke the King's English which didn't hurt.

Crystal was feeling more comfortable with him. She was definitely attracted to him.

"I don't want to go another week without seeing you again."

"Hold your horses. I don't know you."

Her parents had always taught her to be rather conservative in getting acquainted with the opposite sex.

"I plan to spend time getting to know you."

From that moment on they immediately made plans to get together. On the one hand her parents' conditioning told her to take it slow, but her primal desires wanted her to do anything but take it slow.

They would get together and go to a club, a park, a zoo, a movie, a restaurant, a sporting event, a concert, etc., or a museum in Saginaw, Detroit or the surrounding area. They did this for a year, decided they were in love, and wanted to spend the rest of their lives together. So, they decided to get married. They decided they had found what they wanted in a mate and needed to look no further. Crystal was an accountant for a car dealer in Saginaw, and Elliott taught physics at one of the local Catholic high schools in Saginaw.

They planned to get married in six months. They both were involved with other people during the courtship, but they didn't let one another know it. Elliott and crystal both had a lot of repressed desires from their background. I suppose now they thought they could let it all hang out with the wedding being so close. Crystal got drunk at her bachelorette party and had sex with two hired male strippers. She thought what the hell? It was her last night of freedom. Her girlfriends urged her on and swore never to tell. The whole party turned into one big love fest. Elliott got drunk and had sex with two female strippers who jumped out of a cake at his bachelor's party given by his friend Mel. They both begged their friends not to let word get back to their mates. The bachelor's party also turned into one big love fest as well. Elliott considered he was just doing what men do.

Crystal's parents loved Elliott. They figured his discipline as a college graduate and his time in the military would be good for Crystal, and that he was a lot better than some of the possible partners she could have gotten involved with. They had a big wedding at one of the biggest Catholic churches in Saginaw. It's what her mother and father had always wanted. A reception was held at a local hotel.

The next day they left on their honeymoon for Paris and took their favorite couple with them. Betty and Mel were childhood friends of Crystal's. They both thought this was not unusual, and Crystal wanted to share this most important moment with her best friends. She couldn't imagine not sharing this moment with them. During the week they enjoyed all the sights and attractions in Paris.

On one occasion they were sitting around the hotel relaxing and drinking scotch, Elliott asked Crystal, "Why don't we switch partners?"

"Why do you want to do that?" Crystal asked.

"Let's try it, it'll be fun," Elliott said.

Elliott hadn't ever done such a thing before with a partner but thought it might be fun. He had heard people talk about it on many occasions.

"How do you feel about it, Mel?" asked Crystal.

Crystal thought if Mel felt it was OK there was no reason not to do it.

Mel and Betty had never engaged in this type of behavior before either. They had been married for several years.

"It's OK if Betty wants to," Mel said.

All of them had been drinking heavily.

"It's OK with me. What harm can it do? It's just between friends."

Since her alcohol was doing the talking, she agreed to do it.

"If we do it has to stay right here in this room. It must live and die between us and only us," Elliott said.

Elliott knew if such a thing got back to his school he would be in big trouble. The school was a rather provincial Catholic high school.

Elliott got up and took Betty by the hand, and Mel took Crystal by the hand. They engaged in mad passionate love with each other's spouse for the rest of the week.

"Don't forget, what we do is just between us," Elliott said.

They all agreed.

When they returned home from their honeymoon, they seemed to be restless. They decided to go to a swing club where they could exchange partners freely. They went to such a club and seemed to enjoy it. Elliott cautioned Crystal once again that no one should know about their activities. Some people were too provincial for this type of thing. They decided to join a swing club and make it a way of life. They went swinging every weekend. None of his students or colleagues knew about his strange obsession, and none of Crystal's colleagues knew about her activities. They thought it was better to keep this part of their lives discrete. They continued this activity for several years.

After the trip to Paris they didn't even tell Mel and Betty about their continued experiences with swinging. But for some reason Mel and Betty's relationship couldn't stand the strain of swinging. They got a divorce soon after they returned from Paris.

One day they were sitting around at the table having dinner. They both had been thinking about some indiscretions they had been keeping from one another and decided to reveal their secrets. There was no easy way to do it, but they loved each other enough not to keep secrets from each other.

"I've been having an affair with a fellow teacher at work," Elliott said.

They usually didn't keep secrets about these sorts of things, but Elliott had seen no reason to tell Crystal at first. After all, it was just for a few weeks, and he didn't really care about the woman.

"Are you attached to her," Crystal asked.

"It was just a sexual thing. She approached me in the teacher's lounge one day, telling me how lonely she was. I felt sorry for her. She said she wanted to have dinner with me. That dinner turned into a sexual encounter."

"Is it over?"

Crystal thought for sure he was getting ready to ask for a divorce.

"Yes, it is. I won't see her again."

"While we're telling secrets, I have a secret to tell you also." Crystal said.

"What's that?"

"I had an affair with a gentleman at work. He also asked me out to dinner, and it turned into a sexual encounter. We had sex several times, but it's over now."

"When you think about it it's no different than the sexual encounters we've had with other couples," Elliott said.

"I feel the same way," Crystal said.

"But at this point I feel that this activity we've been participating in has gone far enough. We need to find a new place, move away, and start all over."

"That's a good idea."

"Let's look for a new job and a new town. We've been thinking about raising some kids. Maybe you can stay at home and raise the kids for a while. I will put out a search for a new job. It'll be good to get away from Saginaw. We'll forget about our swinging life and start a new life. I'm tired of that life anyway. We simply had some feelings we needed to express. We won't let anyone know about our past."

"Yeah, that part of our lives is best kept a secret."

Within a month Elliott had found a job with an electric company in Southfield, Michigan, a suburb of Detroit that paid him three times as much as his teaching position. This would further allow Crystal to stay at home while he worked. They moved at the end of the teaching year.

They moved and bought an expensive home. They hoped to totally leave the past behind. Crystal became a stay-at-home mom for a while. She stayed at home and raised two boys and a girl until the children were older. At that point she went back to work. The past was completely behind them. Neither their parents nor anyone else beside Mel and Betty knew about their past lifestyle. They never went back to the old lifestyle or saw a need for a sexual encounter outside the marriage.

6

KEISHA'S MOM

I lived in a two-story house within the city limits of Bradford, Texas, a small town of 10,000 in West Texas. We had a family room, a living room, three baths, a dining room, four bedrooms, and a kitchen. We lived on a crowded street. My grandparents and their parents had lived in this same house at 4043 Hazel Street. I attended Bradford High: a small all-Black school. My parents and their grandparents had also attended this school. My uncle in Dallas purchased me a secondhand car for my eighteenth birthday during my senior year in 1966. He thought every teenager should have access to an automobile. It was a maroon 1961 Impala with shiny rims and black interior and seat covers. The car had a 327 engine that purred like a kitten, and a three-speed transmission on the floor. I was the youngest child in my family. I had two brothers, and two sisters, all had moved to larger cities in Texas. They figured better opportunities existed in larger cities. My father worked ten miles away for a munition's factory in Burkshire, and my mother worked for local well-to-do families in the area as a maid. Burkshire was a medium size town of approximately 100,000, 20 miles north of Bradford.

Both had worked at these jobs for the past twenty years. My father caught a ride to work with friends every morning, and those who my mother worked for were glad to pick her up. My parents didn't own a car, but both had a driver's license.

It was April of my senior year, and I had just started to date Keisha. She was a beautiful girl, but until then I hadn't had the self-confidence or self-esteem to approach her. Her parents owned a two-story mansion and drove a 1966 black Buick Electra 225. Her father was a supervisor in a plant in Burkshire. There was lots of competition. Keisha had nice hips, breast, legs, and a pretty face. She was also a fashion play: she always dressed in the latest styles. She had long-flowing-black hair and a swivel in her hips that drove me wild. She was five-six and 120 lbs. Her lips were luscious and tasted like peppermint candy. After I began to observe her, I knew I had to have her. People said a lot of negative things about her, but I didn't let any of it bother me.

The only problem was that she paid more attention to other guys at the school, as well as other guys from Burkshire. She would often be with some of these guys at various activities, and at the same time saying she was my girl.

She refused to give me any respect. I dated her from April through May and couldn't get to first base but continued to date her. Summer came, and I was still seeing her on Sundays. I would come to her house each

Sunday to court her. She still wouldn't go out on a date with me. It was like a bee having a pretty plastic flower before it that it couldn't possibly pollinate. My hormones were raging, and I wanted sex and attention. But I refused to give up on Keisha; I thought there was hope. She seemed to want every boy to be her own special pearl. I wanted to be the only one special in her life. Keisha met me at a restaurant on prom night but wouldn't go out with me on my graduation night. This was embarrassing to me. I figured a guy should be able to pick up his girl on prom night—especially. I put up with a lot just to be able to call Keisha my girl. The summer came, and we didn't break up. I promised her I would be going to college in the fall but would keep seeing her as often as I could.

I took a job for the summer at the Skyline Inn Motel, a small motel in Burkshire. I needed money in order to attend college and was willing to take any kind of job I could get. My parents had no funds to assist me in going to college, nor could my brothers and sisters help me. The only help I could possibly get would probably come from the uncle who purchased the car for me. You were lucky to find any kind of job in the area. I was fortunate enough to get a scholarship, but the scholarship wouldn't pay for the upkeep on my car, and I did want to take my car to school. It also wouldn't pay for miscellaneous items I would need to get along. So, I took a job as a maintenance man. I made $1.25 an hour. The pay was good considering the time and place. At that time, I wasn't going to do much better than minimum wage. My job specifically was to repair and unstop toilets, which kept me busy for most of the summer. On many occasions with my hand in dirty toilets, I started to walk away, but stayed there and toughened it out.

I didn't know Keisha's mother worked at that motel. Keisha had told me her mother worked at a motel in Burkshire, but I didn't know which one. There were several motels in Burkshire. When I saw her working at the motel, I was surprised. One day I walked into a room to fix the toilet and there she was. I had seen her at various school activities and my visits to see Keisha. Mrs. Steel was sophisticated and charming for someone her cohort. She was even prettier and slimmer than Keisha. She looked almost the spitting image of Keisha, except her skin was lighter than Keisha's. I was very familiar with her. She was always friendly and outgoing when I saw her. In fact, she was friendlier than Keisha.

"Hello Mrs. Steel, I didn't know you worked here."

Most folks in Newton took whatever kind of jobs they could get, usually at minimum wage.

"Yes, I've been working here at this motel for the past ten years," she probably was working at the same salary at which she started. That's the way they did it in those days.

"I'm working here for the summer. I'm going to college in the fall."

"Good, I'm glad to see you have plans for your life. Go to college; don't get stuck in one of these menial jobs. I'm trying to convince Keisha to do the same."

She smiled and came closer. Before I knew what was happening, she had her arms around my waist and was hugging me tight.

"Yeah, I have some plans," I said proudly, sticking out my chest.

"Keisha is a young girl and don't know what's going on in the world. She can't be the kind of woman you need. You need some hormone relief. She is too immature. I can tell by the way you carry yourself that you need a real woman."

"What do you mean?"

I wasn't sure what she was talking about. She had to be at least forty-five-years old. I thought she was much too old for a relationship with a teenager. Although, she had taken good care of her body, and looked younger than Keisha.

"A young boy your age and maturity has needs that a sophomore in high school doesn't know how to handle or understand. I can take care of those needs for you."

She had convinced me of this fact in only a few words.

"You could be right," I was surprised by her boldness and forwardness.

"I have to do some work until two o'clock. Meet me in room 132 at that time. That room is currently not being used because it needs some repairs. No one will likely disturb us. I'll show you what I mean by what a real woman can do. If you don't show up, I'll have my answer; if you do—all the better."

I kept thinking about her until almost two o'clock. What would Keisha think? I considered for a while. At two o'clock I made my way over to room 132. I pushed the door open and walked in, it was unlocked; I didn't want to embarrass myself by knocking.

"I see you made it," she said, "You must want some midday action as bad as I do. Lock the door and come on in, it's all here waiting for you."

I wanted any kind of action I could get, whether midday or any other time of day. I was somewhat nervous, but I locked the door, and came on in. She got undressed and got in bed. I hesitated for a moment.

"OK, baby."

"Come on baby, what're you waiting for?"

I knew I was out of my league with such an experienced woman. I came over, got undressed, and got in bed with her.

"Sorry about that. I momentarily forgot that we have limited time."

"You know we don't have that much time. We both have to get back to work soon."

I hadn't had much action, especially with an experienced woman. That is, what she referred to as an experienced woman. She pulled me on top of her in a hurry and guided my penis into her vagina. She acted desperate and began to moan and grown. My penis sank inside her like a bucket going down a well shaft. She immediately began to vibrate like a jackhammer while kissing and holding me. She kept it up until I reached my orgasm and she reached hers.

"Thank you," I said, not knowing what else to say.

"Keisha doesn't know how to take care of a man like I do. There's nothing like young beef; Keisha isn't mature enough to realize that."

We met in room 132 at two o'clock every day for the rest of the summer. Once we decided on the appointed time, we had very little to say to each other, we simply met and had sex. She taught me truly how to make love. I visited Keisha every Sunday. Her mother spoke to me and was very cordial; she was careful not to give her emotions away.

On one of our sexual forays, she said, "Don't you ever mention this to anyone—especially Keisha."

"Don't worry I won't."

"If anyone ever found out I would be in trouble."

"I won't. Don't' worry about it."

"Have you enjoyed the time we spent together this summer?"

"Yes, I have."

"On Sundays I keep hoping you are coming to see me rather than Keisha."

"You could consider me coming to see you."

"Keisha would hate me if she knew her mother was having sex with her boyfriend."

"I doubt it."

"Why don't you think so?"

"Most daughters wouldn't hate their mothers over something like that."

"What about my husband, do you think he would hate me?"

"Probably not."

"Why not?"

"It's all a matter of perspective. Some people don't consider an affair that serious."

"My husband always told me he would leave me if I had an affair."

"Some people say that but aren't serious about it. Lots of people have affairs these days."

"I can't afford to let this get back to my husband. He would either divorce or kill me. Be sure you keep it to yourself."

"I will."

She acted as if she knew it was just a summer fling, and I would be going to college in the fall. Once in college she knew I would meet other young girls.

On one of our forays in room 132 we ran into a boy and girl from Newton whom we knew well. They were coming out of an adjoining room. Mrs. Steel and I thought no more about it until Keisha confronted me. It turned out that Keisha and this girl were good friends, and she figured that something inappropriate was going on. Mrs. Steel had a kind of sordid reputation in the community and was known as a player. The friend told Keisha she should check into the situation. This brought home clearly the idea that somebody sees everything you do. Sometimes you may not be aware they are observing you, but nevertheless sees what you do. Keisha knew I was working at the same motel as her mother but didn't know we had any sustained contact. I went by her house on this particular Sunday.

"What were you and my mother doing coming out of the same room at the motel?'

"We had some work to do in the same room. I had to repair a toilet, and she had to clean the room. It just so happened that we were there at the same time."

"I just bet."

"Seriously, baby."

"My mother denies it also, but you'd better not lie to me about something like that."

"What do you think I am? I wouldn't do that, not with your mother. Your mother is a nice lady, and I respect her tremendously."

She leaned over and kissed me. From that point on I had no problems with Keisha. She started going out with me. When I parked and got in the back seat. She was all over me. She was even wilder than her mother in bed. Keisha felt that going to a motel was something she didn't feel comfortable doing. She would have sex in her living room rather than go to a motel. I cared for Keisha, and we had an excellent relationship from that point on. When I visited Keisha, her mother was still very friendly and courteous, but not showing any emotion.

I kept seeing Keisha's mother when I visited Keisha at her home until my junior year in college. Keisha's mom would often come into the room and say hello when I visited. On one occasion she came in and kissed me, but I quickly pulled away from her. Keisha almost caught us in an embrace. When Keisha and I went our separate ways, it ended my contact with Mrs. Steel. After I went to college Keisha and I eventually drifted apart. Keisha graduated high school and went to college for a while but dropped out of college and got married. I graduated college and went to law school. Something was driving me to contact her. Years later I called and got in touch with her. She had three children, had gotten a divorce, and was getting along fine in Dallas. She wanted me to visit her in Dallas, but I told her I had been happily married for the past three years.

7

A HARD LESSON

I came to Chicago in March of 2000; the month my job with AT&T transferred me from Houston. I was a telephone installer for AT&T. I was thirty-years old, and at the top of the installer's pay grade. I had been employed at this job since I was twenty-one-years old. The idea was to transfer a few of the more experienced installers to other areas. They gave me a 20% increase in salary as an incentive to get me to transfer. They had temporarily trained too many installers for the Houston area. I had never been to Chicago except the time I came to see if I liked the area, and if so to find an apartment. On my visit my wife and I both liked the area and thought it would be a good change. My wife and I were both tired of Houston anyway. She found a job as a nurse within a short period of time in a suburban hospital and was happy with her work.

My son was eight-years old. My son stayed behind with his grandmother in order to finish the 3rd grade in Houston. We thought it would be too disrupting to pull him out of school so close to the end of the year. We soon became adjusted to living in the area. We found a two-bedroom apartment in a Suburb of Chicago called

Matteson, Illinois, and both our jobs were nearby in the south suburbs. It was a nice little community that we enjoyed very much. My son made friends quickly.

My wife and I didn't have a lot of friends at the time, so we took to traveling back to Houston to see our parents whenever we could in order to compensate. We made five trips to Houston within the first two months of being in Chicago. We went to Las Vegas in May. I had never gambled before, except to shoot a few dice and play cards privately for small time change in high school. We went for the entertainment but ended up doing some gambling. My wife and son took a few scenic tours, and my wife and I saw a few shows. On my first trip I won $5,000.00 on a Triple-Cash machine. I won enough to pay all our expenses. My wife was very pleased at my winnings. She won a few dollars and lost a few dollars but never won anything significant.

We went back to Las Vegas in June; it was so enjoyable the first time. This time I won $10,000.00 at the Blackjack table. It must have been beginner's luck, because it was my first-time playing Blackjack at a casino. I paid our expenses and bought a couch, loveseat, and chair for our apartment; and had cash left over. Again, my wife was overjoyed. She didn't have any luck this time either. My wife felt she was unlucky at gambling. I told her the powers up above wanted her to earn her money the old-fashion way.

I hadn't been to the casinos locally before but started going locally. I had been in Chicago a few months, but didn't know the casinos in the area existed. Sometimes I would win, and sometimes I would lose. My wife cautioned me that I was developing a habit, but I didn't pay her any attention. I would go to the casino if I had as little as $5.00 in my pocket, hoping to hit a jackpot. Sometimes I would go to the casino with only a dollar in my pocket. I would sometimes go to the casino without a dime and watch other people play. My wife told me I was wasting time and gas. She got to the point where she would no longer give me money to play with. The only problem was, no matter how much I won, I would play it all back. I would say to myself, when I win a certain amount I'm going to quit. When I won, it seems like I couldn't stop. I would say when I win enough to pay a bill, I'm going to stop, but I wouldn't stop—nothing worked in getting me to stop. I would even have it all planed before I got there, how I was going to quit after I won a certain amount, but be unable to do so. It seems that when I won, I momentarily forgot about the bills I needed to pay and kept playing.

I became upset when I couldn't get enough money to go to the casino. At times I was nervous, agitated, and disagreeable when I couldn't get money to play. I knew I needed help when I would borrow money from a neighbor or anybody I could to get enough money to play at the casino. Sometimes I would even go into my son's piggy bank to get money to play.

My wife suggested that I get some help from Gamblers Anonymous. But I decided to seek help from a private source. I never did like that public atmosphere, but I realized that I needed help. I looked in the Yellow Pages and located a psychologist that specialized in treating gambling addictions. I called and made an appointment. I went to see him on August 18, 2000 at six o'clock p.m. I should have researched to find out what his business reputation was. I walked in and told the secretary that I was Mr. Johnson and had an appointment at six o'clock. He had a cozy little professional office.

"He'll be with you in a moment."

"OK."

"Do you have insurance?"

"Yes."

"Could I see your card? And fill out this form."

She gave me the form, and I gave her my insurance card. She took the information and gave the card back to me.

The doctor came out and ushered me into his office. He was six feet, muscular, slim, dark skinned, and rather handsome. He had on a dark-brown European cut suit, gold watch with diamonds on its face, brown alligator shoes, beige and light-brown-stripped tie, and a classy diamond ring.

"What's your name?"

"Joey Johnson."

"Henry Lewis is my name. Where did you get my number?"

"I found your number in the Yellow Pages."

He had been practicing in the Chicago area for five years.

"What's the problem young man?"

"I think I have a problem with gambling."

"What makes you think you have a problem with gambling?"

"Because I sometimes go to the casino with only a dollar, just enough gas to get to the casino and back, hoping to win a jackpot. I get nervous and agitated when I can't find the money to play. When I win, I can never walk away, I always keep playing until I lose it all. I'm not satisfied unless I walk out with empty pockets. It does no good to win if you are going to keep playing until you lose it all, even I realize that. That kind of behavior is contradictory and makes no sense. I must have some kind of problem."

"Do you take things out of the house to sell them in order to get money to play?"

"No, I've never done that."

"Do you steal from anyone to get money to play?"

"No, I don't, except for taking a few quarters from my son's piggy bank."

"You have a problem, but it may not be as severe as you think."

"We can meet once a week and talk about it. It doesn't mean that you must give up gambling completely, just get it under reasonable control. The key is control."

"That sounds good."

It was exactly what I wanted to hear.

"What do you do for recreation?"

"I don't have any beside the casino; otherwise I go to work and come home."

"Sounds like you just using it for recreation."

"That may be the situation."

"We have a casino in Indianapolis where everybody wins. I live in Indianapolis with my wife, mother-in-law, and son. Why don't you come down with me one weekend? I can teach you how to recognize your limits: when to hold'em and when to fold'em—so to speak. I can teach you more on the floor of the casino than I can in my office."

"Let's plan on that for next weekend after the coming weekend."

"That sounds good."

I was anxious to get out of town and try a new casino. I was glad to hear that you had a good chance to win in this casino. Although I should have known better, this proposition sounded reasonable. To an addicted gambler anything that mentions the word casino sounds reasonable. I should have been able to quickly put two and two together. I didn't give my wife any of the details, only that I was going to Indianapolis with a friend.

"Pack a bag of items that will sustain you for the weekend. The casino atmosphere is very casual. I'll pick you up at five o'clock on Friday after next."

"I'll do that."

I gave him my address and telephone number.

The weekend of August 26 we got on the road for Indianapolis about five o'clock on Friday. We had a short conversation.

"My folks prefer to live in Indianapolis, but I prefer the business in the Chicago area."

"I would think business would be better in the Chicago area."

I didn't know he had ruined his reputation in the Indianapolis area, and had no choice but to move on to a different city. His wife didn't want to move. She said he was going to ruin his reputation wherever he went.

"You'll like my wife, and my mother-in-law's bark is worst than her bite."

"That's usually the case."

"You never said where you were from."

"Houston, Texas. I just moved here in March. AT&T transferred me to the area. I am a telephone installer."

"That's a good profession. I bet you make more money than I do."

I didn't know at the time that no matter how much he made it wouldn't be nearly enough.

"They gave me a 20% increase as an incentive to transfer to Chicago."

I thought that was a lot, but after you considered the cost of living it wasn't that much.

We pulled up finally to a big mansion about ten miles outside Indianapolis. A Mercedes and a Jaguar was parked along a brick-lined driveway, even though it had a four-car garage. The house had huge round pillars. We were riding in a new top-of-the-line Lexus.

The house had plenty of expensive furniture and expensive paintings. Later I saw the pool in back. It was obvious he was living beyond his means. His wife came out and kissed him. His mother–in-law stayed in her room. The fourteen-year old son was at football practice.

"Who is this with you?"

"This is Mr. Johnson. I'm going to teach him something about casino gambling," Henry said.

I don't think he felt comfortable openly describing me as a patient.

"I hope you're going to teach him something besides getting in debt," his wife said.

She knew he had been losing all of his money.

"On the contrary, I'm going to teach him how to be skillful."

I wanted to give it up, not become skillful, but I didn't say anything at the moment. I was anxious to get started, being addicted as I was, I couldn't wait to get to the casino.

"When're we going out to the casino?"

"It's right around the corner, we can go out tonight."

His wife knew he was in debt up to his eyeballs from gambling but didn't say anything. It turns out that his home was in foreclosure. The note on his cars hadn't been paid in several months. They were living from moment to moment and didn't know what their next move would be. It was all from his casino gambling.

We went out that night for a while. I thought we were going to play together so he could teach me, but he went his own separate way. I did win $5,000.00 on a Double-Diamond dollar machine, and he lost $50,000.00 at a Blackjack table. I kept all of what I won and bought it out with me. He acted as if he didn't want to leave, hesitating at the door for a while as if he wanted to go back, then walking on out.

"How did you do?" Henry asked.

"I came out ahead by $5,000.00."

"I lost $50,000.00," Henry said, "but wow! You did well."

I had never played for such high stakes and was surprised to hear him say he lost that much. It was at this point that I figured out he had a gambling problem himself. He only wanted me to come along so that he would have a partner in crime. He didn't say anything to his wife the next day. We had breakfast, and he was anxious to get back to the casino. I thought I would play a grand in the slot machines and still leave with $4,000.00. We left for the casino again Saturday at noon. Before we left the casino, Henry told me he lost another $25,000.00 at the Blackjack table. He didn't say a word on the way back from the casino. He didn't even ask how much I won. I actually won $4,000.00 on a Red, White, and Blue dollar machine.

I went to my room. At six o'clock his wife called me for dinner. I came to the table; and his mother-in-law, wife, and son were sitting at the table. We were having a normal dinner of meatloaf, string beans, yams, cornbread, apple pie and lemonade. Henry was late getting to the table. I had no idea how much distress the family was in. They were on their last leg about to break down. But the family seemed so normal to the last minute. Finally, Henry came in brandishing a .9-millimeter. I thought it was a joke. But he knew what he was doing, and it was no joke. He shot his mother-in-law, his wife, his son, and then shot me. When the bullets started flying, we were too paralyzed with fear to intervene. The bullets hit each of them in the heart. The bullet missed my heart by one inch. He was in the military and was an expert marksman with a .9-millimeter. In addition, he took regular target practice at a local range. After he shot everyone, he put the gun to his own head and pulled the trigger. The rest of them were dead on arrival at the hospital. I was the only one to survive. It took me two weeks to recover. I was lucky.

I was unfortunate enough to choose a psychologist for a gambling addiction that had some out-of-control problems with gambling himself. I learned a hard lesson that day. The shock was enough to get me to give up on gambling. I finally realized that gambling was not the way to prosperity. I haven't been to a casino since that hot day on August 26, 2000.

8

MY SHIP CAME IN

I was born and raised in a small-rural town in East Texas. Before I started school in the first grade, we had no electricity, gas, telephone, or indoor plumbing. There were ten children in the family. If we hadn't raised our own food, we wouldn't have had enough to eat. We existed in a rusty-tin-roof-shotgun shack in what is known as the ARK-LA-TEX: an area bordered by Arkansas, Louisiana, and Texas. We had no road, only a three-mile trail, before first grade. The main road was a curvaceous, hill-ridden, two-lane-blacktopped highway. My first year of school, I had to walk to and from the bus stop at the end of that red-dirt road: it was muddy in winter and dusty in summer.

We got electricity when they built the road, butane when I was a freshman in high school, a telephone and indoor plumbing when I was in college. Even after the road was built it was only a red-dirt road until they finally blacktopped it. But due to failure on the part of the county to maintain it, soon the blacktop wore off. My parents had little education and placed no emphasis on getting an education. The nearest small town was twenty miles away in either direction. Most of my time was spent plowing a mule and other duties on the farm. I had no time for a lot of childhood play. My mother believed *an idle mind is the devil's workshop.*

It was clear in elementary school that I needed speech therapy. Though, my teachers never mentioned it to me. My parents couldn't afford such a thing, nor did they probably know what it was. As far as I know there were no speech therapists within driving distance, and we had no car in my early years to get to one. The school did not provide a speech pathologist, and we were lucky just to get the basic resources. Most people, including my own relatives, avoided communication with me for this reason. It was hard to communicate with me. The majority of people simply snickered about me. Some people would ask my parents questions rather than talk directly to me.

English wasn't heavily emphasized in school. We spent very little time on English in elementary, junior high, or high school. Teachers didn't put emphasis on or encourage us to read: I read one book in addition to my textbooks during my twelve years of schooling and only because we got a new English teacher in twelfth grade. This one and only book was read in twelfth grade. I didn't know enough to pick up a book on my own and read it. There were no libraries or bookstores in towns nearby that we could patronize. I was so tired after my chores that reading would have been almost impossible anyway.

My father once said in reference to getting an education, "Do something with your hands."

"What do you mean?"

"Some people aren't meant to work with their minds."

"I think I can work with my mind."

I figured I was just as intelligent as anyone else.

"Go ahead, if you want to butt your head against the wall."

"I don't like hard work. Working with your hands involves difficult manual labor."

"You can do what you want, but some day you'll find out I was right"

"I can handle it. I have other plans than being a farm boy."

He should have known I was going to do the opposite of what he said. I had passed the point where I seriously listened to my parents. My father was trying to mold me, so he would have a steady-work hand on the farm. I wanted no parts of the farm life. I was tired of digging and plowing in the dirt and feeding the animals. Besides, what did labor on the farm get him? I didn't realize at the time that my education had been vastly neglected. I never discussed with my parents that I had intentions of going to college. I knew they couldn't afford to help me anyway, and probably wouldn't understand my ambition. No matter how innately intelligent I was, my education had been neglected by parents, teachers, and myself. It was my fault I didn't read more in my spare time—no one else's but mine.

I had a close friend that I talked to all the time. We did lots of running around the streets together. I figured if anybody could give me some good advice he could. I met him headed toward the parking lot on a warm spring day.

"Hey Joey," I said.

"What's up Craig?"

"I want to attend college, but feel like I might be wasting my time."

"Some people shouldn't go to college. College is not for everyone."

"I believe I can do it. It might be hard but doable."

"If your parents didn't get an education, and didn't emphasize education, you might not have the background for it."

"What do my parents have to do with it?"

"Do you feel that you applied yourself in high school?"

I didn't understand the true nature of his question.

"I think so."

"Some people didn't apply themselves and are likely to be unsuccessful in college."

I still didn't understand that your background has everything to do with your success in college.

"I have only two options, the military or college, and I prefer college. They say it's going to be hard to get a job in a few years without a college education."

"Do what you feel is right. No one can estimate correctly your motivation."

"That's the way I feel."

"Go to college if you feel that is what you were meant to do. You might be able to make it even if you started out behind the eight ball."

I figured, what did my friend know? I knew he was headed to Dallas—bright lights—big city. He was a fairly intelligent guy, but I knew he had no plans for college. I proceeded to make out applications for college. No one was going to deter me from my ambition. None of my relatives knew about the plans I was making for college. If they had known about my plans, they might have given me more resistance. They would probably have told me it would be best to simply get a job of some kind. I got no help from any of my relatives while in college. This is exactly what I expected. My father did purchase me a secondhand car.

I went to college in East Texas. I avoided English and speech in college. I should have studied English and speech, but knew my background in these subjects were inadequate. I didn't want to get in any situation where I might be seriously challenged. I didn't want my weaknesses to be that apparent. My background was so inadequate in English and speech that I thought I couldn't compete with other students at that level. I couldn't have been more wrong. I made it through college but with these inadequacies hanging over my head. Although, I was able to get through, I should have majored in speech and English, confronted my inadequacies, and put forth my best effort. I found that I was unprepared to major in what I wanted to pursue, so I majored in sociology and made the best of it.

After college I joined the Navy. In the Navy I spent time in Chicago, Boston, and Orlando. When I got out of the Navy, I attended two different graduate schools, and received two separate degrees. My English and speech were atrocious, but I stumbled on through two graduate schools. Students, professors, and secretaries thought I was in over my head, but I kept trying. I wasn't a model student but did my best.

In graduate school one of my teachers asked, "Have you ever considered taking courses in writing and speech?"

"Yes, but I never followed through."

"Maybe you should consider it."

"I will. Thank you."

"It could help you in your long-term career objectives."

The way the school was structured there was not much time for taking additional course work. In addition, I was bold and didn't think too much about what the professors said. My feelings were that they were just trying to sidetrack me in some way. I figured I could make it without that. So, I didn't waste my time with taking extra courses in English or speech. But some students did snicker when I made a presentation. I was extremely aware of my weaknesses; they had been made aware to me all my life. I simply wanted to get my degree and get on with my life.

I got a job offer after graduate school and moved to a Chicago suburb in 1974. Somewhat naïve, it seemed to me that opportunities in Chicago were better because they paid more, I didn't consider the cost of living was greater in Chicago. My wife didn't want to move. She wanted to stay near family and friends. Her mother was instrumental in getting her to follow me to Chicago. Although, she had other ideas about leaving Houston to the last minute. But I wasn't close to family and had few friends. So, we packed and headed for Chicago.

After a few years I enrolled in a Ph.D. program. I wasn't as successful at completing this Ph.D. program as I had previously been in completing other schools. However, I was a very ambitious young man. My inadequacies were beginning to show. I also still had a severe stuttering problem. Since the landscape had changed considerably, I should have invested in speech therapy, but was determined that I could get along without it. I was still weak at both oral and written communication. Again students, secretaries, and professors laughed at me. They laughed at my speech and writing ability. It was obvious they considered my abilities substandard. But I kept trying until I realized it was useless.

I could write and speak well enough to manage, but it still left something to be desired in my work and employment situation. I didn't get a lot of criticism because most of the employees at work weren't any better than I was at writing. They didn't discuss my speech or my writing to my face, but I'm sure they had a lot to say about it in private. Most of them could verbalize at a high level, and that gave them a decided advantage. Most people can verbalize adequately, unless there is some specific defect, but picking up writing skills are a bit more difficult.

I lived in a Chicago suburb until 1991, without doing any serious writing, but began to do a lot of reading. It became clear to me that if I was going to make any progress in my life, I would need to improve in my writing skills. I never gave much thought to my speech. In 1991 I began taking correspondence courses in writing. I took several courses; in the meantime, I read all I could. I had started writing any number of books, but had always reached an impasse and given up on them. I would think I had a good idea, but it turned out to be not such a good idea. I didn't have that killer instinct for writing books. That is being able to get started and to carry them to an end. In 1991 I began to write more consistently and seriously. Before I knew it, I had written several books.

I wrote several books, and the process got easier and easier. I found that all you had to do was write one word, one sentence, one paragraph, one page, and one chapter at a time to get a book written. I kept writing until I had self-published twenty-one books. In my books, I knew I had made a few mechanical errors, but was working on correcting them.

I tried the traditional approach to publishing, but was unable to get anything published, and kept getting rejection letters. I then tried the self-publishing route. When you self-publish a book, if you don't know how to market and distribute it, the going can be rough. My wife told me on many occasions that I was wasting my time, and that I would be better off looking for a job, but I kept writing.

I kept hoping that I would get a call from a publisher any day saying they wanted to publish my books. As long as I publish them myself, they were considered self-published. I wanted wider distribution and marketing for my books. My knowledge of marketing and distribution was negligible. If not publication for all of them, at least one or several of them, just to get my books known to the public. It's hard to get a self-published book into the market place. I was patient, months went by, and I hadn't heard from a publisher.

It was March 15, 2012, a cool-auspicious morning. I was still waiting on some publisher to make me an offer to publish one or several of my books. Finally, one day a neighbor brought me a letter that had been inadvertently left in his box. This was not unusual. Apparently, the publisher didn't have my correct address or simply made a mistake. The publisher put 3802 rather than 3804. The neighbor brought the letter to me.

I opened the door, "Good morning sir."

"The mailman left your letter in my mailbox. It had the wrong address on it," he said.

"Thank you," I said.

The neighbor didn't think anything of the letter. He handed the letter to me and left. It was apparent it was from a publisher, but I didn't think it was a check. I never expected to find what I did in the letter, but it was what I had been waiting for the past year. I opened the letter. The letter read as follows:

> Dear Mr. Matthews:
>
> My company would like to purchase the rights to edit and redo all twenty-one of your books in order to market and distribute them.
>
> Enclosed you will find a check for $200,000.00. If you sign and return the enclosed contract you may keep the check to do with as you please.
>
> If this contract does not meet your approval you may return the contract and the check.
>
> Thank you for considering us.
>
> Yours respectfully,
>
> John Hornstein, Vice President
> Whitehouse Publishing Company

The contract was straightforward. I signed the contract and placed it in the mailbox the following day.

I had to give up all rights to the books except my name would remain on them, and I would receive 10% of all royalties from the sales. I was willing to take a chance on the arrangement.

My wife made a down payment on a new house, replaced our old car with a new one, and promised to help my son to further his education. Life was much better for us. I immediately began writing on my next book.

9

THE BET

I'd broken up with Helen that day and was trying to locate her. Some guys were strolling girls to their buses. Some of them were kissing and holding hands. I couldn't get Helen out of my mind.

It was Friday, October 23, 1964, at 3:30 in the afternoon. I was a junior in high school at the time. The temperature was about sixty degrees. Autumn leaves had turned brown and were beginning to fall. This day was cloudy and overcast, but normal for this time of the year. As usual, the foul odor of paper being manufactured from the mill nearby was in the air. We had experienced the usual rush of traffic that occurs with the final bell of the day. Kids dashed like antelopes being pursued by a lion.

The school was a combined elementary, junior, and senior high. It sat about a mile west of town. There were approximately five-hundred students in the school. As you approached the school there was six-single-story classrooms lined up in a row. Behind this row of classrooms there were eight more single-level classrooms lined up in a row. On the other side of the building there was a small home-economics building. To the right of the home-economics building was a shop building. We also had an auditorium, a gymnasium, and a field house for football. In addition, there were a baseball and a football field. There was grass in the back of the school, but the front was completely blacktopped.

Every turn I made I could see Helen scurry through my mind. I could feel her warm-sweet lips on mine while groping her curvaceous body. Her Evening in Paris seemed to be in the air. I could visualize her smooth skin, pretty face, and almost taste her hot-candy breath. At night I ruminated about her constantly.

Helen was what the boys in the community and at school referred to as a "Yellow Hammer"; because her skin was so light. Helen had it all, light-smooth skin, big hips, a pretty face, nice legs, a body that wouldn't quit, and long-flowing-black hair. I wanted her badly.

My cousin Steve lived four miles from me. He met me coming out of the school building, "Hey, bro."

"How's it going, Steve?"

Steve was light skinned with an Ivy-League haircut. He wore horned-rim glasses, was rather handsome, and intelligent. Steve was six-feet-four and weighed two-twenty—all muscle. I never understood why Steve didn't play football. He probably was more inclined toward academics, because his parents didn't encourage athletic prowess.

"I missed my bus. Can I ride home with you?"

Last year my brother had given me his 1959 Chevrolet Impala, Coupe for my birthday. It was Black with red and white interior and bubble-plastic covers for the seats. It had some shiny moon hubcaps that you could see your picture in and ran like a well-oiled machine. I liked driving to school rather than riding the bus. It gave me a feeling of independence and autonomy.

"Sure." I patted him on the back. "If you had to walk it would be a long one."

Steve was my cousin. My father was his uncle. We were a close family.

"Are you going to the game tonight, bro?"

"Yes, I think so."

"Do you have to go home first?"

"No, Dad isn't working today, and he usually takes care of the chores on his day off."

I had a lot of chores to do every day when I got home: feed the animals, gather wood for the fireplace, sometimes plow during growing season, bring up the cows for milking, and fix anything that needed fixing. Steve knew I lived a difficult life compared to him. He would sometimes ask me how I did it. I often wondered why Steve's father had a much more prosperous style of life than my father. I understood part of the picture. His father had more education and earned a higher income. My father was only a laborer while his father was a professional; he taught school during the week and preached on Sundays. Still I couldn't understand how two brothers could grow up in the same household and have such different outlooks on life.

"At least you get some relief."

"Let's get something to eat at the Dairy Queen, and get a beer before the game tonight," I said.

"That sounds good."

"The Dairy Queen has some good food."

We went to the Dairy Queen in Hallsville and we both had a cheeseburger and a root-beer float.

"How're you and Helen doing, bro?"

"We broke up."

"What happened?"

Helen was in Steve's class and a close friend of his. He told me once he liked Helen, but they were opposite in personality types. He also said that her being in his class put her too close to him, and that made him know more about her than he wanted to know. Sometimes he saw her react in ways he didn't like.

"She doesn't want to give me any."

"I hear lots of people are getting it, why won't she give you any," he rolled his eyes.

I had seen Helen react to other guys and heard too many stories about her. She wasn't a saint by anybody's imagination. I just couldn't figure out why she wouldn't be nice to me. My concern was that there was something wrong with me, and she didn't want to hurt my feelings by telling me. On many occasions I'd caught her in compromising situations, yet she denied anything but being pure and sanctified. I've also heard some wild stories about her and several guys from Longview. She swears they were her cousins, but I caught her kissing one of them in the school's parking lot.

"I guess she just doesn't love me enough. Are you still seeing Amy?" I asked, wanting to change the conversation.

"Yes."

"How're things going with you guys?"

"Things are working like a charm with us, bro."

"Is she giving you any?"

"All I can handle."

"Great."

"I wish it had worked out with Helen and me," I said.

"I know you really liked her, bro."

"Yes, I did."

"Do you think there's any hope left, or are you quitting for good this time? This is about the tenth time you guys have broken up and made up," he said, smiling.

"It's all over now."

"Let's go get the beer," he said.

I had developed a habit of having a few beers as a way of dealing with what I saw as problems at the time.

Hallsville was a "dry" town. We had to go to Longview to get beer. It was a ten-mile drive to get the beer.

We arrived at the liquor store on the outskirts of Longview. I always went in to get the beer since I looked older than Steve. "What kind of beer do you want?" I asked.

"Get me a quart of Budweiser and whatever you want for yourself. Here's five dollars."

We got the beer without any problems and headed back to the game. I never had any problems buying liquor. When they saw how tall I was and sporting a full beard, they always gave me whatever I wanted. Sometimes seniors would take me along to buy the beer. We opened our beers and started to drink. It didn't take long for the beer to saturate our brains. We gulped down the beer and drove along with our minds on the game. We sucked on some breath mints and used air freshener in the car, so we wouldn't be so obvious. We didn't expect to get stopped by the Highway Patrol. All of a sudden, we heard a siren and saw a red light flashing behind us. We pulled over.

"Let me see your driver's license," the state policeman said, holding out his hand.

"Yes, sir," I handed my license to him.

I thought for sure he would get us for drinking, but since we had disposed of the bottles, he couldn't say we were drinking for sure. He took the driver's license and went back to his car. In a few minutes he came back.

"I'm gonna' give you a warning ticket. Your taillight is out," handing me the ticket.

"I didn't know, sir," I said, taking the ticket.

"Get it fixed as soon as you can."

"OK." I nodded.

"You boys take care of yourselves."

"Yes sir, we will."

We definitely thought we were goners and were glad to get away with a warning ticket. I guess he completely overlooked the smell of the Budweiser. Although we sucked on mint lifesavers and sprayed the car with air freshener, there was still a slight odor of beer in the car. We slowed down to avoid getting stopped again and eased on toward the school.

We both had gotten high from those two quarts of beer. I could feel my reaction time getting slower as I placed my foot on the brakes. As I jammed my foot on the brakes I felt as if I'd flow through the dashboard. We were both feeling good just as we wanted to.

We pulled into the parking lot and danced up the hill to the game. We were walking on air. Even though we had only drunk a quart each we felt self-conscious and wondered if anyone could tell we'd been drinking. The fresh October night air was cool and invigorating. We went to the game and our team was winning by ten points. The school had a good team that year. It was depressing because Helen was parading her new boyfriend around in the stands.

Steve and I were seated at the game, coming down from our highs, and not saying much. A guy who lived not far from us named Samuel, but had gone to a different school, and dropped out about a year before, came over to where Steve and I were sitting.

"Hello, fellows," Samuel said. He had a rough and tough appearance. He was dark skinned with kinky hair, sported a goatee and had keloids on his arms and neck. He walked as if he owned the world: big, bold, and Black. This guy was six-feet-five and weighed two-hundred-forty pounds. He was three years behind in school when he dropped out. He had gone to a school twenty-miles south, because he lived in another school district.

"How's it going, Samuel?" Steve and I chorused.

"It's great, fellows," Samuel said, looking and acting as if he had something crafty on his mind.

I didn't know him well but could tell by the smirk on his face that he didn't care for me. "Sure is, we're winning," I said.

"Would anyone care to put a wager on the game?" Samuel asked, reaching for his wallet.

"Sure." Feeling that I couldn't let people think I didn't support my team, and have school spirit, besides I still had a little buzz on.

"I bet a five that Hallsville lose by five points," Samuel said, taking out his money and holding it in his hand.

"OK, you got a bet," I said.

We were still winning by ten points in the beginning of the fourth quarter. After he saw there was no way for Hallsville to lose, he said, "I'm changing my mind.

I don't want to bet any more." He placed the money in his shirt pocket.

"You owe me five dollars," I said.

"See me after the game," Samuel said, taking the money from his shirt pocket and putting it back in his wallet.

By this time our highs had completely worn off. Steve and I went to the dance but stood around like wallflowers. Steve's girlfriend had been ill all that week. I was mostly watching Helen and her date while they were affectionately holding each other close. She was being coy, acting as if she didn't notice me. This made me even more upset. Usually I enjoyed dancing and being at dances.

I said to her, "Hello, Helen."

"Bye, Cool." She turned away from me.

"What's wrong?" I asked, "I was just trying to be friendly."

If I couldn't have Helen, I didn't want anyone.

"You know what's wrong," she said, "I've told you what time it is."

A song by Jerry Butler started to play, "I Stand Accused." It brought up feelings of loving and good times I had with Helen. It made me want to cry.

"Can I have this dance?"

"You're spoiling my fun," she said, "goodnight, Cool."

"If you insist," I felt like I wanted to regurgitate when she turned me down.

"I do."

I walked back to where Steve was standing and motioned to him that it was time to go. I was still feeling dizzy.

"You ready, bro?" Steve asked.

"Yeah, I can't get anywhere with Helen."

After the game and the dance, Steve and I were standing out front of the school building watching the cars leave.

Samuel came over to where we were standing. "You want your money, punk?" He took a defensive stance.

"Yes, punk," I said.

He threw up his fist. "Come and get it."

"I will if you don't pay me."

I had seen too much violence and would do almost anything to avoid a fight. Samuel advanced toward me. Steve got between us. Samuel simply wanted to make trouble. He was known for his fighting, stealing, and getting in other kinds of trouble.

"Never in a million years." His eyes turned red, and he stood erect with his fist in greater position to do battle.

"I'll get my money over your dead body," I said, shaking my fist in his face.

"That's the way it'll have to be," he stated.

"If you have a beef with Charles you have a beef with me. Unless you're prepared to fight us both you had better get out of hear," Steve said.

Samuel got in his car and burned rubber getting out of there. It was a classic 1955 Bel-Aire Chevrolet. His rims were shinning, and his fresh, midnight-blue paint job blended in with the night. He yelled out his window, "Another place another time." He burned rubber so hard that the tires and gravel smelled like metal scratching against metal.

"Thanks, Steve."

"No problem, bro. I was going to show him who's a punk."

"Let's go," I said.

Practically all the cars had vacated the parking lot. We left and headed home.

I let Steve off at home. My house was further down the road. After I let him out and was driving home, a car passed by me, I could see it was Samuel. It was that midnight-blue 1955 Chevrolet Bel-Aire. He stopped on the side of the road and waited until I passed him. He was playing a cat and mouse game. Samuel quickly got behind me and followed me until I got almost home; driving a few car lengths behind me while blowing his horn. When I sped up, he would increase his speed, and if I slowed, he would slow down. I could hear Samuel laughing and yelling as he mashed his accelerator. His pipes were loud, and you could hear the motor gunning. The bright lights blinded me from behind. I kept going until I got closer to home. I was scared. Meanwhile the car got closer and closer. He was so close that if I had suddenly hit my brakes there was no way an accident could've been prevented. Finally, when I got closer to home, he turned off and went another direction.

I never saw Samuel again after that night. I heard he got married, and later spent some time in prison for murder. It was a one-of-a-kind experience during my lifetime. As far as Helen was concerned, I went on to find other love interest, it was only puppy love.

10

WHAT KIND OF FOOL?

It was a Friday night. I had the habit of going to the little café in Johnsonville on Friday nights. I was feeling down about a girl named Dora, felt like I needed to be around some other people, and clear my head. Johnsonville only had a café, bank, Dairy Queen, post office, several general stores, and several gas stations. Johnsonville was ten miles north of where we lived in the country, approximately 5,000, the place where we went to a small segregated school. Crimson was a city of 100,000, approximately ten miles north of Johnsonville. Most of the buildings in Johnsonville were unpainted and single story. There were several other people there in the café, the usual crowd. We were sitting around doing nothing but talking. Two people were playing Blackjack. I decided to play one of my favorite tunes on the juke box. The song was, "What Kind of Fool?" by Major Lance, a popular hit tune in those days. The others in the café were all boys from the local Black high school, except several of the waitresses were taking a break. The boys from my school knew I was brooding and sulking over Dora, the love of my life. When I played the song, one of my classmates mumbled under his breath, "A big one." Everyone knew I was in love with Dora, and how stupid I was being for her.

The portion of the café reserved for Blacks was a little unpainted room added on as an afterthought on the side. It consisted of broken-down furniture discarded from the main café. They placed it in that section only after the main part of the café couldn't use it any more. Everything was mildewed. When I thought about the situation it increased my sadness and depression. But I kept thinking about my classmate indicating I was a "big fool" for Dora. I sat there for a while and thought about Dora and what she meant to me. Nothing he could have said would have turned me away from Dora. I had to make up my own mind that she was no good for me. I thought back to the events that occurred during the past week with her. I kept thinking how love could really hurt if you weren't careful. Especially when the person didn't care for you like you cared for him or her. As they say, "It's not good loving somebody when they don't love you back." Also, if the person feels he or she can make a fool of you, the person will frequently try. It's in some people's nature not to be satisfied with one person. No matter what the other person does the individual is going to reach out to someone else to fill what the person perceives as an empty void in their lives. I kept thinking about the events that occurred during the past week.

It was a warm-sunshiny Friday in rural East Texas 1964 in April. In fact, it was hot—who am I kidding.

All I knew was hot Texas weather. I didn't know the difference between hot East Texas weather and any other kind of weather. I hadn't been anywhere except Ft. Worth, the Gulf Coast, and Shreveport, Louisiana. I hadn't been around enough to know much about how to relate to the real world, or to people in general for that matter. Even for a rural area we were especially isolated. I didn't have well developed interpersonal skills.

I waited at the front entrance to the school for Dora. I was waiting for her in order to walk her to her bus. I walked her to her bus everyday, sat with her during school events, and visited with her sometimes on Sunday evenings. Sometimes I met her at county fairs, sporting events, and special events in and around Crimson.

When she came out of the building I said, "Hello Dora, how was your day?"

"Fine," she said, "It was a good day. We're taking achievement test on Monday."

"That should be a lot of fun."

"Not for me."

"Do your best."

"I almost forgot, Steve, I'm having a party for my fourteenth birthday. I would be pleased if you could make it."

"How could I not make my best girl's fourteenth birthday party? I'll be sure and make it."

Ever since I saw Dora coming out of the elementary school building, when she was in sixth grade, and I was in eighth grade, I had been in love with her. I spent a lot of time wandering around the school, not doing anything constructive in those days. She had a step like a prized show pony, and was built like a Clydesdale, except more well proportioned. She was just developing, and her breast stood at attention. She had pretty, smooth legs, and her face was cute. She was about five-three with caramel skin.

"Be sure you don't forget."

"OK, I won't forget."

I walked her to her bus and got on my way. She seemed so anxious to have me come to the party that later I wandered if she didn't have her little scene planned for me.

Occasionally I couldn't walk her to the bus, because someone else would be walking her. All I could do was put my head down and walk away. It was a special privilege for a guy to walk his girl to her bus. Sometimes I would go to an activity in Crimson, expecting to be with her, and one of her friends would have her occupied. There was a sense of constantly having to compete with all her other friends. I never got a sense of having priority over her time; that she was available to me only. I got the feeling that anyone could replace me, and I was expendable; that I occupied no special place in her heart. Henry, her cousin, said she was too young and immature to understand what was involved in adult more mature relationships; that I was trying to get blood from a turnip. She was still special to me, and I didn't think I could give her up. Dora was like a drug to me, she kept me feeling stable.

That Saturday morning, I picked up her a gift and started getting ready for the party about three o'clock p.m., the party started at six o'clock p.m. I was in the tenth grade, was sixteen, and had a driver's license. I could drive the car practically anywhere I wanted to go. I was the only child at home, and my mother and father had never learned how to drive a vehicle. Dora was in eighth grade and couldn't even officially date as far as I knew. We had a truck that my father had purchased to use for work on the farm, and a car that my brother had given me. The truck was a 1958 green Chevrolet; and the car was a 1959 black Chevrolet Impala, Coupe. I got dressed, got in my car, and headed for the party. I didn't make a practice of riding a group of boys with me when I went places. My brother had warned me about doing this when he gave me the car. He said riding a lot of boys around with you was one sure-easy way of getting in trouble. He said the car was strictly for my transportation needs only.

I left home about 5:30 p.m. and got to the party at six. They lived a few miles north of Johnsonville. There were a number of cars parked in the yard and on the street. People were gathered in the house and yard. Dora was sitting in the living room on the couch talking to a young man when I walked in. He looked to be about six feet and 180 lbs., and his complexion was dark. I handed her my gift. When I gave her the gift she got up from the couch and placed the gift on a table with the other gifts. She hadn't bothered to open any of her gifts. She came back and walked over to the stereo. I had a problem in talking to Dora. Whenever I was away from her all I could think about was what I was going to say when we got together. Yet, when we got together, I couldn't think of anything to say. Though I loved Dora, I had trouble looking her in the eyes and talking to her like a man. Dora spoke to me and resumed her position on the couch beside her friend. I went over to where they were sitting on the couch, and she introduces him to me. She told me it was her cousin, Luther, from Crimson. She sat there for a while then both got up and disappeared among the cars in the dark. She had absolutely no respect for me. It was my conclusion that she wanted someone who was self-confident, smooth, with a good personality, and was good at sports. I was too insecure, vastly lacking in self-confidence, and never given an opportunity to play the sports I might have been decent at. My interpersonal skills certainly left something to be desired. I thought about confronting him, but realized it would be senseless, since I was only five-five and 125 lbs. I thought Dora just didn't like me that much; I didn't know she actually needed a variety of men. She would even do what I perceived as neglecting me for other boys at school. She seemed to have a problem with monogamy. Dora wanted *to have her cake and eat it too.*

I was just sitting there, afraid to make a move, too afraid I would see something I didn't want to see. Someone played "What Kind of Fool?" on the stereo. Then someone put on a song by the Jerry Butler, "I Stand Accused." After that someone played, "I'm so Proud of You," by the Impressions. I wondered if someone played these songs for my benefit. I couldn't take any more. I was sitting there with tears in my eyes. Her brother came over and asked me what was wrong? He knew what was wrong. Even though it was a birthday party, and everyone was trying to have a good time. I couldn't say anything just kept my head buried in my chest.

One of my classmates, Henry, came over and said, "Find you another girl, man. Dora is just like her mother; she likes to play the field."

"OK, maybe you're right."

I still didn't want to give up on Dora. There was nothing like Dora. I loved those big luscious thighs and everything else about her.

Henry's mother and Dora's father were sisters and brothers. Henry kept telling me Dora was always going to like a variety of men. If I couldn't adjust to that I should get to stepping and move on with my life.

"Why don't you go out there and see what they're doing? If she was supposed to be my girl I would," Henry said.

I wasn't conscious of the fact that everyone was aware that Dora and Luther were outside in a car. This was even more embarrassing.

But I couldn't handle the truth.

Everyone looked at me in a way to suggest they felt sorry for me. I sat there on the couch almost paralyzed, afraid to move, not wanting to know what was really going on. Here, an eight grader was taking a sophomore to the cleaners. It didn't look good. Dora came back in approximately an hour later. Luther had gone back to Crimson. Her hair was out of place, her clothes were disheveled, and her stockings fit loose on her legs. Not her usual immaculate self. None of her relatives had anything to say, at least not at the time. She acted as if she was looking normal and didn't pay any attention to her own appearance.

I left in a hurry after saying good-bye to everyone. I finally realized there was no hope for Dora and me. I kept thinking "What Kind of Food?" and, "I Stand Accused."

Once I caught her at the county fair in Crimson with another friend of hers. I walked right up to her and the person she was with.

"What's going on, baby?"

"Oh, how're you doing Steve. This is just a platonic friend of mine," she must have felt she was out of order.

"I thought you said we could be together tonight."

"We can be together any time. I see you at school everyday, and sometimes on Sundays. Let me be with my friend tonight. Don't you think we need some time apart?"

"But we have planned to attend the fair all week."

"We did, but there'll be plenty of other activities for us to attend."

"I thought it was just you and me from now on."

"It is, but tonight I want to be with my friend."

"You're not treating me right, baby."

"Sometimes I like to be with other people. I thought you understood that by now."

"OK, baby. I understand. Do we still have a date for Sunday?"

"Sure, it's still on for Sunday."

Again, I hung my head and walked away.

She always made a rationalization for her negative behaviors, and I always allowed her to make them. I think she thought she could put anything over on me, because I cared so much.

Luther wasn't the only one Dora had an interest in. I finally had gotten my emotional fill and was ready to tell Dora what I thought. That Monday I walked her to her bus as usual. I'm sure she thought I was going to keep being her fool.

"I can't take it any more, Dora. If you are going to be my girl, I at least have to have priority on your affections."

"I told you Luther was my cousin."

"You must think I'm a fool. Girls don't get in cars and make out with their cousins."

"How do you know what I was doing at my birthday party?"

"Just a guess."

"You guessed wrong."

"This isn't the first time you've gone astray; I just wasn't paying attention before."

"You're wrong."

"What about the time you spent with Luther at the homecoming game?"

"What do you mean?"

"You know exactly what I mean."

"Well, if that the way you feel."

"This is good-bye Dora. I've done everything I can. I'm leaving my heart with you."

I had made up my mind after the birthday party.

"See you around, Steve."

She saw she couldn't hoodwink me any more and gave up.

"Good luck"

I figured she would need it at the rate she was going.

I soon found other love interest, and learned when you fall in love, not to fall so hard.

The next day another fool was walking her to her bus.

It was the following Friday night in the café in Johnsonville, and I was still thinking about her. I figured it would take time to get over her, but I figured I had time to invest, but it wouldn't be easy.

11

A LAPSE OF MEMORY

My wife had been cautioning me about gambling for a long time. She had chastised me severely and consistently. I had a habit of going to the casino and spending everything I had in my pocket, and everything else I could get my hands on—no matter how much that was. Of course, there was always a limit on what I could spend. I would go to the casino and win, but keep playing until I lost it all. I didn't seem to have any control. She didn't care so much about my gambling, but my losing all sense of control.

My wife would say after I lost all my money, "You need some help."

"I know baby."

I was enjoying my spree while it lasted, and I had no intentions of giving it up.

"Well, when are you going to get it?"

"I'm thinking about it."

"You need to go see Gamblers Anonymous or somebody. We're not going to get anywhere until you get some help"

"I will look into it."

My very reason for gambling was to support my family, but I was blocking myself from being able to do this by persistent and uncontrolled gambling.

But I paid her little attention and kept gambling whenever I had the cash. I told her I was only using gambling as a form of recreation. She said there was something else to it: she implied that I had psychological issues which I needed to resolve. She would sometimes go to the casino with me but had just about decided that the casino wasn't going to let you win. She is one that recognizes her limits and knows how to walk away. We had both decided that the casino was nothing but a losing proposition, especially if you couldn't walk away after you win. I had always heard that gambling was for suckers, and the house always win. If it was any other way the casino could not stay in business. I knew the end results, because I couldn't walk away after winning, but each time I felt depressed and guilty for being so stupid. It doesn't make sense to spend all your money, and afterward spend a great deal of time being concerned about it—why not keep your money in the first place. There is something incongruous about such behavior. I kept feeling I was going to hit that big one, and could then walk away once I did that, when in reality, a small win is probably the best I was going to be able to do. The small wins have never been sufficient for me to walk away.

One day I got some money from some books I had sold, $4,000.00 to be exact, and I decided to go to the casino, hopefully to add to my good fortune. As a matter of fact, I couldn't wait until the money came so I could try for the big one. I should have put some of it away for a better day, so I wouldn't spend it all, but I kept the full amount in my pocket, knowing I wouldn't have enough control to stop until I had spent every penny. Of course, I would always persuade myself that I could maintain control, but in reality, I knew I couldn't. I would always tell myself, this time I'm going to have control, but I never could exert that needed control. If I only could learn to leave after winning, my problem would have been solved.

I got to the casino and found a machine to play. I usually picked a machine based on my intuition about the machine. I'm not sure how one should go about picking a machine, but don't firmly believe that one can win by intuition. I wasn't winning on that one fast enough, so I decided to move to another one. I was spending hundred-dollar bills like they were confederate money or going out of style. I'm sure staff members must have been in awe at seeing how reckless I was spending my money. Finally, I decided to play another machine. I played for several minutes, and hit for seven times 180, on some off-brand machine, it turned out to be $1,800.00. Instead of going home I kept playing. I had a long dry spell before I won again and had had a long dry spell since I had won anything at the casino. After a long dry spell, I'm more inclined to keep playing after a decent hit. I lost several more $100.00 bills before hitting for $1,080.00, on a Triple-Strike machine, but I couldn't quit. If I had quit, I would have been way ahead. I had to have more action. I knew deep in my mind that I was going to play until I lost it all. I always knew the end results but didn't want to admit it. I seemed to be programmed to lose every penny once I started playing. I was like a drug addict going for that ultimate high. This situation is similar to that monkey who would overdose on cocaine if he could continue to get it. What I didn't understand, even about myself, was how much was enough.

I had always felt that the staff in the casino can control the machines. If you happen to win, they watch you, so that you don't keep winning. They simply call central control and say regulate machine 22135. I still believe this is so. I believe they watched me and cut off every machine I played after my first wins. It seems that no staff wants you to win on their shift. It's like they get graded by how much they keep you from winning. I ended up losing the rest of the $4,000.00 and the $2,900.00 I won. It took me the rest of the night to lose it but I lost it all. There was something driving me, I couldn't seem to quit. Once I started playing, I lost all rational thought about what was logical to do.

I kept thinking about how big a fool I was for losing all my money but couldn't seem to help myself. I kept processing my losses over and over in my mind, but it was too late, I had lost it all. I had gone through this type of behavior over and over in my mind on other occasions as well. The casino wasn't going to let me win it back, unless I had more money to spend. If they indeed can regulate the machines to decide who wins, then the whole process was useless. I thought about my losses until the next night. I went to bed early still thinking about my losses.

I drifted off into a restless sleep and kept going in and out of consciousness. I found myself back on that dirt road where I was raised in East Texas. I came from a small town in a rural area of East Texas where we owned a small-dirt farm. Consequently, I have never gotten over my feelings of deprivation and want. This is one reason why I keep playing the "sucker's game," of trying to hit the big one. This kept me playing after I won a decent size jackpot. Growing up, I never had enough of anything, so I keep struggling to obtain things and resources.

I came from a background where men were only able to provide scarce resources for their families. I am therefore motivated to provide the full compliment of resources that my family might need. I was always afraid that I was not going to be able to measure up to my family's needs. Realizing that any edge I can get on providing resources to my family would put me ahead of the game. I went to school, but most of my early education was a plough and a mule and working in the field. Part of my drive to accumulate resources has to do with my early deprivation as a child. I suppose these are some of the qualities gamblers are made of. Though, I realize gambling is a losing proposition, especially if you can't walk away once you have won.

Back on the farm, my brother had just bought me a car for my sixteenth birthday, and my mother was getting older and needed much medical attention. She would occasionally have me miss school in order to take her to the doctor; there was no one else to take her where she wanted to go. There were no taxis or busses to take her.

It seems that one man who would have me take him places, and lived right down the road from us, had a niece who had lived in the city, and she had come to live with him and assisted him with his care. He had purchased her a car, and I no longer had to worry about taking him places. The niece and I became great friends. We went to school together, and she was very independent and enterprising. Other people in the community would use me as a cheap form of transportation but would never think of having me miss school. This ran through my dream briefly for some reason.

Today my mother had an appointment with a doctor in Shreveport, Louisiana. I had taken her to Shreveport to see this doctor on a number of occasions. In the middle of the appointment I got tired of looking at the magazines, drifted off to sleep, and had a memory lapse. At first it seemed I was back at my old high school in Burkshire, Texas. I started off trying to get my bearings. I was caught up between my old school and a strange new school. This occurred as I was sitting in the doctor's office waiting on my mother. I was sitting there having a dream. It seemed as if it would take forever for my mother to finish her appointment. It seemed that I had come back to school the next day but couldn't find my classroom. First, I couldn't find my classroom at my old school. Then I found myself in a strange new setting. I was at two places simultaneously. I wasn't familiar with this strange new setting. I went to my homeroom but couldn't find where I belonged, everyone was missing from homeroom. I went to the gym but couldn't find where I belonged. I didn't see any familiar faces at either school. It's like coming to school one day and being unable to find your class, you wonder if they got some information the previous day that you had no knowledge of.

I didn't see the faces of any of the old students I was familiar with. It looked like a completely new school environment. I saw that half the students were white at this school. At my old school all the students were Black. I figured I must be at a different place. I couldn't figure out this strange environment. I couldn't seem to understand this momentary lapse in memory. I couldn't understand why I didn't have my briefcase that I carried with me everywhere I went at school. I kept looking for it but couldn't seem to find it. I thought if I could find my briefcase it would solve part of my problem, but after going back to my homeroom, I still couldn't find it. Again, I peeped into the gym, but the people I saw gave me no hint of a familiar environment. They seemed to be having a P.E. class of some sort, while some students were observing. They were cheering loud and whistles were blowing. Normal things seemed to be going on. Part of this scene was at my old school and part was at the new-strange school, the scene kept switching back and forth, but it was all different and new. I looked in several classrooms, but no one looked familiar. I wanted to ask a teacher where my class was being held but felt I would be too far out of place.

I considered there was something wrong with my mind, and that I had a psychiatric problem of some sort that caused me to lose perspective on who, what, and where I was. The school was a strange and different place for me. It seemed that I had lost myself. It seemed that I wasn't going to get any place in the school, so I walked out on the street, still not seeing any familiar faces. I asked one child that looked to be about ten-years old, what town was this? He looked at me in a rather strange way but said nothing. Seeing young children at the school made sense, since my old school was 1st through twelfth. I asked an older female who looked as if she was a teacher of some kind, what town was this? She said this is Williams, Louisiana.

"How do I get to Burkshire, Texas from here?"

"You go to Interstate 20 and keep north for about 40 miles."

I finally figured out that I had brought my mother to Shreveport, had had a memory lapse, and found myself wandering around the local high school in a dream. It all came back to me. I woke up out of my dream and found myself in the waiting room waiting on my mother. The nurse noted that I seemed to be in a daze.

"Is everything all right," the nurse asked.

"Everything is fine," I said, as I woke up.

"You mother is ready," the nurse said.

"Thank you," I said.

I was glad to get out of there. She was finally ready, so we left for home. I tried to keep the number of days I missed school to transport my mother to a minimal from that point onward.

I woke up in Chicago and found myself in a comfortable bed in a Chicago suburb. Glad to be alive. So, I figured I could worry about what I would do about the problem at a later point. When I woke up, I found myself lying there wondering what I was going to do about my gambling problem. It felt good just to be able to get out of bed and be in my right state of mind. I guess for some things there are no easy solutions. I kept thinking that

I definitely had to find some solution to my gambling problem, either a private psychotherapist or Gamblers Anonymous. Certainly, solving my gambling problem won't be as easy as waking up from a dream. Whatever the situation, I have many things to be thankful for, and there's no reason yet to give up on life.

12

SEIZURE IN THE YELLOW MELLOW COMMUNITY

It was a cool-rainy Friday evening, November 13, 1936. A storm was brewing out of the east. The sky had been clear all that day, but it rained cats and dogs later that evening. About all we had to look forward to was the Christmas season. We lived in the rural area of a small town in East Texas. I was in the fifth grade. I had recently experienced my tenth birthday in October. My sister was in eighth grade. We both enjoyed school and loved to read. It was shortly after the Depression, and a few years before World War II. We live five miles off State Highway 192 that ran through the heart of the community. It was a blacktopped, meandering, uphill road that led to two small towns in either direction. It was called the Yellow Mellow community. Why it was called that is anybody's guess. My parents didn't know how the community got its name. I suppose it was named after some famous persons, or an event many years ago.

We had our own school, and had several general stores scattered throughout the community. We were a self-sufficient community, and turned to members of the community for everything we needed. Highway 192 to the south led to Hemingway, Texas (30,000), about 20 miles away; and the road to the north led to Berkshire, Texas (100,000), about twenty miles away. Crosby was 1,000,000 in population and was 125 miles away to the north; Bluebell, Louisiana was thirty miles to the south, and was approximately 500,000. One other town was Crystal Lake, about 30 miles to the north, a little north of Berkshire.

We had finished harvesting our crops for the season, including digging up our sweet potatoes, and placing them in the potato cellar. We had butchered a 400 lb. hog and a 400 lb. calf only a few days ago. We had peanuts, potatoes, and my mother's canned fruits and vegetables. We were set for a long winter. We had a small log cabin at the end of a five-mile trail. My father and a local jackleg carpenter had built it themselves: including cutting down the trees from our property, measuring, and fitting them. There was no road for the five miles off the highway, only a trail. This trail had ditches, tree limbs, and tall grass along the way. When it rained, and the creeks overflowed, you never knew what you might find along the trail; soon after a rain we sometimes found fish, at other times turtles—still alive. We ate whatever we found. It was also difficult to make our way to school soon after a rain, because of the flood plain. If you were very ingenious and creative, you possibly could manage to drive a truck or wagon over this trail. The rain made it even more difficult. That's the way it was in those days. We hauled everything we needed in a wagon. We owned 200 acres of good farming land. My paternal grandfather left it to my father. There were four children, and he left each of them 200 acres of prime land. Most of it we didn't use for crops, just enough to feed the family and sell food to neighbors. The rest of it was used as pasture for raising our cattle. We didn't have modern transportation, only a wagon and several horses.

We always thought we were safe from marauders, thieves, and highway robbers—especially living that far off the main highway, but not that night. We went to bed about nine o'clock, early as usual. My parents would let me go to bed only after I finished my homework. I was studious and spent a great deal of my time doing homework. The log cabin only had four rooms: two bedrooms, a kitchen, and a family room. We didn't have electricity or indoor plumbing. The kitchen entrance was never locked; you could just push the door open easily. Anyone who seriously tried could simply walk in the house through the door. My father kept putting off placing a lock on it. Again, he thought we didn't have to worry, being so far off the beaten path. We had a smokehouse and a rickety-old barn out back of the house that required no special ingenuity to open. The smokehouse sat along side the barn. There were plenty of meat in the smokehouse, and most of mom's summer canning was on shelves in the barn. Some of the meat was hanging in the smokehouse, and some of it was packed in salt in a box in the barn. That's what you did when you didn't have electricity in those days.

We woke up about 11 p.m. and found that someone had entered the house through the kitchen, and they were rummaging through the kitchen, the smokehouse, and the barn. We all had drifted off to sleep and didn't hear them approaching. Two of them came in the house brandishing guns. There was only my father, my mother, my sister, and me. I was ten, my sister was thirteen, my father was forty, and my mother was thirty-eight. The nearest neighbor was three miles down the trail. Yelling or screaming wasn't going to help, and there was no way to alert anyone. It was four white men. They were driving a 1934 truck-like vehicle much like the one depicted on the "Beverly Hillbillies." The truck was parked in the back yard. At the time I couldn't understand how they drove the truck through the impossible trail. It was the first four-wheel-motor vehicle I had seen come back that far. We all were frightened to death. My father didn't show his anxiety as much as the rest of us. My mother fainted and fell to the floor like a house of cards folding. They searched the house and gathered us in the family room. They said they were on their way to California from Memphis, Tennessee. They were all close relatives. They assured us they would not hurt us, but simply needed food and some sleep, in order to continue on their journey. I thought these white men must really be poor to be robbing us. I thought we were worse off than anyone I knew. Three of them had shotguns, and one of them had a .45 caliber pistol. They were disheveled, with dirty clothes, scruffy beards, and had an odd odor that I couldn't quite place. They raided the smokehouse and the potato cellar. They also found where mother stored her summer's canning in the barn. She had worked all summer canning fruits and vegetables: she had peaches, okra, corn, pears, tomatoes, wine, pickles, beets, etc. The only thing we bought from a store was a few spices and household furnishing, and some of our household furnishings were homemade. A man in the community specialized in making furniture. They took only what they needed for their journey. They were careful to selectively take only some of each of the items we had. They took what they wanted and began to question my father. They seemed to know where people like us kept our food. They were poor folk themselves and knew how folks like us did things.

"Boy, do you people have any more food in the house?" the older man asked.

None of the other men said a word the whole time they were in our presence. The older man did all the talking.

My father had watched them as they gathered food from throughout the house. My mother kept some of her canning in the house.

"You've taken some of everything we have," my father said, we were so frightened that my father did all the talking for us.

"Don't lie to me, boy. We don't want to hurt you, but we need food to take on our trip." The older man seemed to doubt my father's sincerity.

"We've nothing else," replied my father.

"We also need to stay here until morning. If you cooperate everything will be fine. We just want to sleep on the floor until then. It will be too dangerous trying to negotiate that trail at night in the storm and the rain."

"How long you people been living here?" the older man asked.

"Since 1924," my father said, proudly.

"You've been here a long time."

"I guess so," my father replied.

"Have you ever thought about moving further west? I hear opportunities are better for everyone."

"I have 200 acres of good land here, I wouldn't want to leave it," my father said.

The only kind of life my mother and father knew about was farming, and they weren't going to give that up.

"Why haven't you folks had a road built?"

"We've been too satisfied with the way things are."

"A road would make transportation so much easier."

"You're probably right. I've been too busy struggling from day to day to think about anything else."

"It reminds me of where I lived in Memphis; but we got together, went to the county, and petitioned them to build a road."

"It's easy to do, all you have to do is get everyone on the trail to sign a petition and take it to the county administrator."

"We have to see about getting that done."

In spite of what they told my father it was many years later before he followed through with getting it done.

"How do your children get to school?"

"They walk to a local school nearby."

We were afraid to let down our guards. He was still holding his gun. Here he was robbing us and talking to us like a neighbor. Even though these men were robbing us, I could empathize with them.

It was odd that none of the other men mumbled a word. The older man was about forty-five, wore blue jeans, red-flannel shirt, heavy-work boots, his hair was beginning to gray, and he carried a shotgun. One of the men wore overalls, red-wool-flannel shirt, with dark hair, was about forty, and also carried a shotgun. Another man wore kakis, blue-work shirt, work boots, was about thirty-five, had a monstrous nose, and carried a shotgun as well. The other man wore blue jeans, brown-work boots, and red shirt. He had a tinge of grey in his hair, looked to be about thirty, and carried a .45 caliber pistol. They all carried their heads high, like a young girl's breast, as if they were trying to maintain their dignity.

"Would you cook us something to eat," the older man held his head down at that point.

"What would you like," my mother asked, after she awakened from her faint, even then looking and acting as if she felt sorry for them.

"Anything you fix will be fine," he said.

"Would you like some macaroni and cheese, ham, and biscuits?"

"That'll be fine."

The men sat down to eat, and my father showed them where they could sleep in the family room on the couch and the floor until morning. He even gave them some blankets and pillows.

Again, the older man said, "Thank you."

"Why didn't you just ask for food if that's what you wanted," my father asked.

"We didn't think you would be this cooperative. Some people wouldn't give up their food. Most of them have been hit badly by the Depression. The Depression wiped all of us out, and diseases killed the rest of our families," the older man said.

"Sorry to hear that," my mother said, again speaking up.

"We'll just sleep here until morning. In the morning we will leave for California and won't bother you again.

We don't know what lies ahead, but it's got to be better than where we came from. Where we come from people are eating horses and even considering dogs."

"Good luck!" My father said being the good-natured person he was.

They told us to go back to bed and not to try and contact anyone about what happened. My sister was in too big of a shock to say a word. We all had a hard time sleeping, but in the morning, they had hit the road before we got up. My sister and I got up, had grits, fatback, biscuits, and fresh milk. We walked the muddy trail to school; and my father and mother got on with their chores. We had a hard winter but were able to make it with the help of neighbors and friends. It was a close-knit community and we relied on one another in hard times.

Right away we butchered another large hog and calf. We found out several days later that our family was not the only one that was robbed. Several of them weren't as cooperative as we were. It was only years later after reading about the Great Depression and its after effects that I was able to appreciate what drove certain people to desperation during this crisis. Before that there had been no discussion of the Great Depression. We were so poor that we weren't affected too greatly by it. We didn't have anything to lose except our land. It helped us during this period that we at least grew our own food.

My father didn't want to involve the police, but my mother finally convinced him to report the offense. He and several other people from the community who was affected rode a wagon for at least twenty miles to make the report. The police said it was nothing they could do, since the men would be halfway to California before they could locate them, and they had other life and death issues to work on in the community. That's all they had to say about the matter.

I graduated from that small elementary school in the community, went to high school in the city, and was then lucky enough to get a scholarship to college. I kept thinking about what these men said about California for a long time and decided I would do like these men and head in that direction. I had heard so much about opportunities for advancement in California. I had always been fascinated with the law. I moved to California, did an apprenticeship as a lawyer with a cousin who was a well-established lawyer, took the Bar exam several years later and passed it, becoming a lawyer in 1956 at thirty years of age. I had a long and productive career as a lawyer in private-practice. I specialized in the area of divorce law.

It was 1954 before the county finally converted that five-mile trail to a dirt road, with my urging. My father finally heeded what that older man told him about getting a petition signed and taking it to the county administrator. Until that time, they were happy with their isolation in their own part of the world. Eventually they even blacktopped it. My father bought a car and had a new house built once the road was constructed. Things were easier for my parents and the whole community.

13

THE PRINCIPAL AND HIS WIFE

We had just finished harvesting our crops on the Westinghouse plantation: mostly corn, cotton, sweet potatoes, peanuts, and peas—the standard crops for the area. It was a plantation right off Highway 165 in East Texas near Marshall, Texas. An area located in proximity to Arkansas, Louisiana, and Texas. It was a 1,600 acres plantation with twelve Black families doing sharecropping on the place. There was plenty of good fishing and hunting on the plantation, but we never had time for such activities—too much work to do. This plantation had existed since the early 1800s. Generations of my relatives on my father's side went back to the beginning of the plantation when Blacks were bona fide slaves.

My father had been ill during the harvest. He hadn't done any work in several years. We got the news that my father wouldn't make it through the night. He was dying of kidney failure and heart disease. That night he passed away in his sleep. He passed away on a cool-ominous night in early September. The funeral was held but not many people came. My father isolated himself and didn't have many friends or relatives. His philosophy was that *you are born in this world alone and when you die, you'll die alone.* It almost came true for him. He died at the age of sixty-one.

With our father gone we could no longer hold our own on the plantation. We were barely making it to begin with. We didn't have enough individuals in the family to do their necessary share of the work. The owner had complained many times about us not carrying our share of the workload. The owner believed in three things: work, work, and more work. With my father's death he saw this as a good opportunity to be rid of us for good. We had to move. At first, we didn't know what we were going to do, but eventually moved to a little shack further up the highway, right off 165, closer to Marshall. This place had no indoor plumbing or gas.

There were six children in our family, four boys and two girls. My mother wasn't old enough for Social Security. We survived on welfare and what jobs my mother could get cleaning houses for white folks. My two older brothers also helped out by obtaining various types of odd jobs. I had two brothers who were old enough to find occasional temporary work. One of my older brothers was seventeen and the other was nineteen. I was eight and another brother was twelve. My two sisters were fourteen and sixteen—even they would help with odd jobs.

Then my mother became ill soon after my father died. The doctor told us that she had cancer which had metastasized. That she probably had about a year to live. Everyone in the family felt that she lost her will to live after my father died. Word got around that we would soon be orphans and would be looking for a home before the end of the year. This prediction turned out to be accurate. The principal and his wife at Lincoln Elementary were looking for a child to nurture, they had been looking for a child for a while. This was the elementary school that I attended. It was convenient that I would need a family soon. They said they were looking for a boy that they could offer their home and resources. The principal's wife had tried for years to conceive and thus had finally given up. They had tried everything imaginable with no luck.

At the end of that year my mother passed away from cancer. She died a year to the day that the doctor said she would. There is a saying in the Black community that when one parent dies, the other won't be too far behind. Primarily this occurs because the other parent loses their will to live, after living with them for so long. They can't live without them. She died at the age of sixty-one. My father was one year older than my mother. People from all over came to the funeral, from as far away as California. My mother was more gregarious than my father, and she had more relatives. There was a great deal of screaming and shouting. The principal and his wife had already heard about the family situation and paid us a visit. My nineteen-year old brother was in charge of the family now. We all were still in shock over the recent death of our mother and father. Someone had to carry on the business of the family, since Henry was the oldest, the responsibility fell on him.

"We want to give Sammy a home," the principal said to my brother Henry.

"He needs a good home," Henry said.

Henry had already heard about the principal and his wife, and how they could provide Sammy a good home. He knew this was the best opportunity Sammy was going to get.

"We have a nice home not far from here," said the principal.

"Can I visit him when possible? I'd like to keep in touch with my brother," asked Henry.

"Sure, you can visit any time you like," the principal said.

"I'd like to see one of us go to college and become something worthwhile. It seems that Sammy will have that chance," Henry said.

"He will have as much opportunity as he is able to take advantage of," the principal said.

"Take care of him," Henry said.

Henry was pleased that at least Sammy would have an opportunity to be all he was able to take advantage of.

I was a student in the principal's wife class and she knew my situation. I was in third grade, and frequently came to school with no lunch. The teacher would share her lunch with me. I believe that she soon started to bring an extra sandwich everyday just for me. On occasions, she would provide me with school supplies, when it was evident, I had none. She could see that my clothing was inappropriate and sometimes tattered and torn. Once I came to school with ringworms in my head. The teacher took it upon herself to buy medicine and apply it to my scalp herself. It got better within a matter of days. The teacher told my brother I was exactly what she was looking for in a child and would be delighted to take me as her own child and take care of me. The teacher was looking for someone who was exceptionally needy, and they didn't come any needier than I.

My seventeen- and nineteen-year-old brothers were going to make it on their own—regardless of the situation. The seventeen-year-old had picked up some carpentry skills on the plantation, and the nineteen-year-old had been to automobile mechanics school in Dallas. They both took jobs in Marshall. My twelve-year-old brother was adopted by a working-class family in Texarkana, Texas. My sixteen-yea-old sister thought it best if she tried to make it on her own as well. She was a bit old to play at being somebody's child. So, she lived with the other two brothers and took a job in Marshall also. My fourteen-year-old sister was adopted by a working-class family in Longview, Texas. None of them would get a similar opportunity as I would.

The principal and his wife picked me up in their brand new, red, 1954 Chevrolet Bel-Aire. It was clean and polished. He kept it that way. I had no idea what I was in for. They took me to a Georgia Colonial, red-brick home on the outskirts of Marshall. It was a ranch with horses and cows, and some other farm animals. They had live-in staff hired to take care of the animals. All I had to do was to eat my meals and take advantage of the activities—there was no work or chores for me to do. The house had twelve rooms—six bedrooms. For a farm everything was neat and well ordered. The lawn was neatly manicured. Huge trees lined the driveway. They had no children. The principal and his wife said that everything they had one day would be mine, as they were officially adopting me. The principal was about six-feet tall, light skinned, and one-hundred-sixty pounds. He was an immaculate dresser and an excellent communicator. His wife was five-six, one-hundred-thirty pounds, caramel in color, and also an immaculate dresser and excellent communicator.

They took me to a clothing store and bought me some appropriate clothing. All I had were a few torn rags that I had managed to collect in a bag and bring with me. They also bought me toys appropriate for my age. Until that time, I had very few toys. Toys were considered luxury items and expendable. They introduced me to music, horseback riding, and fishing; and some of the other finer things of life. They even purchase me a new-shiny-red Schwinn bike. When they adopted me, I was in third grade, and reading at the second-grade level. At the end of that year I was reading at a sixth-grade level. They bought me all kinds of age-appropriate books to read. They also had a large library in their house that I had unlimited access to. I read constantly day and night, and during my summer vacations. However, my reading didn't get in the way of other activities, for there were many activities that we engaged in. They even had a fishing pond on the premises, and you could hunt on the property as well. The principal and his wife took me to visit my brothers and sisters, when they didn't come around to see me. When I got my driver's license, I would visit them on my own.

We went camping, went to basketball, football, and baseball games; and went to museums in Dallas, Houston, and Shreveport. The principal got me involved in football as soon as I came to live with them. I subsequently played football in elementary, junior high, and high school. I made All-State in my junior and senior high school years. Football turned out to be my sport. The principal and his wife kept me close at hand and taught me how to survive in the world. When they felt it necessary, they would sit down with me and give me some good parental advice. They never left me hanging out there by myself but made an attempt to be a real family.

In high school I was a member of the Honor Society, the debate team, and was always president of my class. I was also valedictorian of my senior class. When I was old enough the principal taught me how to drive and purchased me a Black 1962 Impala Chevrolet. It came time to make plans for college. I had accepted the fact that the principal and his wife wanted me to attend college. I accepted this plan for my life as if it was the normal and natural thing to do. In high school I had a 4.0 grade point average on a four-point system. There was no reason why I should not go to college. I also had a football scholarship to Grambling College in Grambling, Louisiana; and one to Wiley College in Marshall, Texas, as well as several other possibilities. I could have gotten a scholarship to just about any college I so desired.

When it came time for college the principal sat down with me and discussed the issue.

"What college do you plan to attend?" asked the principal, as if going to one or another was the only option.

"I hadn't made up my mind yet," I replied.

"Take your time and make a good choice," he said.

"Two of them have offered me scholarships in football. But I'm not sure which I will accept."

"You are the only one who has to live with your choice, so I won't give you any suggestion," he said.

"Thanks dad."

"I'd like to think we have prepared you to make the right choices," he said

I read all that summer before entering college. The principal bought some books specifically designed to help prepare me for college. I was going to get a job, but the principal told me it would be better to spend my time preparing for college rather than making a few dollars on a minimum wage job. He told me to relax and enjoy the activities on the farm, I had earned a little free time. He said if I needed any extra money in college, he would provide it. I took the full scholarship to Grambling. They were supposed to have an excellent football program. I was not only interested in the football program but interested in the academic program as well. I was a running back and was good at it. The principal said I was one of the best he had ever seen.

The principal even allowed me to take the car he had purchase for me to college, being careful to make sure it was in the best working order, so I wouldn't have any problems out of it. I went to college, kept up my average, and graduated magna cum laude. I even pledged Alpha Phi Alpha. I also made All-American my junior and senior years. I was headed for the pros, but hurt my knee in the last game of the season. Before that the pros were scouting me heavily. Needless to say, I was extremely disappointed. My future in football had come to an abrupt end.

After that I wasn't quite sure what to do, but the principal had prepared me for such eventuality. He had told me never to put all my eggs in one basket. I wanted to play pro football, but knew I had other options. The principal advised me if I couldn't play pro football, another option was to attend law school. I applied to Texas Southern University Law School in Houston and got a fully paid scholarship. My knee injury left me with a hobble, but I was able to get around on it without any problems.

I graduated law school and went to work for Williams and Jones, a law firm in Houston. I did get married about a year later and had two children. The principal and his wife were just like my real parents rather than adoptive parents. They also considered my children their grandchildren. They were serious about their commitment to me. I was always grateful to the principal and his wife for rescuing me when they did. I couldn't have been successful on the same level without their help.

I maintained contact with my brothers and sisters and provided them with financial assistance when I could.

14

DARLA IN MY LIFE

I attended a rural-segregated school in East Texas. It was much like the one-room schoolhouse of traditional-historical literature, except there was a classroom for each grade. It was cold in winter and too hot the rest of the year. It was located in Hallsville, Texas, a small town between Longview and Marshall. One day I was roaming around my school campus as I usually did. I frequently wandered aimlessly around the campus. Nothing much was going on inside the classroom as I could remember. We would sit there for hours engaging in horseplay and staring out the window—daydreaming. We had a tremendous amount of downtime. I would go to the bathroom to relieve the monotony, and wander around the campus for long periods of time. The teachers seemed disinterested, so I developed the same attitude.

All of a sudden, I saw the girl of my dreams. She was walking on the sidewalk port of the elementary section of the campus. The elementary, junior, and high school were physically on the same campus. She was about five-two, one-hundred-ten pounds, youthful-erect breast that stood at attention, big-rounded hips, smooth legs, and a pretty face. She was moving like a show pony in a horse show. As my cousin from Dallas says, "She had an ass like a horse and a waist like a wasp." Her hips tended to swivel as she moved. Later I found out that she moved this way because of polio as a child. I was immediately smitten with her. I would sit and admire those beautiful-long legs for extensive periods of time. I'm sure some people must have thought I was psychiatrically ill. No one could be that captivated by another person.

She was in sixth grade and I was in the eighth grade. She was seemingly very physically mature for her age. Some would have considered that I was robbing the cradle, but I felt perfectly justified in pursuing her. I hadn't noticed her before. They say everything has a first time. From that point onward, I would try to talk to her. I had a speech impediment which made communication difficult, but that didn't stop me from trying. Later, I got the idea from her behavior that she wanted someone who was smooth, self-confident, athletic, and with a good personality. I didn't have any of these qualities. My personality was underdeveloped, and I didn't get an opportunity to play the sports I wanted to play. I also felt she didn't like me because of my speech impediment.

I would sit with her at various events at school, walk her to her bus, and see her at school on other occasions whenever I could. On Sundays, once I got a driver's license, I would come to court her at her grandmother's house. My brother bought me a car once I turned sixteen and was able to get my driver's license. At this time, I could go wherever I wanted. It took a lot of convincing, but her father finally allowed me to take her out. She didn't want me to come and see her at her house. Later, I figured out that it had something to do with the condition of her house. This is only an assumption because I never saw more than the outside of her house. From the outside it looked to be in a deteriorated condition. Her grandmother's house was in a little better condition, although it was nothing exceptional. I couldn't see what the big deal was; none of us lived a luxurious type of lifestyle. In any case, I kept seeing her at her grandmother's house and never questioned why she wanted me to visit her there.

As time would have it, we moved on. She would give favor to other boys from Longview. I would go places and she would be there with these boys. These boys would sometimes come to our campus and boldly walk around with her on their arms. I didn't quite know what to do. Once I caught her kissing one of them in the parking lot. These boys caused me a great deal of frustration. I was nonviolent, so violence wasn't an option. My friend who lived near her and was her cousin said she was going to be just like her mother, and that her mother was a sport of a woman. She was supposed to have enjoyed relationships with a variety of men. My father had a similar type orientation. All I knew was that I loved Darla; I didn't have anyone to give me fatherly advice. My father worked out of town—coming home twice a month and wasn't around enough for me to ask him what I should do. When he was home, I figured he didn't want to be bothered with such foolishness. My father was a no-nonsense person. I had no brothers or cousins to confer with, and no close relationship with other men in the community. No one else thought enough of me to give me any advice.

On one occasion my so-called friend Thomas was walking Darla to her bus. I met her and Thomas at the front of the building as I usually met Darla.

"What's going on?" I asked.

Thomas spoke up.

"I'm taking over your girl," Thomas said.

"Is this true?" I asked Darla, seemingly taken aback.

"I have to decide which one I want."

"What do you mean?" I asked.

"I'll let you know next week which one I want," Darla said.

I walked away like a dog severely chastised by its master. I knew I loved Darla and didn't know what to do. I was stupid and in love enough to accept this kind of behavior from Darla. I should have simply left Darla alone, but the next week I met them again coming out of the building. I suppose I thought if I kept pressuring her, she would give in and say she wanted me.

"Which one did you choose?" I asked.

"Thomas is my choice," Darla said.

I was out of my mind for allowing her to take the situation that far. I should have either knocked Thomas out, or told her she didn't have to bother about making a choice. The choice had already been made. But I wasn't about to defend my manhood in a violent way. If she felt I needed to defend something then it wasn't worth it to begin with, I knew that someone had put Thomas up to it. Who ever put Thomas up to it probably figured, if he took my girl, I would get disgusted and drop out of school. Some people had that strong of a dislike for me. I knew Thomas liked his girls with a bit more class. Darla was cute but not classy enough for Thomas. He had a classy girl in Hallsville, Marshall, and Longview; and every other town he thought to visit. I had seen several of them and they were some real stars. Someone put him up to it just to disturb my equilibrium. I put Darla out of sight but not out of mind for several years. I kept thinking about her. She was constantly on my mind as I would see her walking about the campus, and at various events at the school.

But after Thomas we broke up. We had few encounters at the school or any place else until my senior year. I got back with her and gradually began to have a better relationship with her during my senior year. My love for her was too strong to completely give up on her. At this time, she was a sophomore, and a bit more physically and psychologically developed. I started back visiting her at her grandmother's house. It is said that a man will seek out someone who has similar characteristics as his mother. I must admit she was similar to my mother in many ways: light skin, big hips, and plenty of meat on her bones. I still had competition from other boys in Longview. I guess it's hard for a leopard to change its spots. Thomas had moved on to other girls.

I graduated and took her to my senior prom. We went out to dinner at Johnny Casey Sea Food Restaurant in Longview on my graduation night. I hadn't had sex with her at that point. She had kept me at a distance, saying that she was trying to save herself. On graduation night she broke down and went to the Holiday Inn with me. For me it was the night of a lifetime. I was finally getting something I had been denied all these years. She had denied me so long she didn't quite know how to act, pretending she didn't know what to do once I got her in bed. On this night I fell in love with her all over again.

On this night we dreamed and planned for the rest of our lives. We discussed it right down to the two kids and the two-story-white house with the white-picket fence; the Mercedes, Jaguar, and the poodle. We also discussed colleges. I informed her that I was going to Stephen F. Austin. She said she wanted to go to Princeton, but Stephen F. Austin would do just as well. In her preference I detected a note of sarcasm, but I didn't push it further. I didn't get her home until Monday morning about five o'clock. Her father and mother were sitting in the car in their yard about to come looking for us, her mother didn't say much, just said she was glad we were all right. Her dad cursed me for everything he could think of and raised holy hell for about an hour.

We made plans that when she graduated, she would go to whatever school I was attending and work and support me until I could graduate. Then I could work and support her until she graduated. Once we both graduated, we could get married. For some reason she wanted to spend a few years together before we got married. I was ready to get married right away. But her idea sounded like a good plan in theory.

I graduated and went to Stephen F. Austin State University in Nacogdoches, Texas. I came back to homecoming and several other games and functions. It seemed that we were on our way again. Only once did I have a problem with another male letting me know that he had a claim on her as well. However, she quickly diffused the situation and put him in his place. Apparently, she also had another secret high school sweetheart. I figured this was only natural behavior, especially since I wasn't around, I'm not sure if my being around would have changed that situation any. *When the cat's away the mice will play.* On several weekends she visited the campus, and we got a room at the Holiday Inn. These were the best times of my life. I was just about willing to share Darla or do whatever I had to do just to keep her.

Her parents were against it, they felt we should get married when she graduated high school. When she did graduate, I secured an apartment near the campus. She moved to Nacogdoches and took a job at the Safeway Grocery Store as a cashier. I took a part-time job at Kentucky Fried Chicken to help pay for the apartment, groceries, my tuition, and whatever else we needed. I didn't want her to feel she was working all by herself. She supported me until I graduated in the next two years. She was saving most of her money because my job paid most of my bills—including school bills. But she did help a great deal. Her support came just in time. I couldn't have made it without her working to help me get through school. I'm not sure what happened to get her to change her mind about our dream of spending the rest of our lives together. Some things are just not meant to be, and it is not for us to reason why.

Things were going fine until near the end of my senior year. I should have known it wouldn't last. Darla was into socializing a lot. All she was doing was working; and all I was doing was working, going to class, and studying. She had met a student who was working at Safeway as a cashier also. She had developed a relationship with him over the past year. Two of my classes got cancelled in the same day and I came home early that day. I caught them in my apartment in bed together. They were moaning and groaning, having the time of their lives, they didn't even here me when I walked in the apartment. I could have pulled an O.J. on them.

"What's going on?" I asked.

"I thought you were in class," Darla said.

"You mean this goes on when I'm in class," I said.

"That's not what I meant," Darla said.

The young man put on his clothes and ran out the door. I didn't try to stop him.

"What do you mean?"

"It gets lonely with you working, studying, and going to class all the time."

Even at that point I wasn't ready to give up on Darla and was thinking how we could adjust the situation to meet both our needs.

Her explanation sounded logical, but I saw it as a leopard having difficulty changing its spots. Maybe she had been conditioned by her mother to be a certain way, a way that I couldn't change. But I kept thinking that maybe I could recondition her.

But after all was said and done, we decided that this arrangement wasn't the best solution to our problems after all. It took us several weeks to reach this conclusion. She decided it was time to make other plans, and that going to school wasn't her ambition any more, that she was moving to Memphis to be close to family and friends. This was the sadist time of my life. I had hoped to repay the favor and support her while I took a full-time job in Nacogdoches. I had already been offered a job in Nacogdoches. I loved Darla, but she had other things on her mind. She didn't think she could live, work, and go to school in that small town. I tried to convince her that we could move to some other place, but she had definite plans of her own. She packed her things and headed for Memphis. I took a job in Chicago as a high school economics teacher.

On occasions I hear from her at special times such as Christmas and Thanksgiving. I will never forget Darla.

15

THE BUS RIDE

We are sometimes conditioned to want certain things without understanding the reasons why. Sometimes the reasons for our being attracted to these things are because of our lack of exposure to them. We must constantly re-examine the reasons for our behavior.

I was born in a small-rural-segregated town called Hallsville, Texas. There weren't many activities to participate in, but what there were they were all segregated. Mostly we engaged in activities like sports, gambling, drinking, and chasing women. The schools and the little café in town were segregated. These were the centers of attraction. That's about all there were to participate in this town. The town was approximately 1,300 in population in 1965. The town consisted of a post office, several gas stations, several general stores, a Dairy Queen, a café, and a bank. Most of the buildings were single story and unpainted. There was only one policeman in the town that was legendary for being abusive to Black people. There were several cities close by that weren't much different than Hallsville—only larger: Longview was ten miles away to the north (100,000); Marshall was ten miles to the south (45,000); Shreveport was forty miles to the south 200,000; Tyler was about thirty miles to the north (60,000); and Dallas was 125 miles to the north (1,000,000). To my knowledge even the libraries in these smaller towns weren't available to Blacks. They all maintained distinct patterns of racial segregation and separation.

Therefore, there wasn't much opportunity to get to know other so-called races—unless done in clandestine fashion. We very seldom saw folks of other races. The only times there was mixing was if you happen to work for a particular organization and came in contact with other races while you were on duty. I grew up and decided to go to an integrated university. I had no idea what school would be best to attend. I wasn't prepared for a Black or white university, but decided to jump into this university with both feet. My educational background had been deprived. I had a speech impediment; and had poor math, English, and social skills. There was no history of attending colleges in my immediate family. My relatives were working-class individuals who barely got by from day to day. They didn't have high-minded things on their minds like going to college. They were simply lucky to get out of those woods alive. Other people in my community didn't often attend college either, a few did but it was rare to do so. When they did attend, they usually dropped out after the first few semesters. Most of them were just concerned with getting a job of some kind—whatever they could get. They had no such illusion of being able to choose their occupation. I was on my own with regard to making decisions about college. I was lucky to even be considered by any college, especially a traditional middle-class university. I thought I knew what was best for me, but my decision ended up being haphazard and ill advised. When I look back on it, I would probably have been better off to start with a historically Black college and take it from there.

I heard a friend talking about Stephen F. Austin in Nacogdoches. He was one of the more intelligent students at our school. I had passed by the campus on my way to Houston on any number of occasions, and I knew my brother's wife parents lived in this town. You could see the picturesque campus from the highway as you passed going down Highway 59. For some reason I thought it might be the school for me. The only other colleges I knew about were Texas Southern, Wiley, Grambling, Bishop or Prairie View. Most of the students from my high school had gone to Prairie View. I wanted something different for my education. It was the age of integration, and civil rights' leaders were fighting for the right to attend integrated schools. I wanted to do my thing for integration. It was the only contribution I could conceive of making to the Civil Rights Movement. There was a strange force which pulled me toward this particular school, as if it was my destiny. I knew it was about eighty miles from Marshall, Texas, and would be not far from home. At the time I didn't want to be far from home. I figured it wouldn't be so hard trying to get home during holidays if I stayed close to home. On the one hand I wanted to get away from home, and on the other I wanted to stay close. My friend said it was a good school, and he was thinking about attending the school. I made up my mind to attend the school. The friend changed his mind about the school and went to the Army instead. I am not sure why he changed his mind.

I took the necessary admission test, filled out my application, and had no problems being accepted. I guess the school was meant for me. I did have some help in filling out the application from a teacher. Without her help I probably wouldn't have been accepted. I was lucky to get admitted since it was the only college I applied to. They say a student should apply to several colleges rather than just one, in case their first choice falls through. I went even without the assistance of a scholarship.

An individual from a nearby community had gotten a basketball scholarship and came by to give me a ride to the campus. I didn't even know he was going to attend that college and didn't know he knew I was planning to attend—talk about fate. We had gone to high school together during our junior year. I had planned on catching the bus and hadn't expected a ride to the dorm. The best I could hope for was that my brother would drive me to the campus.

I had been on the campus for one semester. I liked the campus even more than I thought I would. The food was good, and the dormitories were nice and clean. The campus was neatly manicured and pleasant with magnificently tall picturesque pine and oak trees. It had skyscraper dormitory and classroom buildings. Most of the students both black and white were decent.

It was time to go home for Christmas break. I hadn't done that well but managed to stay off academic probation. I was looking forward to the next semester when I could work on improving my grade point average. I headed to the bus station to catch a ride to Marshall where my brother would pick me up and give me a ride to the country. We lived 10 miles north of Marshall in a rural area. There was no transportation except personal transportation to the country where we lived.

The school had plenty of girls most of them were of other so-called races. There was a lot of competition for the few Black girls. The girls from other races were considered off limits to Black males, yet, you were constantly in their presence. It was hard to be around them constantly and not at least desire a relationship with some of them.

I went to step on the bus headed for Marshall, and a vision of loveliness caught my eyes, or was it just that I was deprived of social and physical contact. It was the age of the miniskirt, and this girl had on a tight mini which she wore well. She was about five-five, one-hundred-twenty pounds, nice hips, long-smooth legs, and an angelic face. She had on silk pantyhose which made her legs look even that much smoother. When she stepped on the bus that mini seemed to rise higher and higher on her thighs. I wanted her in the worst way. All the girls I had seen and wanted tended to run through my mind in quick succession.

We both headed for the back of the bus. The bus was filled to capacity, and there was only one seat available on the bus. We both gravitated toward that one seat. I was ahead of her and made it to the seat first. I thought she would not want to sit on the same seat with me, but she had no problem in sitting next to me. We made it to Henderson before either of us opened up with some conversation. In the meantime, I had my eyes on those long-sleek legs, and how high that mini rose on her thighs when she sat down. The longer she sat in the seat the higher her skirt rose.

I couldn't take my eyes off those legs. They were perfect. In Henderson the bus stopped for a few minutes. It was still crowded. A lot of the passengers were students headed for Marshall, Tyler, or Longview.

"Would you like something?" she asked.

I was surprised by her sudden question.

"No thanks," I said.

She came back with a coke and a bag of potato chips. When she came back, she began to engage in conversation. I was again surprised.

"Have some chips."

"No thanks."

"I insist. Take a few chips."

"Thanks."

She wasn't going to let me get away without at least sampling her potato chips and I didn't want to disappoint her.

"Do you go to Stephen F. Austin? I noticed you got on in Nacogdoches."

"Yes, that's where I attend. Is that where you attend also?"

"Yes, I'm a freshman," she said.

"I am too, but I hadn't seen you before," I said.

I knew there were very little chance of us attending the same activities, and therefore little chance of us meeting. Even at the same activities there was little chance of us being able to associate with one another.

"It's a big campus. If you're not careful you can go there for a semester and miss a lot of people."

She was trying to be kind.

"I guess you're right."

"Where're you headed?" she asked.

"I'm headed to Marshall," I said, "I live in Hallsville, but my brother is picking me up in Marshall. I live about ten miles out on Farm Road 165."

"I live in Marshall in the heart of the city," she said, "My parents are picking me up at the bus station as well."

I still had my eyes on those luscious legs all the while. Somehow, I wanted to touch them. Her breast stood at attention as if they were attracted to something in the atmosphere. I was attracted to her, and she must have been attracted to me for some reason.

"Are you seeing anyone on campus?" I asked.

"No, I'm not. I dated a few times, but it's hard to find someone of quality, and the competition is stiff."

"I found the situation to be similar."

"Why don't we get together over the holidays?" she asked.

"Do you think we can get together without having obstacles get in our way over the holidays in a small town like Marshall?"

"I know a little place where we can get together without being interrupted."

About that time, we pulled up into the bus terminal in Marshall.

She caught my arm and looked deep into my eyes, "Call me at this number. It's my private number. You don't have to worry about my parents picking up the phone."

She handed the number to me on a piece of note paper.

I was at home for two days. It was Sunday afternoon and I kept thinking about those legs. I decided to give her a call.

"Hello, this is Sharon,"

"Hi Sharon, we talked all that time and I didn't get your name."

"I know, I didn't get yours either. At the time getting acquainted was more important. What's your name?"

"Freddie."

"Why don't you meet me later on tonight at the Pack and Sack on North Street? We can go from there. I'll be in a Black 1966 GTO Pontiac. It's my car, but my mom wasn't ready for me to bring it to school. I'll have it next semester."

"That sounds good."

"I'll be there at eight o'clock. Don't be late. I don't want to be sitting there in the parking lot waiting on you."

I drove to Marshall and pulled into the parking lot of the Pack and Sack. I spotted the Black GTO Pontiac. The car was also sleek and beautiful with shiny wheels. I pulled up to her car and she saw me. I motioned for her to come over and get in and she did so. I was driving my brother's 1966 Toyota Camry. She gave me directions to a little hide-away motel. At first, I couldn't figure out where she wanted to go, but then I remembered where the motel was located.

"This is the only way we're going to be left alone and have some privacy."

"You're probably correct."

I went in, got a room, and came back to the car. I understood why she chose a little out-of-the-way Black motel. We both enjoyed ourselves, and there was an immediate bond between us. We came back to that little motel on many occasions during the holiday break. We were satisfied being alone rather than being in a crowd of people. It was inappropriate of us to parade around in front of the good citizens of Marshall. After that we spent a great deal of our time talking on the phone.

The time came for us to go back to the campus. We caught the bus on the Sunday after the first day of January and headed back to the campus. We had made plans to catch the same bus. We didn't say anything to each other until we got close to the campus.

"How do you feel about me Freddie?" she asked.

"I feel better about you than I have ever felt about any girl I have met."

"Can we continue to see one another at Stephen F.?"

She gripped my hand tight, and we got off the bus and caught a taxi to our dorms.

From that point on we went to sporting events together, as well as all other events. The next semester she brought her car on campus, and I didn't have to worry about transportation. She let me drive her car wherever I wanted to go. She even took out special insurance so that I would be covered in case of an accident. We relieved our stress by going to Houston or Dallas for an occasional weekend. We dated until we both graduated in May of 1971. She told me that her heart was with me, but her parents had made other obligations for her that she couldn't avoid keeping. My heart was with her also, but I hadn't seen or heard from her since that warm Friday night in May of 1971.

16

BEFORE THE AGE OF SIX

I didn't have many friends, mostly because I didn't have the time or the personality to cultivate them. Bucko and I spent much time roaming the hills and roads together in our early years.

Bucko was my most enduring friend, and I would always think of him with great respect and admiration whenever I thought of my childhood days. I first met Bucko when I was in the third grade, and Bucko was in the first grade. I had remembered seeing Bucko when my sister, Sarah, and I had visited the Larson's, and I was a few years younger. I had heard my parents often speak of the Larson family.

"That Larson family has never gotten a break in life," my mother said. "They've always been dirt poor, without enough food, clothing or shelter to keep the family going."

"They do about as well as anyone else in these parts," my father replied.

"Most people have their own land. The Larson's have always sharecropped on some white man's place."

"I would say they work as hard as anyone else. Lots of people work hard and still never seem to get any place."

"They want everything given to them. They aren't willing to work hard for anything."

"Most Blacks people are in the same boat. They all struggle from day to day."

"Look at those good-for-nothing boys, lazy and won't work. They lie around on their mother, eating her food and stealing her money. They leave home but always come back to lie around on their mother. When they get some money, they spend it until it's gone before they'll work again."

My mother felt that Bucko's parents were lazy and didn't have a desire to get a foothold on bettering their condition, but my father spoke sympathetically of them. He had always felt that way toward individuals who seemingly had more misery than he did. I couldn't understand how any family could have more misery than mine.

"These boys have been beaten down by the system," my father said. "They have no education, no skills, and can't get a decent job. Some people just aren't going to work on any kind of job. I wouldn't work some jobs they offer Black men."

A chance meeting provided me with my first lasting impression of Bucko. One day I missed my bus but was able to catch a ride on another bus that went by Bucko's house and let me off at a nearby bus stop. When I saw Bucko, I remembered him from the time before when I had smart-mouthed his grandmother.

To me Bucko seemed a pitiful frame of a boy. He was about eight-years old and had a very sad look on his face, as though he had been through hell and didn't get burned but was greatly affected by it. We both probably had that pitiful look in common, for it was impossible to look any more pitiful than I. Part of my feelings had to do with the picture my parents had painted of Bucko's family. I instantly took a liking to this pitiful little boy whom I had been told was so poor and needy. We greeted each other and didn't get very friendly at first.

Bucko seemed to have a certain coldness and reserve about him, which usually comes with being treated with indifference over a long period of time and being exposed to poverty and neglect. He worked hard at trying to mask his real feelings. We both had developed a similar approach to life, and we used it to mask the hurt that we had already experienced at such a young-tender age.

Bucko and I would visit each other at least once or twice a week, especially during the summer months. Sometimes he would spend the night at my house or I would spend the night at his. We would walk and talk for miles. One bright, sunny Saturday, we walked almost twenty miles to and from a nearby town. We had sporadic conversation along the way.

"One of these days, man, I'm gonna' travel around the country."

"Yeah, man, I want to go to California," Bucko replied.

"What've you heard about California?"

"People are friendly, there's lots of water, and my uncle tells me it's easy to make a living."

"I'm not sure where I want to go yet. I'm gonna' travel first and see some places, then I can make up my mind about where I want to live."

"Where've you been so far?"

"I've been to lots of small places in Luzana and Texas. But the largest places I've been are: Dallas, Ft. Worth, Houston, Shreveport, and New Orleans. Where've you been?"

"I haven't been any further than East Texas."

"Don't worry we'll both see the world one day."

"Maybe we could do like Budd and Todd in 'Route 66.' Get us a Corvette and travel around the country," said Bucko.

"That would be great," I replied.

"It really would, man."

"You've got to have money and a nice car to travel around the country."

"We can get a job, save our money, buy a car, and hit the road."

"I get tired of walking across these hills and valleys. I'll be glad when I can get a car. If I had a car, I could go just about any place I wanted. When I get older, I'm getting a car and leaving East Texas for certain."

We were both silent for a moment, then the conversation shifted to a new girl in the neighborhood who had come from Detroit for the summer.

"I really like Tonya, man," said Bucko.

Tonya was Mrs. Cooper's granddaughter, an older woman who lived across the way.

"Tonya is mine, man," I said.

"We can both share her, man."

"I like her a lot. She's cute and has a nice body for someone her age. She's the kind of girl I would marry. But I have to be careful you know what happen with John and Shelly."

John was my older brother, and Shelly was Tonya's aunt. John was supposed to have gotten Shelly pregnant but never did admit it.

"John almost had a shotgun wedding," said Bucko.

"Don't talk about that, man, I don't like to talk about it. I'm still going by to see Tonya tomorrow."

The sun was hot, and our thoughts drifted to the weather.

"How the hell did it get so damn hot?" asked Bucko.

"It's hot in East Texas, that's one reason why I want to get away from here. I'm tired of plowing that mule every day in the hot sun."

"I'd get tired of that myself. I don't see how you stand it."

"I've no other choice."

We talked about one subject and then another. Mr. Crayton the school bus driver, passed then stopped about fifty feet headed in the opposite direction. We ran and got on his truck, happy to get a ride.

"Where're you boys going?" Mr. Crayton asked.

"Just taking a walk into town," I replied.

"It's a long walk back to your house. I have to pick up something, but I'll be returning home in a few minutes. Would you boys like a ride back?"

"Thanks, sir. Sure, would appreciate a ride. It's hot out here," said Bucko.

Mr. Crayton lived a few miles down the road from me.

I was fifteen and Bucko was fourteen-years old at the time, not regretting a moment, and delighted to be young bucks that were vibrant and alive with energy. Each weekend we would get together to walk and talk. I tried to show Bucko a different side of life by taking him places and sharing anything I had with him. Bucko accepted some things but not my values. I finally figured out that I couldn't convert Bucko into a studious individual who was interested in school.

Once, I felt sorry for Bucko; my brother John had come home for the weekend and was angry about something. Bucko got in the car slowly and had his hand in the door. John closed the door before Bucko could remove his hand. The door crushed several of Bucko's fingers. John took him home and apologized to his grandmother for hastily shutting the door. His fingers healed normally.

Bucko was the closest thing to a brother I had in my day-to-day relationships. Most of my biological brothers were away from home; they were grown up and had lives of their own. I had nephews and nieces, but they were many miles away, and we would only see each other on rare occasions. There were other boys in the neighborhood, but they always, as boys will do, tended to have some kind of fight brewing. No matter what activity they became involved in, it always ended in a situation where they had to demonstrate their fighting prowess. Since I was small for my age, I tried to avoid such situations. I was always peace-loving and didn't care to fight. Bucko and I had something in common: we both admired and respected each other's sister. Bucko liked my sister Debra and I liked his sister Gloria. Neither girl paid either of us any attention. Neither situation amounted to more than a teenage crush. Gloria and Debra both probably felt that we were too immature, ragged, and tattered for them. Gloria probably never saw me as anything but a young, immature, retard who could barely talk. One day we had a conversation about it.

"Debra is pretty, man. I'd like to marry her."

"I want to marry Gloria."

"Gloria has lots of boyfriends."

Bucko knew I didn't have a chance, and this was his way of sparing my feelings. He didn't want me to talk about his sister, but he wanted to talk about mine.

"Debra has a boyfriend too. Besides, what kind of game are you playing?"

"I believe I can move them out of her life. All I have to do is turn on my charms."

"Get real."

"Gloria's five years older than you."

"Don't blame me for wanting her."

"You know that we're both wasting our time. We had both better go and see Tonya," Bucko said.

"I'm afraid you're right," I said.

Gloria lived in Marshall with the woman English teacher at my high school. This English teacher had taken Gloria into her home when she was in her early teens, and she had lived with her since. Prior to that, Gloria had known mostly poverty and distress. The English teacher provided for her needs in grand style. She eventually went to college. It was as if Gloria was the teacher's own child, as far as I was concerned, though the teacher did have several older children of her own. The teacher had a beautiful home in one of the best parts of town and could offer Gloria a better way of life than her own parents.

Gloria went to the same school as I did, and though she was much older, I admired her grace and beauty. She was everything I thought a young girl should be: tall, light skinned, well-built, with a beautiful face, and long-straight hair. One day I asked Gloria to help me with my science homework. I knew how to do my homework but wanted to be close to her and hear her voice.

"Gloria, what does photosynthesis mean?" I asked, nervously.

"That's when plants take in sunlight and make oxygen."

"How does that work?"

I wanted her to think I was helpless. I didn't care how dumb she thought I was, as long as she wanted to help me.

"It's difficult to explain."

She didn't take the bait, and I didn't know what else to say. She was the dream of my life. I was fixated on white or light-skinned women for much of my youth. Like many Black men, I had been brainwashed: too much televisions, movies, and magazines that showed cultured white women. I finally figured out that color served no useful purpose except as a basis on which to discriminate. I used to enjoy looking at Gloria's yellow thighs and her light skin. Gloria was a close friend of my sister Sarah. I engaged in many fantasies about Gloria. When she was around my heart would flutter. All I could do was stutter in her presence. I wanted someday to be close to her, though deep inside I knew the opportunity would never come.

I was sure that since Gloria had lived with this teacher, she had been introduced to some of the finer things of life. Not only was I too young for her, but I was also beneath her in grade level and social class at that point, never mind the humble situation in which she had originally existed. Gloria graduated at the end of my freshman year. The last time I saw her was the day she graduated from high school in May of 1963. I was too shy to tell her what I thought of her. I would have liked to have seen her again, but never did.

I was too stupid to know that my uncle was her father, and we were also closely related on the other side of the family. My parents never thought to tell me who my cousins were. Bucko lived with his grandmother. His real mother had remarried, and as happens in many cases, it was easier to let grandmothers keep the children by a former relationship. It was a practice in those days and still is a practice to cast such children off to a grandmother or aunt. His mother changed men frequently but visited him on a regular basis. Practically every Sunday she would come and visit with Bucko and his grandmother, and Bucko often spent time at his mother's house. Bucko's mother spoke so rapidly that she was almost unintelligible.

I wanted Bucko to have my values: that is, to take school seriously, to be ambitious, and to stay out of trouble. I tried to instill in Bucko my concerns for getting an education and staying in school, but to no avail. I felt deep inside that I would achieve something in my life, and wanted to help Bucko amount to something too, so I tried to help Bucko understand that his life should have some direction. When Bucko missed school, I would challenge him, make him explain why, and tell him how important it was for him to go to school.

"Bucko, why did you miss school yesterday?"

"I had to go to town with my mother."

"Watch what I tell you, man."

"I'll be here from now on."

"You better not miss anymore. It's hard to do anything without an education."

I was repeating some words I had heard somewhere. I didn't even remember where.

"I'm going to get mine," Bucko said.

"Don't you want to get a good job and get out of East Texas?"

"Yes, I do."

"Then you had better begin to apply yourself to your schoolwork." Again, I was mimicking words I wasn't even applying myself.

"I apply myself."

"To what?"

Bucko didn't know what it meant to apply himself.

"Everything I do."

"If you're going to hang with me, man, you had better get your act together."

"My act is together."

"OK then, if you want to be a smart ass."

Most of our disagreements came because I was always on his back trying to get him to straighten out his life. I continued to labor, day after day, trying to advise him of the benefits of an education. Bucko simply refused to listen to what I had to say and would skip school whether he had a reason or not. He was hard, cold, and made up his mind that he was going to have his way in spite of what I admonished him to do. As Bucko grew older, he used the excuse that he needed to make money. Bucko wasn't interested in my values; he had his own. Bucko kept getting into trouble with the police and was accused of stealing many times. I was so embarrassed that I didn't want to discuss the details with Bucko. I didn't want to hang with someone who had such a reputation. Bucko never spent any time in reform school, or jail for that matter, but everyone thought he was headed down a very broad and loose path. He was very intelligent but had no interest in school. He usually missed many days out of the school year, sometimes because he didn't have the clothing he wanted to wear.

All but a few of the boys in the area followed a pattern of dropping out of school in junior high and going to work. Most of these boys were intelligent, but their families encouraged them to quit school and go to work to help support the family. I tried to keep Bucko from following that crowd, but he seemed drawn to them more than to me or my style of existence. Bucko ran with many of these boys and developed some of their habits. I could not seem to convince him that hanging out with these boys was a bad thing for him and would only get him into trouble.

"Why do you hang with these chumps? They drink, steal, and they're gonna' get you in trouble."

"They're good people, man."

"You know Gene and Wilson were put in jail for burglary and rape last week, and you're going to get in the same kind of trouble if you hang with them."

"They were framed by the police."

"According to whom?"

"That's what they said."

Now and then Bucko allowed his naiveté to show through.

"Sure, they would say anything to get out of trouble."

My reasons for saying some of these things were because I was jealous. I still didn't like some of their behavior and felt that Bucko shouldn't associate with them. Most of their pranks were normal for boys their ages, but since I was not a fighter and was so easy going, I felt intimidated around them, though I never had a problem in taking Bucko on when his temper flared.

I could remember one incident where Bucko and I had a physical confrontation. One day we were walking through the woods during one of our regular outings, and Bucko kept teasing me about something that happened.

"Didn't I tell you not to play with me?"

"What do you mean play?"

"Don't do it again or I'm going to hurt you."

He did it again, and I picked up a tree limb and walloped him across his head. Bucko was more adventurous, aggressive, and persistent about some things than I. Bucko didn't have any farm chores to do, and consequently had more time to spend in the streets than I did. As he got older, he began to get out of control, and his grandmother couldn't manage him. I could recall several instances of Bucko's grandmother trying to whip him, and it looked as if Bucko was whipping her. I always respected my mother, though I knew she was fixated on an earlier period in time, and after I reached the age of fourteen, she gave up on whipping me.

Bucko and I were usually intelligent enough to fight only at the verbal level. On occasions I would get sick and tired of his behavior and lash out at him. Usually Bucko would not challenge my authority. Part of Bucko's reasons for accepting my authority was because I had all the resources: transportation, money, and the knowledge of how to get what I wanted. Most of the time Bucko relied on my resources. At times I would get angry because I felt Bucko was relying on me too much. I was willing to help him but didn't want him to become too dependent.

On many occasions I tried to get Bucko to work with me on our farm and would pay him.

"How about helping us with gathering and selling our produce to the market?"

"Are you going to pay me?"

"Sure, I'll pay you."

"How much?"

"The same as every other farmer pays their hands. Why don't you come by at eight o'clock in the morning? We can begin then."

Bucko worked once but never came back again to work. He wasn't willing to exert himself on a consistent basis and was unreliable. I never could count on Bucko being there when it was necessary to get work done. Bucko was just like they said about his uncles. He would work only long enough to get a few dollars in his pocket and not show up again until that was completely gone.

I was not sure why Bucko and I never associated at school—possibly because our school interests were so different, and I was several years ahead of him. Bucko eventually got tired of wearing the same clothes every day, never having enough money in his pocket, and started cutting school more and more often.

When I started to drive, I went my own way, and Bucko found other neighborhood boys to hang out with. There were a number of factors involved in why we went our separate ways. One of them was because one day I put Bucko out of my car. We had both worked all that evening hauling hay in my truck. I knew Bucko had money because I had paid him out of the money I received.

"Can you give me some money on the gas?"

"I don't have any money."

"I just paid you for hauling hay. I know you have money."

"I don't have any to spare."

"OK, then get out."

"Man, you gonna' put me out?"

"Yes, and don't try to get in my car again."

I made it a practice never to take anyone anyplace unless they helped with the gas. I did this because my parents weren't paying for repair bills or supplying me with gas. I had to pay for this myself. I wasn't giving away any freebies. I put Bucko out of my car in a town twenty miles away from our homes in the country. Later I regretted it, but decided I couldn't carry Bucko any more, we weren't children any longer. That was the last time I saw Bucko. I went away to college and lost all contact with Bucko.

One of my sisters said Bucko died of some type of seizure and couldn't get to the doctor in time to save his life. We lived twenty miles from the nearest medical facility. My other sister said he was killed in a robbery attempt. I'm not sure what happened. In any case, Bucko actually lost his life before he was six years of age.

17

THE ANGUS BULL

It was June 20, 1970. It was a clear, hot, muggy Saturday— not a cloud in the sky. It was hotter than a cayenne and jalapeno peppers' pie. It was about 105 degrees. You could see steam in the air. We lived in a small-rural town in East Texas called Hallsville, on a mid-size ranch about five miles outside town on Highway 165. The landscape was a combination of rolling hills and flatland. On a clear day you could see for miles. Hallsville was approximately 1,300 in population. Longview was ten miles to the north and Marshall was ten miles to the south. Dallas was 145 miles to the north.

Many people were retiring and moving back to this part of the country. In the 1930s, '40s and '50s many of them had moved away. They moved away in the latter part of the great migration into larger cities: some move to industrial cities of the North, Midwest, West, and Northeast. Many felt that things had improved in this part of the country and were coming back to reclaim the land. It was truly beautiful country. The sun shined constantly except for intermittent rain. Usually the weather was balanced. There was plenty of good fishing and hunting. I loved the vast array of wildflowers in spring that could be seen as one traversed the countryside.

Last year my father had employed a construction company from Shreveport to build a beautiful two-story log cabin with four bedrooms, a family room, a living room, two bathrooms, a library, and a laundry room. This replaced the old makeshift house that sat on the property, which was nothing more than a barn that could be lived in. We had all the modern conveniences in our log cabin.

My father retired from teaching agriculture in a town called Springdale, about 70 miles north of Hallsville, and wanted to follow his dream of having a ranch. My dad loved ranching and everything it involved. He taught agriculture in a large high school for over 30 years. I think he wanted to assume a more relaxed life style. He never did like larger cities. Owning a cattle ranch was big business in Texas, and many used it as an independent business. He said he wanted something he could pass down through the generations. Passing it on to me wasn't such a good idea, but he figured maybe he could pass it on to one of my sister's children. She was the mother of two boys. Her two boys were doing well in sixth and seventh grade. If not her children, maybe her husband would be interested. My sister's husband was an auto-mechanic and was raised on a farm not far from where we lived. I wasn't that crazy about ranching but could take it or leave it. I wanted to be a professional, not always stepping in cow manure, all day, every day of the rest of my life.

My father already owned a hundred acres of land, so there was nothing left but to buy the livestock and get his ranch started. The ranch was already started for the most part. Most of this land had not been cleared, he planned to clear all of it that it was feasible to clear, plant a favorable variety of grass for the cattle, and cut and bail the rest as hay for winter. We already had 20 prized Black Angus cattle that he had acquired in recent years while anticipating his retirement but didn't own a bull. The only bull he had died mysteriously last year. He decided to purchase a bull. We also owned a few pigs that we raised and sold to the market, several prize ponies, some chickens, ducks, and had a fish pond about one-hundred yards from the ranch house. The horses were strictly for riding only. We also grew a variety of vegetables for ourselves to eat.

During the past year, prior to my father's retiring, we had a foreman who cared for the ranch. The foreman was no longer necessary. My father, mother, and I would come to the ranch every weekend. We now lived on the ranch permanently. My mother had taught English at a high school in Springdale for thirty years while I had attended high school. My mother also retired and was satisfied with a more relaxed way of life. I graduated in May of this year. I planned to attend Howard University in Washington D.C. in the fall and study dentistry. I had a 3.8 grade point average and made a 30 on the ACT. I attended great schools in Springdale. My grade point average could have been better, but I would always read the latest books, newspapers and magazines, instead of concentrating on my homework. I had applied for several scholarships and was waiting to hear from them. My counselor assured me it was just a matter of time before I heard from them. The counselor also told me that it would be harder for me than some to get a scholarship because of the annual salary of my parents.

A man several miles up the road from us had a number of magnificent purebred bulls that weighed at least 2,500 lbs. each, and was sleek, shiny, and black. All of them stood about four-feet high and broad in the shoulders. He also had 100 head of prime Angus cattle. My father picked out the bull he wanted. To my father the bull seemed like an excellent seed bull. The man we bought the bull from said he was well mannered. My father paid $1,000.00 for the bull, bought him on sight, loaded him on the trailer, and brought him home. My father thought he had gotten the bull rather cheap, and figured he only gave him such a deal because he was a neighbor. The bull gave us no problems and did seem good-natured.

We got up early today, had breakfast—some eggs, sausage, pancakes, grits, and apple juice. My sister had come in last night. She drove in by herself. She said her husband had some business to take care of, and her sons had a Little League game today. My parents and my sister engaged in some chitchat about life in general, and my sister struck up another conversation with me.

"What're you going to do with your life," she asked. I'm glad she was concerned. My sister had always been right there in my corner. It didn't matter what I needed she would be right there to help me out. She and her husband bought me a nice-gold watch and a briefcase for my graduation. She had always been there to support me. She frequently bought me clothes and books, or whatever I asked for. Books were one of her favorite gifts. I loved to read, and she knew what good books did for the mind. She and her husband wanted to purchase me a good secondhand car as soon as I obtained my driver's license, but I asked her to wait until I was situated in college. That's when I would really need a car.

"I'm going to Howard University and study dentistry."

"What makes you want to study dentistry?"

"I just always wanted to be a dentist."

"That will take a lot of study and hard work."

For a while there she acted as if she doubted my ability to pursue a degree in dentistry.

"I know that already, but no pain, no gain."

I knew she didn't doubt me in reality. My sister was trying to warn me not to get in over my head. She wanted me to do something I could be successful at, and not something that would stress me out.

"If you need any help feel free to call on me. You shouldn't have any problem with your grades and score on the ACT."

"Thank you. I do hope to get a scholarship."

"It's kind of hard to get a job around here for the summer, why don't you come to Dallas and try to get a job for the summer."

"I promised the old man I would work for him during the summer and earn some money for college. He is going to pay me more than I could earn on a job in Dallas. Besides, the job with Dad is guaranteed."

I figured I'd rather help my father than work for someone else. I would also be investing in something I might have ownership in one day.

"Let me know if you need anything when you get to college."

"Thanks, I will."

I was glad to hear her say that. I knew in college there would be times when I would need to call on her for help. There would be lots of things I would need in college. Besides my parents, she and her husband were the only people I could count on. In fact, I was waiting for the appropriate time to bring up the idea of the car we had discussed earlier in high school.

We kept the bull for only two weeks, and at that point it began to act out on this Saturday morning. It was out of the blue and totally unexpected. On this particular Saturday morning my father told my sister he wanted to show her his prize bull. My father was proud of his ranch and his cattle. She had attended Grambling University, studied art, and was an art teacher in Dallas. She had never spent time around any kind of animals. She had been teaching for the past four years. The barn was about 100 yards from the house. She didn't really want to go see the bull, just did it to humor my father. My father, my sister, and I walked up to the barn where all the cattle were gathered. There were only two children in the family. My sister was eight-years older than myself.

I just graduated from high school in May, weighed 140 lbs., and was five-feet-eight inches tall. My sister weighed 130 lbs. and was five-five. My father weighed 165 lbs. and was five-feet-nine. None of us were prepared to handle a 2,500 lbs. bull or had any idea about how to handle such a bull. Neither my sister nor I knew anything about bulls or what to expect from them. Helen, my sister, had on a loud color red blouse.

From a distance the bull seemed perfectly calm until we got close. As soon as we opened the gate, got about 10 yards from the bull, it charged after us. Luckily, we were close to the corral. All three of us jumped inside the corral and closed the gate. The bull acted as if it would charge right into us. My father had to push my sister into the corral; she seemed unaware of the danger. I don't think she expected the bull would follow through with his threats. We had no idea what was wrong with the bull. The bull made a beeline for us. The bull was humping its back and snorting as if it had gone mad, it again snorted, made a loud noise, and jumped on several cows and rode them for about ten yards. The bull jumped up on the side of the barn and humped his back as if it was inseminating a cow. The bull's penis kept protruding and retracting, as it butted its head against the fence. It tried to break into the corral, but it was recently built, and was sturdy and strong.

The bull kept pawing in the dirt with his feet and attempting to jump over the corral. The bull stumbled a few feet, fell to its knees, and quickly got to its feet. Foam appeared to be coming out of its nose. My father, sister, nor I could understand what was wrong with the bull. My father knew a lot about the behavior of animals, having studied animals for most of his life, but he couldn't understand it.

The bull soon began to calm down. We stayed in the corral until the rest of the cattle ventured off for the pasture, the bull followed them making loud noises while trying to mount one then the other.

We then closed the corral gate and went back to the ranch house. Father decided to get rid of the bull and get another one. He didn't want to keep a bull like that around.

"What made it act like that Dad?" I asked.

"Darn if I know, but I'm getting rid of it as soon as I can."

"Maybe it was just a one-time thing."

"Whatever it is, I don't need that around here. I'm gonna' trade it for one of the other bulls. All of them can't be this neurotic."

I couldn't believe, as much experience as my father had with animals, he didn't have a clue as to what was wrong with the bull.

"Yeah, what's wrong with it Dad?" my sister asked.

Again, he said, "I don't know. I've never seen a bull act like that before."

The man he bought the bull from was glad to trade for another one. My father wasn't willing to give the bull another chance, acting out once in a major way was enough for my father. My father said the next time it might injure someone. This bull had put a scare into him. He was able to trade the bull for another one just as magnificent. A bull that weighed 2,500 lbs. could be dangerous when out of control. We never knew for sure what got into that bull on that particular day. When the man came to pick up the bull it was as gentle as a lamb. He quickly loaded the bull on the trailer, and the next day my father picked up another one that was better behaved. My father never mentioned to the rancher exactly why he wanted another bull. He said he gave him some "cock and bull" story as to why he wanted to trade for another one.

"Do you think the color of Helen's blouse had anything to do with the bull acting out?" I asked my father.

"I don't know son. I have heard people say that a bull will charge the color red, but I thought it was just superstition."

"I have heard also many times that bulls will charge something with a loud red color. That's supposedly why the matador used a red cape to intimidate the bull."

Somehow, I didn't feel comfortable suggesting to my father that my sister's blouse was what upset the bull. I didn't want to seem unorthodox. But I suggested it anyway.

"There just may be something to that old superstition."

My sister never went near another bull again. My father eventually increased his herd to over fifty head and achieved his dream of being an authentic cattle rancher. Eventually he owned several magnificent Angus bulls. He never encountered such a problem again.

I did get a full-ride to Howard. In the fall I went to Howard and did eventually become a dentist. Helen was correct. It took a lot of hard work before I obtained my degree. My father willed the ranch to both me and my sister's two boys. We carried on his legacy.

18

MY BEST BRANDY AND SCOTCH

I grew up in the Chatham neighborhood on the South Side of Chicago. I attended the University of Chicago Lab School and had a 3.9 grade point average. I belonged to a variety of clubs and social organizations at the lab school. My parents and I attended church every Sunday and Wednesday. I had a normal middle-class upbringing, was a model student, and never got into gangs or other kinds of trouble. Gangs tried to recruit me, but I somehow avoided them. My parents were fully middle-class citizens who seemed socially, educationally, politically, economically, and psychologically well adjusted. They were very political and were always involved in one campaign or another. As a youth I was never that involved in politics. My mother was a high school teacher on the south side, and my father was a supervisor for the Department of Streets and Sanitation. They made sure that I was inundated with middle-class values.

Henry, my best friend, also went to the lab school. He had a 3.4 grade point average, and we both participated in the same clubs and organizations. His father was a preacher of a medium-size church, and his mother was a guidance counselor. Henry's parents weren't that involved in politics. Neither of us was that involved in sports, except to occasionally play on the playground, and watch it with our fathers on Sunday afternoons. The lab school didn't sponsor any sports teams. We had been close friends since the first grade. He lived two houses down from mine on the same side of the street. We both lived in well-built-sturdy brick bungalows— built during the 1950s, but still nice houses. We did everything together: wherever you found me, you could be sure he was around somewhere. We made a pact that whatever happened to one would happen to the other.

I remember my father questioning me in high school about what I wanted to study in college.

"What're you going to do with your life, son?" wanting to be sure I got on the right track before it was too late.

"I'm going to major in business and sociology," speaking like I was sure of myself.

"What made you decide on business and sociology," curious about my decision.

"I want to help myself first and then help other people," demonstrating that I was definite about my plans.

"Be sure it's something in which you can make a good living. Don't major in something minor," he was trying to provide me with fatherly guidance.

"What do you mean?" not clear what he meant by something minor.

"Some people go to college and are never able to practice what they study or make a good living. Be sure the field you study will support you financially," not wanting me to waste my time in college.

"I think business will do that Dad. If not, I can always think about going into business for myself."

"What college do you plan to attend?" never having discussed it with him before.

"I'm not sure yet. I thought about going locally, but felt it might be better to have a change of atmosphere," assuring him that I had given it some thought.

"Think about Morehouse. It is one of the best Black colleges. It will develop you socially and intellectually, as well as academically," wanting me to know my options.

"I'll consider it," letting him know that I valued his opinion.

"Look into it and let me know what you think."

When it was all said and done, Henry's parents had the same idea, so we decided to go to Morehouse. In addition, the minister at my church, whose opinion I valued highly, suggested Morehouse. The Black counselor at the lab school also suggested Morehouse. They had a major in business as well as in sociology, so we decided to go there. Henry decided to take the same major, though he wasn't quite as enthused about business as I was.

We graduated from the lab school on an eighty-degree sunshiny, clear day at the beginning of June. There wasn't a cloud in the sky. Henry said it was a sign for good things ahead for the both of us. Family, relatives, friends, and others wished us the best. Henry and I never left each others side. Neither of us had a girl to leave behind. We didn't get that serious about girls in high school. We were too serious about our studies. So that was one hurdle we didn't have to overcome.

The day came when we went off to Morehouse College. We said good-bye to our parents, relatives, friends, and significant others. The situation didn't change that much. We both pledged Alpha Phi Alpha and were members of several other organizations. We were also roommates for four years. We were inseparable on the campus and did everything together. We always participated in the same activities: even went to chapel and traveled around the South together during our college years. Henry and I were as close as two peas in a pod. We had a habit of attending lectures at other colleges in the Atlanta area for pleasure and recreation: we thought this would be good for our overall development.

It was at Atlanta University that I met Althea. I happen to be at a lecture with another college friend when I met her. Henry was too busy to attend that lecture. We made a date for pizza, and I fell in love with her right away. I invited her home for Christmas. Before we went home, I told Henry I was bringing a girl home for the Christmas Holiday. I remember he wanted the details about her. My father and mother had combined resources and bought me a 1972 Malibu that was practically new. Henry and I shared the expenses as we traveled around the country on vacations.

When Henry found out I was dating her he wanted to know all about her.

"When did you meet her?"

"I met her at a John Henrik Clarke's lecture on the Atlanta University campus."

"I'm surprised I haven't heard more about her," thinking I was keeping things from him.

"You know how it is, some thing you keep to yourself," beginning to define some borders.

"Not from your best buddy."

"She is a beautiful girl, about five-feet-five, one-twenty-five, with nice legs, and a wonderful personality."

"It'll be good to meet her."

"You'll have a good opportunity to meet her on our trip home during the holidays."

"That sounds good."

Henry hadn't met her and didn't meet her until the day we left (it was 1973), and all three of us drove home in the same car. Henry liked her and felt that she was the girl for me."

Prior to my meeting Althea, Henry and I both had dated any number of girls in the Atlanta Complex. Henry continued to date girls from other colleges.

We laughed, talked, and sang all the way to Chicago, until our vocal cords got fatigued. I've never had more fun. I was glad that Henry and Althea got along well together.

Henry and I graduated from Morehouse in 1975. Althea graduated from Atlanta University at the same time. We had thought about getting married, finally I asked her to marry me, and she said yes. It was the happiest moment of my life. Again, all three of us took the ride back to Chicago in my 1972 Chevrolet Malibu. Neither of us had anything but the clothes in our suitcases. We were careful to get rid of anything that was outdated, so we could all fit our things in the trunk. Henry was going to live with his parents until he could get a job. Althea and I were going to stay with my parents until we could both secure a job, then we would get married. It had all been worked out.

I got a job as administrator of a social agency in about a month, and Althea got a job as a teacher on the south side the following September. Henry was slow to get a job but finally got a job as a counselor in the Department of Mental Health working for the city. My father helped him to get that job through the precinct captain. Althea and I were both able to hold on to our jobs, but Henry couldn't seem to hold on to his. I guess he felt easy come, easy go. Althea and I found a nice apartment in Hyde Park, and took up residence there. Henry was still living with his parents. It was two years after graduation from college.

Practically every day when I got home from work Henry would be at my apartment, crying his eyes out, and giving Althea and I a sad story about his job situation; and the woes, trials, and tribulation of an unequal society. He thought he should be able to get a better job and didn't feel it was fair for a college graduate to have to put up with some of the things he had to put up with. I liked to drink Brandy and Scotch now and then. I didn't have a habit but did like to drink socially. I also liked to keep Brandy and Scotch around for friends when they came over. I noticed that I couldn't keep Brandy and Scotch in my cabinet, and it wasn't just any Brandy and Scotch, it was the best. I thought it was just my wife drinking it, but it was her and Henry both doing the damage. I got the habit of drinking good Brandy and Scotch from my father. He liked nothing but the best.

I guess I was naive. I would leave Althea and Henry alone while I went to the store. I would ask Henry if he wanted to go with me, and he would say he would wait until I got back. What could I say? I didn't want to force him to come with me. Since Henry wasn't working most of the time, he would come by as soon as Althea got out of school. Usually she got out of school about two-thirty every afternoon. Most days he would be there when I got home. It was easy to do since he barely kept a job. I should have put a stop to it, but we all had been friends for five years. I didn't think their relationship could do any harm. I had always shared what I had with him. I thought the relationship was good for Henry since he seemed to be having an adjustment problem.

One fine day I came home and caught him having sex with Althea in the bedroom. They were so carried away that they forgot that it was about time for me to come home, and were so intense in their lovemaking that they couldn't think about anything else.

"What's going on Henry," looking at him very intensely.

"I thought you knew what was going on, and was just willing to share with your friend," trying to put on his shirt.

"Why would you do this to a friend who has always been there for you?" I tighten up my fist.

I started to hit him, but then considered that it wouldn't do any good. The damage had already been done.

"It's been going on for the past two years. I thought you had to know," finally fastening his belt.

I have never seen a more disgusting sight than the two of them in bed together.

I told Henry to get out, and that I didn't want to see him again. Our friendship was over. I hated to say it but felt that was best for all of us. Althea tried to tell me that he needed us, and wanted to know how I could treat a lifetime friend that way. I was going to give Althea another chance, because I cared so much about her.

However, she came to me and told me, under the circumstances, she was moving in with Henry. She had tears in her eyes.

"But Henry lives with his parents," I said, seemingly outdone.

"Can you give me two weeks to find a place," looking sad. "I've got to go baby."

I didn't want to give up on our relationship.

"Do you know what you're doing?"

"Yes, it's too late for us baby."

"Why don't we give it another try? Bad times occur in every relationship."

"It wasn't just Henry. It could've been anybody showing a little affection."

"Didn't I show you affection?"

"You're more concerned about your job than me."

"It just seems that way baby. I love you."

"I have been around you for several years. If I thought you could change, I would stay, but you can't change. What you are is a part of your DNA."

"OK, baby, if you feel that way."

She said Henry needed her. I wished her my best and didn't think I would ever be happy again. Why would she leave me for a man who couldn't hold a Job? Her bags were packed, and she walked out the door. She was ripping my heart right out of my chest. My heart walked out the door with her. It was the saddest day of my life. Althea and Henry got married on a hot night in July 1979. They invited me but somehow, I didn't have the heart to attend. I did pass by the reception several times just to see if I could get a glimpse of them. I couldn't believe my best friend since first grade, who had shared and done everything together, in the end drank my best Brandy and Scotch, and stole my wife.

Henry never was able to keep a job. He would obtain a job and pretend to try, but he just didn't have it in him. He became a chronic alcoholic, and at times would beat Althea as well as emotionally abuse her. Althea eventually ran off with the TV cable man and took up residence in Atlanta. There relationship was doomed from the start.

I would never be quite the same but somehow managed to survive. It would have been more difficult to make it had it not been for the strong background that my parents gave me, and the experiences received from the educational system. It was that and the counselling received from a minister at my church that helped me to survive. What happened to Henry to cause him to go astray? I will never know the whole of it. His background was just as good as mine. Of course, there could have been something in his background that I didn't know about, as close as we were supposed to be. As they say, *everyone won't get to the promise land.*

I continued to be an administrator for the same social agency. I haven't heard from Althea and Henry since they sent me that invitation to their wedding. Friends kept me informed about some of the things happening in their lives. I heard that it took hitting rock bottom for Henry to change his ways. Last I heard he was a counselor for an alcoholic rehabilitation program. I harbored no hard feelings for either Althea or Henry. Althea left me because of my own naïveté, and my overly exuberant efforts to provide a living for my family. I had a good background, went to good schools; but I wasn't prepared for my best friend to drink my best Brandy and Scotch, and steal my wife.

19

CHRONICLES OF A BUS TRIP: FROM CHICAGO, ILLINOIS TO NORTH CHARLESTON, SOUTH CAROLINA

I came to Chicago in June 1974 from Houston, Texas, seeking better economic opportunities. Most of my early life was spent in East Texas. After graduating from college, spending time in the Navy, and graduating from a Masters' social work program, I was looking for the best opportunity I could get. I held various jobs between 1974 and 1991. My career had come to a standstill, and I was looking for something else to get involved in. I had worked at a chronic disease hospital; a mental health center; and was a private therapist, as well as several other minor positions.

I became interested in the Black family prior to 1991: my interest developed after reading Jewelle Taylor Gibbs book concerning the Black male as an endangered species. Making presentations at conferences had become one of my favorite things to do. My academic side was beginning to manifest itself. I began to participate in various Black family conferences around the country. Among the many Black family conferences I participated in, was the Black Family Conference out of the University of South Carolina, and the University of Kansas in Lawrence, Kansas. Generally, the workshop in South Carolina was held in different parts of the state. In 1991 it was held in North Charleston, South Carolina.

Under normal conditions I would drive, fly, or maybe catch a train to where I wanted to go. But this year I decided to go by bus. The truth of the matter is I was trying to conserve on funds. I hadn't worked in several months. So, I packed my bags, got together the other things I wanted to take, and got on the road. Usually I tried to sell some books at the conferences to offset my traveling expenses and make some extra money.

My wife and I were having an argument, so I got a friend to drive me to the bus station in Chicago. It was a cold night in April, and the wind was sweeping clean like a new broom off the lake. I had never taken such a long bus trip before, didn't know how stressful it could be, and was actually looking forward to it. So, I loaded my luggage and books on the bus, and the bus pulled off for North Charleston, South Carolina.

During the entire trip the bus was never crowded, but at times was almost filled to capacity. Since I was the lone stranger, usually the seat next to me was vacant. Most people are a little leery of sitting next to a complete stranger. People would get on the bus and seek out the one remaining seat. I got an opportunity to meet a lot

of interesting characters in that way. We pulled into
Louisville, Kentucky, and had to wait six hours for a
connecting bus. I didn't bring a book to read and had all
that time on my hands. I hadn't considered reading as a
possible activity on the trip, though reading was another
of my favorite pastimes.

We got back on the road and drove for miles and
miles over open highway, occasionally pulling into a
small town. We made it to Bowling Green, Kentucky. A
young Black man with an African accent got on the bus,
accompanied by a young white female. They sat at the
back of the bus. They were kissing and trying to make
out on the bus. The young woman kept screaming and
moaning. I couldn't see what they were doing, but you
could smell the aroma of sex on the bus. The bus driver
stopped the bus and walked back to the back of the bus
to see what was going on with them. He then threatened
to put them off the bus. The bus driver turned the lights
on, so he could see what was going on. The Black man
asked the bus driver to turn the lights out. The bus
driver became enraged. The woman tapped me on the
shoulder and asked if I wanted to join them. She said
she could make it worth my while. It was tempting, but
she was two thick around the middle for me, wearing a
cheap wig, didn't seem to care about her hygiene, and a
little too promiscuous for my taste. At the time the bus
wasn't filled to capacity. I said no thanks. My conception
was that anyone would do for what she wanted them for

had they been available. Finally, the couple reached their destination in Nashville, Tennessee and got off the bus. They were joyful and cheerful as they exited the bus. The bus driver seemed relieved.

In Knoxville, Tennessee, a young man got on the bus. He appeared to be about fourteen-years old. He had long-blonde, well-kept hair and kept staring at me. He had a soft voice and wore a military uniform, as if he went to military school. His uniform was neat, cleaned and pressed. He had the qualities of a pubescent teenage girl. I got the idea his school was not far away, and he was going home for the weekend. It was Friday night. He kept trying to make conversation, but I was reluctant to engage with him. You never know what kind of characters you're going to meet on such a trip. Eventually the young man got off the bus in Ashville, Tennessee. I was glad, because there was something freaky and strange about him. Observing him would cause any individual to be deeply introspective about their own behavior. I could see why his parents sent him off to military school. They probably didn't want to be reminded of the idea that they had partially failed as parents.

A young girl got on the bus in Ashville, Tennessee. She had three children in tow. The children appeared to be stair steps in ages: like 3, 4, and 5 years of age. When she bent over in her tank top, you could see the word BUTTER tattooed across her backside. She had a pretty face but was a little overweight. She was about five–five and 145 lbs. She said she was on her way to Atlanta, Georgia. She was twenty-five-years old, she and her husband lived in Atlanta, and she had been visiting relatives in Chattanooga, Tennessee. She and her husband had moved to Atlanta from Chattanooga several years earlier.

In Clinton, South Carolina, three people from Sweden got on the bus: a man and two women. One of the girls was a brunet and the other a blonde. The blonde was cute, about five-five, 120 lbs. Smooth skin and a pretty face. Her personality seemed above reproach. The blonde sat on the seat with me, and kept looking over at me, until finally we started a conversation. I couldn't see a reason not to engage in conversation with her. I had heard her say to someone else that she and her two friends were touring the United States, and that she was a student at the University of Stockholm.

"So, you're from Sweden?" smiling as I looked at her.

"Yes, I'll be touring the United States for three months. I'm trying to get a good perspective on what America is like. In the meantime, I'm writing a paper on this country for my Masters' thesis," she seemed proud of her accomplishments.

"What kind of school is the University of Stockholm?"

"It's a Liberal Arts University."

"That sounds like fun. Are you doing it in collaboration with your friends?" I noticed the man in front of me staring at me as I talked to her.

"We're writing the paper as a collaborative thesis," trying to explain why they were traveling together.

The bus pulled up to a station in another town called Newberry, South Carolina.

"How exciting that must be," indicating such a venture would be exciting for me too.

"Would you like something from inside the station," she asked, she got her purse and headed into the station.

"No, I don't want anything," pleased that she would ask me, as she left.

She didn't ask anyone else if they wanted anything, not even the people in her group.

She came back from inside the station.

"I'm getting off the bus in Columbia. Have to make a connection for Columbus, Ohio," as if she hated to leave me so soon.

"It was nice to have met you," I said, letting her know the feeling was mutual.

"See you later."

The bus pulled up to the station in Columbia.

We had ridden together until they were able to make their connections. She got off the bus, and obviously I never saw her again. She was the kind of person I would like to get to know.

In Richtex, a young Chinese girl got on the bus with two Black men. The men near the back of the bus kept getting out of their seat and going to the back of the bus where the girl was. You could hear loud noises coming from the back of the bus. I thought the driver was going to run off the road trying to keep his eyes on the girl and her companions. After about two-hundred miles, all of a sudden, the girl jumped up from her seat and started crying. She said she had missed a connection to Charlotte that would put her on a flight to China, and if she missed it, it wouldn't be traveling again for several more days. To top all that off it was 2:00 a.m. She got off in Columbia in order to make her way the best she could for a connection with her flight.

In Orangeburg, South Carolina, a young lady got on the bus. She was approximately nineteen years of age, smooth-long legs, and a pretty face. She was probably around five–six and 125 lbs. There was only one seat left on the bus, so she sat on the seat with me. I started a conversation with her.

"Where are you headed?" looking directly at her.

"To Summerville," she failed to make eye contact.

"Are you coming from school?" trying desperately to engage her in conversation.

She looked intelligent, and I figured she was in somebody's school.

"Yes, I go to the University of South Carolina," beginning to make eye contact.

"What's your standing?" I turned toward her in order to get a better look at her.

"I'm a junior. Where are your from?" finally giving me her full attention.

"Chicago," I was fully focusing on her.

"Where are you headed?" beginning to be interested in what I was saying.

"To a Black family conference in North Charleston, South Carolina," hoping it would impress her.

"Are you making a presentation?" Getting more involved in the conversation.

"Yes, I'm making a presentation on, A Black Family Model for Counselling the Violent Offender," identifying with her academic situation.

"You have a long trip."

"Yeah! I do"

"See you later. It's time for me to get off the bus."

Her home wasn't far from where she got on the bus, about 100 miles back. She got off the bus and said good-bye. She got off the bus in Summerville. Her family was waiting for her at the bus station.

By this time, I was tired and sleepy. We pulled into Hanahan. The bus driver said the next bus to North Charleston would arrive around six o'clock in the morning. It was running late but would be there. At the station café I had a cheeseburger, French fries, and a coke; came back and read the local Hanahan paper. I lay around on the bench, careful not to close my eyes for fear of predators. I lie there in a half-awakened state until the next morning. Finally, the attendant made the announcement that the bus to North Charleston had arrived. Somehow, I hadn't expected such long layovers, although I should have known there wouldn't always be smooth connections.

We made it to the bus station in North Charleston. I was sitting there waiting on a taxi. A woman or what looked like a woman sat next to me. She probably cased me out as a mark. I started a conversation with her until my taxi came. I thought it was a woman, but it was really a man dressed like a woman in order to run one type of con or another on unsuspecting travelers. The woman's skin was smooth, she had on a wig, carried a purse, dressed in high heels, and it was difficult to know her true identity. When my taxi pulled up, I shook her hand and headed for my taxi. In talking with her I was trying to get a flavor for the culture of North Charleston. I felt the way to get to know a place was to talk to the people. After I shook her hand, and got in my taxi, I noticed my gold ring was missing from my finger. That ring cost me five-hundred dollars. The ring always fit loose on my finger. It was easy for a smooth con man to take such a ring without my being aware of it. I tossed it up as a lesson well learned.

When I walked out of the bus station, I met the police coming in. There sirens were blaring. As my taxi pulled away from the station, I saw the police lead the woman who had took my ring, out of the bus station. Her wig had come off in a struggle with the police and she was carrying it in her hand. It was too late for me to retrieve my ring, so I let the taxi driver continue on his way.

The taxi took me directly to the hotel where the conference was held in North Charleston. I had arrived in North Charleston after the long trip from Chicago.

I had a wonderful time in North Charleston, South Carolina. I made my presentation, sold some books, and enjoyed the scenery. I sold enough books to pay for my return trip. I also met some old friends who generally traveled the circuit.

I decided to fly back to Chicago instead of riding the bus. I booked a flight back to Chicago as soon as the conference was over. The trip from Chicago to North Charleston had spoiled my taste for buses.

I have continued to travel over the years, but usually either fly or take a train. Traveling by bus is a little too downscale for me. Of course, it's six in one and a half dozen in the other: any form of transportation has its own drawbacks—especially in modern times.

20

COUNTRY BOY IN THE CITY

I was born in Nutbush, Tennessee in November 1985, a small town with a population of 259. I got tired of plowing a tractor on a medium-sized farm and wanted to find greener pastures. I wasn't keeping up my grades in school, and my overall school situation left something to be desired. My relationship skills were poor, because there were many social problems in my family, causing me to have difficulty getting along with the other children. My father drank too much, would frequently beat my mother, and was often unemployed. Mother had been in mental institutions on several occasions. There were six other children in the family, and I felt my parents had enough mouths to feed without me.

They could barely keep us in food and clothing, there was never any extra money, or anything else extra for that matter. On top of all that I didn't get along with my parents; they constantly harassed me. There was no alternative for me but to leave. I was the oldest of seven. Biologists and some others say when an eagle gets ready for her babies to leave the nest, she will make the nest uncomfortable, while trying to nudge them out of the nest. I got a strange feeling they were trying to have that effect on me. There were too many kids. Somebody had to go. Why not me? So, I dropped out of school in the tenth grade—at fifteen and ran away from home. When everyone else was asleep, I left in the middle of the night, without saying good-bye. I was six-feet tall, muscular, and had a premature beard. I thought I was a man and was feeling my oats. My parents probably felt the same way. I caught the first thing moving, a freight train that only stopped in Chicago, and that's where I got off.

At first, I roamed around Chicago, sleeping in run-down hotels, flophouses, and doing day work. Many times, I wanted to give up completely. On the streets I was robbed, beaten, and misused on numerous occasions. I was out there for three years, and figured it was time to do better with my life. I have many horrendous stories I could tell, but they wouldn't be the main point of my overall story. After being in Chicago for this period, I heard the Salvation Army was a good place to start, so I went there for counselling. I didn't have high hopes for the Salvation Army. So many other leads didn't work out. The counselor and I hit it off right away, and he sincerely wanted to help me, especially after I told him my story. It turns out that he had had similar experiences to mine. He referred me to a job as a maintenance man at a local hospital in Harvey, Illinois. He said he knew the head man personally, and that this was a sure thing. I was hired at the first interview. I worked at the hospital for three more years before I was able to get a decent apartment in Matteson, Illinois, leaving the flophouses and run-down hotels behind. My salary made it possible for me to purchase a good used car. I kept it in good condition, because I had developed some good auto-mechanic skills.

At the hospital I met Cheryl, and we became close friends. She liked gambling and asked me to go to the riverboat with her. She worked in housekeeping. I met her one day I was changing burnt-out florescent lights. I had seen her before but hadn't paid her much attention. She initiated the conversation.

"How're you doing?" Cheryl asked, smiling.

"I'm fine, how're you?" I asked.

"Are you working hard, or hardly working?"

"Neither."

"I would stop and talk to you if I had time, but I have to get back to work."

"We could have lunch in the cafeteria sometimes," I said.

"Let's do that."

I was getting the feeling that she liked me. From then on Cheryl and I were thick as thieves. I would have lunch in the cafeteria with her when I had time, and would drop by her apartment for dinner. Sometimes I spent more time at Cheryl's apartment than I did at mine. Gambling was the only form of recreation that she really enjoyed. She was a very pleasant young lady, approximately twenty-one years of age. She was plain but sexy, and smooth as silk. The only form of recreation I enjoyed was going to bars. I decided to expand my horizon and give the riverboat a try.

Cheryl and I went to the boat on a cool Friday night in October 2006. I had never been to such a place before. I got hooked by all the music, lights, bells, and whistles. There were drinks and food readily available at your fingertips. There were pretty waitresses serving drinks. You could be in solitude yet be around other people. It took care of both an individual's social and solitary needs. I think that's why so many people get hooked.

There were too many people at the crap and blackjack tables, and I didn't feel like being social. Playing blackjack and craps required a certain amount of interaction with others. With the slot machines you were at it alone. I picked a slot machine at random. It was a Triple-Double-Diamond machine. The machine was a dollar machine in which you could play up to three coins, so I was actually playing three dollars with each pull of the handle. I pulled the leaver approximately ten times, and two triple diamonds and a double diamond came to rest symmetrically on the line. I sat there momentarily spell bound as the sirens, bells, and whistles blasted. I didn't know how much I had won.

A passerby said, "That's a good one."

Another one said, "That's the best hit I've seen tonight."

Someone else said, "Great hit."

Lots of people gathered around me, one of them said, "Quit while you're ahead. Don't give it all back. Take it home."

The slot-machine attendant came over and told me I had won $4,000.00. I almost lost my cool.

"How do you want this, cash or check?" the attendant asked.

"Check," I said, as she opened the machine and made some type of notation on some kind of record sheet, worried that I might get robbed it the wrong element knew I had won that much money.

She took my driver's license and gave me a piece of paper that she had written some information on, and said, "We'll be back in a minute with your check. Congratulations."

I came back the following Friday and won $1,600.00 on a Double-Diamond machine. I decided not to play the same machine, feeling that lightning would not strike twice in the same place. It was a two-coin, Double-Diamond machine. I got essentially the same feedback, and the slot attendant went through the same procedure. I must have been having beginner's luck. Again, my girlfriend from work came with me.

My girlfriend thought playing dollars was being too extravagant. She just enjoyed the atmosphere. She usually played a few credits on the 2 cent and penny machines.

"You're lucky," she said.

"Some people have told me that," I replied.

"What're you going to do with it?"

"Buy you a nice present and put the rest in the bank."

"You don't have to buy me anything."

"But I want to buy you something."

Two weeks later I won another $4,000.00 on a Red, White, and Blue machine. This time I didn't bring my friend but was there by myself. She had to go out of town to visit her sick father in Michigan. One young lady who came over and congratulated me took a seat next to where I was playing while waiting for them to bring my check. She started a conversation.

"You did well," she said, "Congratulations."

"Thank you."

Not paying her much attention, I kept playing my machine.

"I just won $10,000.00 on a five-cent machine, playing 60 credits at a time," she handed me a receipt for the $10,000.00 that she had received from the slot attendant.

"Oh! You really did well," surprised that someone had won that much money.

"Where are you from," she asked.

"Nutbush, Tennessee."

"I've never heard of it."

"Not many people have who're not from Tennessee."

"I like you. Why don't we split a motel room," she said, smiling.

"But you don't know me," the country boy coming out in me.

"You just look like a good person."

"Let me think about it," being careful.

I didn't like the idea of going to bed with a strange woman, but felt it would be OK if I used a condom.

"I'll watch you play while you think about it."

I thought about the pros and cons of the proposition for another hour while she watched me play.

"Aren't you going to play any more?" it was nerve racking for her to watch me play, even though I knew she had good intentions.

"I can't possibly do better than what I've done. All I can do is lose what I've won," demonstrating plain old common sense.

"That's a good way to look at it. I have lost $300.00 in the past hour. I had better quit while I'm ahead if I don't want to lose any more."

"On the way here, I saw a sign for a Red Roof Inn off Larkin. We can get an inexpensive room for little or nothing."

I noticed the motel because on my last visit to the casino I was thinking about what I would do if I met someone.

"That sounds good."

I thought to myself that I couldn't do much better. She was smaller than a plus size, was impeccably dressed, and her hair was well done. Her legs were smooth and long though she was slightly hefty on top. She had on a pink dress with some type of flower pattern. She wore the latest glass frame, four-inch heels, and black pantyhose. Her hair appeared to have some kind of weave but was better than her having a wig. For some reason I didn't care for women who wore wigs very much. I would say she was about my age and was the type of woman any man would want to date, especially on a short-term basis.

We left the casino and went to the motel. We engaged in foreplay for about an hour, and then we both got undressed and got in bed. After making love for about ten minutes she began to quiver, shake, and jerk. I thought that was part of her lovemaking act, but all of a sudden, she stopped and quit moving. She was lying there motionless as a dead horse. I didn't know what to do. I thought for a minute and decided to call 911. The ambulance came and took her to the hospital, but she was dead on arrival. I didn't know at the time what epilepsy was or that she had had a seizure and died. This was all perplexing to me, but I still didn't know she had had a seizure.

The police arrived and took me to the police station. After we got to the station, they took me in a room and began to question me.

"The girl was dead on arrival. What happened?" a bright light was in my face.

"I met her at the casino. We had a little luck and decided we could afford a motel. We were having sex when she began to shake, quiver, and jerk. I didn't know what was wrong. I thought I was doing a good job of pleasing her, and this was causing her to react that way. But then she stopped moving at all and was lying perfectly motionless."

"You didn't do anything to cause her death."

"Not a thing, sir."

"Did you two fight or have any harsh words?"

"No, we didn't"

"Who decided to get the room?"

"She asked me if I wanted to get a room."

"And you agreed."

"Yes, I thought it couldn't do that much harm."

"Be more careful the next time in deciding who you want to get a room with."

"I will be more careful, sir."

I thought he was getting personal, but all I could do was to answer his questions.

"Was tonight your first time meeting her? You had never seen her before?"

"Yes, it was."

"OK. We'll get this processed and get you out of here as quickly as possible."

He put me back in the cell. They said the situation had to be further investigated. They placed me in a cell for the night. I had a long restless night. Fortunately, I was in a cell alone, I didn't have to worry about other characters harassing me.

The police went through her wallet, found her parents number, a $10,000.00 check from the casino, and some other cash. At lest they were sure there was no robbery motive on my part. Both her parents told them that she was an epileptic and was prone to seizures. The autopsy revealed that she died of a grand mal seizure. They came to my cell the next day and told me I was free to go, but in such a situation they had to investigate before letting me go.

I had learned something about picking up strange women at bars and casinos. I went to the casino on several other occasions but never picked up another strange woman again. I soon learned, as all intelligent and self-disciplined people do, that you can't beat the house. If you play long enough, you are going to lose.

It was time to advance my situation in life. I was twenty-four years old and it was the year 2009. I decided to try and make something better of my life. I went to electrician school and soon became an electrician. I didn't have too many problems.

In 2011 I asked the housekeeper at the hospital to marry me and she said yes. We got married and moved back to Nutbush. She had for a long time wanted to meet someone who would get her out of the Chicago area. In addition, I never liked the city, and wanted to get as far away from it as I could. My uncle was a builder in the area, and I went to work for him: wiring houses he built in Nutbush and the surrounding area. I never thought I would go back to Nutbush, but I finally felt at home and at peace. My father and mother owned 100 acres of family land that was just sitting there. This same uncle built us a nice house and we eventually had two children. My wife got a job working for a large hotel chain in the area. You can go back home! I was glad to be back.

21

DREAMS AND READING

I was born in the small town of Brownsville, Texas, in 1970. My mother was a history teacher, and my father was a brakeman for the Union Pacific Railway. My mother had a Masters' degree in history, and my father only graduated high school. Neither of them ever missed a day of work. With the hard work of my mother and father, we had practically everything one could ask for. We were a traditional middle-class family. I can't remember ever asking for something I didn't get, and we got the best of whatever we wanted. There were four children: two boys and two girls. We had plenty of food, a nice home, good schools, and all the education we wanted. Neither of us even had to get a loan for college, my dad and mother paid for it all from their salary. In fact, my parents pushed all four of their children to attend college and gave additional encouragements along the way. They couldn't have stood the thought of one of their children not getting a college education. In addition, we seemed to be self-motivated and self-conscious in most ways. Three of them received Masters' degrees, one got a Ph.D.

When it came time for college, there was no doubt I was going to somebody's college. The only question was would I go away to college or attend a local college? One of my sisters attended Spellman and Howard; the other attended Atlanta University and Howard, and my brother attended Howard and New York City College; while, I attended Broadmoore University and the University of Illinois. In the end, it was a conjoint decision that I would attend a local college, my second choice was Howard. I had read all my life and was prepared for college. I had even read every volume of *Great Books of the Western World* by the time I graduated high school. Folks would tease me by saying I had read every book in the local public library. I made 34 on the ACT and had a 3.9 grade point average. In high school while the other children were attending activities, I would be reading on subjects that extended far beyond high school. Even in elementary school I was big on reading. My cousins told me *all work and no play make Jack a dull boy*. But I never was interested in extra-curricula school activities. I spent my extra time preparing for college. My friends never understood why I didn't attend activities at school.

For Christmas and my birthday, I generally asked my mother, father, sisters, and brother to buy me a book or two rather than any other type of gift. They had done this since fifth grade. I left home for college with only the basic essentials in clothing and my computer.

In 1987 I went off to college. I attended Broadmoore University in Broadmoore, Texas, a small town in the Southwest. I had trouble deciding on a major but finally decided on business and economics. There were so many subjects I was interested in; one of my favorites was history. I didn't encounter any major obstacles to my education, but I was slightly awkward socially. Being used to spending most of my time studying, I continued to spend most of my time in that way. I had an active fantasy life. I graduated with a B.S. degree in business and economics in 1991. I then moved to Chicago and took a management job with Texaco. They offered me more money than any of my other offers. I came to Chicago strictly for the money.

I had a fully functional dream life. One night I went to sleep about one o'clock and had a succession of short dreams. I was walking an old friend to her bus after school. I can always remember having restless nights and dreaming a lot—even in high school.

Susie said, "What's Joey going to say about this?" as we walked along to her bus.

"What Joey doesn't know won't hurt him!" I said, confident in what I had to say.

"He'll find out," wanting to cooperate with me, but a little unsure of the situation.

"He'll just have to deal with it," indicating that *all is fair in love and war.*

"Why are you walking me to my bus?" she asked, unsure of my motives.

"Obviously, I'm interested in you," trying to establish myself as a friend and lover.

"You may have to pay a high price for that interest," again, letting me know that Joey wouldn't like what I was doing.

Joey came out of the building and saw me walking with Susie.

"What's up homeboy?" he became hostile and angry.

"I had to tell your girl something," showing less confidence.

"Did you have to walk her to her bus? That's my job. Don't do it again!" he seemed to get angrier.

He hit me and left me lying on the pavement. Susie was my girlfriend before she started dating Joey. I always wanted her back and saw this as an opportunity to pursue her. The security guard told the principal, he got suspended from school for two days, and couldn't participate in extra-curricula activities for a week. It had to be a dream, because it wasn't like me to interfere with another guy and his girl.

I woke up from the dream and the scene shifted to another scene. I then went into another dream. I had met an East Indian girl named Tabitha at school. One day I was talking to her at the mall.

"Why can't we go out for a Coke or pizza sometimes?" I asked Tabitha, looking at her seriously.

"I can't go out with someone not of my religion," she said, smiling.

"But I'll treat you right," taking a sip from the drink in my hand.

"That has nothing to do with it."

"What does it have to do with?"

"It's a cultural thing."

"Haven't I always respected your values?"

"You still don't understand. It's not about respect."

Her mother walked from around the corner, "Why're you associating with a Christian boy?"

I noticed that both of them had on the traditional Moslem headgear.

"He's a nice guy," Tabitha said, lowering her head in deference to her mother.

"Nevertheless, you shouldn't waste your time talking to Christian boys."

"OK, Mother."

"Don't ever forget that we're Moslem and are not to associate with Christians," she frowned as she spoke.

Tabitha was smooth and beautiful, I really liked her. I thought it was a plus that she was from a different culture. The way she dressed made her even more beautiful.

I continued to dream. The scene shifted again. I then dreamed that in some cities the buildings had been almost overtaken by the undergrowth of vines, shrubs, and trees. It happened all of a sudden since I had been in the mall for about an hour. I tried to leave the mall by the back entrance, but the undergrowth was too thick. For miles and miles there was nothing outside the city but dense undergrowth. I tried to leave the city but had to return, the undergrowth was too thick. I was able to call my wife on the phone. She said it was the same way every where you went. It was in every major city that was in the news.

My wife said some of the highways were still open, and if I could make it to one of the main thoroughfares, I might be able to get home. That we could figure out what to do after I made it home. I made it to my car and was able to make it to a main thoroughfare. I drove until I reached home. Everything on the way was covered in dense underbrush except the highways and the buildings. Some of the buildings and highways were covered.

The next night I had another strange dream. I was married and was living in Chicago, in an apartment on the south side. My wife had gone to work, and I was sitting around home that day, apparently, I had a day off. I came into my living room and there was a guy sitting there sewing his shirt.

I asked him, "What're you doing in my apartment? Get out. What's wrong with people these days?" hostile and angry.

"I'm sewing my shirt. What does it look like I'm doing?" confident that it was OK to confiscate someone else's property.

He had walked in off the street and was going to make my home his.

"You can't just come into someone's apartment and sew your shirt," outdone by his attitude.

"I can do anything I want," overcome by a false sense of power.

I knew something was wrong with this guy. His whole attitude was out of place. He came toward me, and I moved toward him. He pulled out a twelve-inch butcher's knife from under a pillow on the couch, and I grabbed a butcher's knife from the kitchen. For a while there we were cutting each other until we drew blood from one another. When the blood started flowing, I woke up. I managed to somehow call 911 on my cell phone, got the police, and got the guy out of my house.

The scene changed, still dreaming. The Black alumni from Broadmoore decided to have a ten-year reunion to coincide with Homecoming. We had three days of activities starting with a cool Friday night in October. It was to last until Sunday morning with a meeting at the old church that we all attended while in college at Broadmoore. We won the game by twenty points. I saw a lot of people I hadn't seen in ten years or more.

My wife's friend told her we could stay with him. They had dated for a short while during college. He liked the Broadmoore experience so much that he stayed in Broadmoore and bought a house near the campus. I was glad to not have a hotel bill and readily agreed to this arrangement. He taught at a local high school.

After the football game we went to the Sadie Hawkins dance. My wife and others said they enjoyed the festivities. Later we came back to Henry's house. We had driven from Chicago to Broadmoore. He noted that I might want to get some rest for the long drive back on Sunday. My wife Della said she was going to stay up for a while and have a drink.

I lay down for the night but woke up after about an hour wondering where my wife was. I didn't like rambling through another man's house, but felt I had a right to look for my wife. After looking in every room, I finally found Della and Henry. They were in one of the bedrooms, and he was trying to kiss her. I stood there listening for a minute. They didn't hear me when I pushed open the door and peeped inside.

"He's in the bedroom at the end of the hallway. He won't know what's going on in here," Henry said to Della, placing his drink on the nightstand.

"He'll get upset if I don't come to bed soon." Della said, lowering her head.

"He never suspected us of having a relationship, did he?"

"No, but I don't want to give him any ideas."

Henry tried to kiss Della again. I walked in and surprised them.

"Get your things Della. We're going to a hotel," I was outraged and angry.

"Why, we have a room here?" seemingly satisfied with the situation.

"The only reason he let us stay, is so he could carry on a relationship with you.'

"All we were doing is talking, brother Jay. You're wrong, brother Jay, nothing is going on," surprised at my sudden insight.

"I didn't expect you to tell me the truth."

"You don't think I would misuse your friendship, do you?"

We left that night about two o'clock and went to a hotel. We really did have a friend in college named Henry, but I never said anything to him about the dream.

Once I had a dream about my last day of class at my old university. I was to graduate on May 6, 1991. It was May 1, 1991. I stayed up late studying for a class. I even took some NoDoz. I was up until late that morning but went to bed about four o'clock. The test was to be at eight o'clock. I didn't wake up until eight-thirty that morning. I grabbed some clothing, didn't have time to take a shower, and went to the building where the test was held. The professor opened the door but wouldn't let me in. I explained to him that my graduation depended on my successfully passing the test. But he said it was too late, I would have to take the course over, by coming back in the summer or the fall. Broadmoore had a strict and definite policy about being late for exams or class. There was no way I could graduate without this class. It was hard to wake up from this one, but I finally woke up and was happy that this hadn't actually happened.

I had another dream once that I was late getting up for a class. Again, it was at Broadmoore. The test was at eight, and I didn't get to the class until ten o'clock. It was the final exam for the class. This time I was up late having a few drinks. The professor and the other students had gone, and I didn't know how to contact the professor. When I finally made contact with the professor, he told me my only option was to take an "F" for the test and probably for the class. Again, I was pleased to wake up and find this too hadn't actually happened. I had many dreams about being late for class or exams after I graduated from Broadmoore. It was the worst possible academic infraction at Broadmoore.

I had read broadly so I did some elaborate dreaming. I had taken trips through my books to many strange worlds. I am thankful for my reading habits which gave me a rich fantasy life. There were many more nights of colorful dreaming until I died in a car accident on November 10, 2010. Some people will try to talk you against reading, but anything you ever want to know can be found in a book—somewhere. Reading broadens your horizons of the world.

22

SILK PANTYHOSE FETISH

Freddie began to have a fetish with pantyhose in elementary school. He didn't know he was developing one at the time, or that it would have such a powerful influence on his early life. His brothers would bring home girly magazines, and he would find them and look at them very intently. He spent a great deal of his time looking at these magazines. This progressed to looking at women in pantyhose while masturbating. Once his brother brought home a sexy-girly magazine, and Freddie took it and masturbated right in front of his older brother. His brother didn't know what to say but didn't try to chastise him. His brother even encouraged it, feeling that it would help him to grow up to be a man's man. His favorite color in pantyhose was black with lots of embroidery, the more the better.

It was 1970, and Freddie and his girlfriend lived in Marshall, Texas, and they attended Marshall High School. This fetish continued until in high school he would sit and stare at his girlfriend and other girls in their shiny-silk pantyhose. In high school his girlfriend wouldn't give him sex. The greatest source of pleasure he got from her was seeing her in pantyhose. She would wear the shear shiny ones. To him the pantyhose seemed to give the legs a sense of perfection: made them look smooth and without flaw. He could see something in the pantyhose that he couldn't see by looking at her natural legs. When they attended school programs all he could do was stare at those long-smooth legs in black-silk pantyhose. He would go places and adore women in their pantyhose. As a senior in high school he broke up with Gwendolyn because all she would do is let him touch and feel her pantyhose, nothing else, and he so badly wanted to go further.

Freddie came back to his high school when his former girlfriend was a senior. It was a cool-cloudy night in September. He was a sophomore at Grambling University at the time. He hadn't seen her in two years. Neither of them had made any attempt to contact the other. He saw her in the stands and it was like magic. Even she wanted to go some place where they could have some privacy. She expected him to come back to the school on a white horse and save her. He expected her to contact him, since she was the one mostly responsible for the breakup.

When she saw him, she yelled out loud, "Freddie! Where've you been?" she jumped from the seat as if to give him a standing ovation.

He walked over to her, "Hello baby," he said.

They immediately left and went to his car without any provoking conversation. Someone told her boyfriend, who was working with one of the teachers in the concession stand, that Freddie was in town and he and Gwendolyn went to his car in the parking lot. You know how spies are in high school. Craig immediately dropped what he was doing to see about the matter.

In the meantime, while they were sitting in the car.

"I expected you to come back for me," she said.

"I was waiting on you to get in touch." he replied "Baby, I still love you."

"Don't forget about me just because I'm away at school. You are still in my heart."

"I'll try not to forget."

In the earlier part of her high school years she boarded on being a plus size, but had now slim down, and had curves in places he couldn't even imagine—except on those women in his magazines. He collected those magazines and had probably the best collection around. She had shed much of that baby fat. This development made her whole body more attractive. His family had combined resources and strained to buy him a 1970 GT mustang, they purchase a new one, so he wouldn't have to worry about repair bills, and would have transportation. He was sitting in his car touching her pantyhose and kissing her when her boyfriend banged on Freddie's car window, opened the door, and smacked him several times before he could even respond—he was caught by surprise. Freddie lost the fight. Her boy friend gave him a fat lip and bloody nose.

Freddie called her the following Sunday night and spoke with her. He could barely speak.

"Why didn't you tell me that Craig was your new boyfriend?"

"You didn't ask if I was seeing anyone."

"Can't you get rid of him, so we can get back together on a permanent basis?"

"If you're serious I'll dump him, we can get back together, and you won't have that problem again. Have a safe trip back to Grambling and keep in contact."

"I'll call you as well."

"Bye-bye."

"Yeah, see ya'."

Once he came home and was riding around in his car. He passed by the local high school. He got overly excited looking at young girls walking around in their pantyhose. He masturbated while driving down the street and looking at them. Young girls in pantyhose put him in Heaven.

Gwendolyn graduated and went to East Texas State University outside Dallas. They wrote to each other but seldom made contact. She told him that she had broken up with her boyfriend. One of Freddie's friends was going to East Texas State to visit his girlfriend who was attending there. Freddie decided to go along and visit with Gwendolyn.

Freddie and Luther decided to get rooms at a local hotel. They picked up the girls and both got separate rooms. In that way they wouldn't interfere with the other's privacy. Freddie still hadn't gotten any further with Gwendolyn than touching and feeling her pantyhose. When they got to the hotel Freddie and Luther took their girls to the rooms. When they got to the room Freddie and Gwendolyn began kissing and making up for lost time.

"I have a surprise for you," she said, acting and looking mysterious.

"What's that," he asked curiously.

"Do you remember how you liked to see me in pantyhose?" She laughed.

"Sure," I still do like to see you in them, reassuringly.

"Well, when you make love to me, I want you to wear pantyhose as well," looking as if she was serious.

Freddie had never thought about such a thing before but felt it couldn't be too bad. In addition, he would do almost anything to get into Gwendolyn's panties.

He had no idea that Gwendolyn had a fetish similar to his.

"That shouldn't be too difficult for me to do."

"Here I brought an extra pair just for you. Mine and yours are both crouchless, so you can relax and take in the view."

They both got undressed, put on their pantyhose and made mad-passionate love. Neither Freddie nor Gwendolyn had had a better weekend. They parted and again promised to see each other on a more regular basis.

On the campus there were girls of all sizes and shapes, most of them wore either silk stockings or silk pantyhose. Freddie dated some of them, but never revealed his fetish. He did sometimes get carried away with touching and feeling their pantyhose. If his behavior was queer to them, they never mentioned it to him.

Freddie graduated with a degree in sociology from Grambling in 1975. They decided to get married. Two months before the wedding Freddie picked her up at school and took her home for the weekend. Freddie felt he had to perform the traditional ritual of asking her father for her hand in marriage. Some families never forgave you if you didn't carry out this ritual.

When he got her father alone, he approached him, "Mr. Carter, I want to officially ask you for your daughter's hand in marriage," he looked as if he was overwhelmed.

"That's fine with me, son. I hope you guys are in love. It'll last longer if you're in love."

"Yes, we are, sir."

"Son, always remember, when you get married you have got to take the good with the bad," looking off into the distance, "Most women have an Angelic and a Devilish side."

"Yes, I know that sir," trying to say it in such a way not to alienate him.

"You have my blessings, son."

"Thank you, sir."

Gwendolyn wasn't doing well in school and decided to drop out of college as a sophomore. Freddie would take Gwendolyn any way he could get her. They had a small church wedding in her parents' church in Marshall. Lots of people came and it was a festive occasion. Most of Freddie's relatives came: his mother, father, two brothers, and his one sister came, in addition to numerous other relatives. Gwendolyn only had one sister who served as one of the bridesmaids, and one of Freddie's brothers served as the best man. It was a glorious occasion.

When her mother got some time alone with Freddie, she said, "Take care of my daughter," as if she had her doubts about him.

"I'd hurt myself before I hurt her," looking steady, comfortable, and self-assured.

"You know she's not perfect but deserves to be treated like a human being."

"I'll take good care of her."

"If you feel you have to hit her send her home first."

"You can depend on me."

"If she deserves anything it is respect, dignity, and love."

"I know that."

All her father said was, "Be good to my baby-girl. If you love her half as much as we do, you'll take care of her."

"I'll do my best, sir."

"If you need anything let us know, we don't have much but are willing to share what we have with you."

We spent the night at her parents' home, went to church that Sunday morning at a small-intimate Baptist church, and departed for Dallas that evening. They already knew we had contracted for an apartment in an area of Dallas called Oakcliff. Their departing words were for us to come and see them as often as possible. Her father said he liked for the family to be as close as possible. He suggested that there weren't many Carters left, and what there were should stick together.

They moved to Dallas and took a one-bedroom apartment. Freddie took a job at one of the state schools in Dallas. Gwendolyn took a job as a cook in an upscale restaurant. She still wasn't making much money and decided to quit after six months of it. She would get out the old crouchless pantyhose for the both of them whenever they wanted to get intimate. There wasn't a lot of money to spare, but the old Mustang was still running well, and they had money to buy what they wanted, even though she decided to quit her job.

He came home one day, and noticed she had a long scar on her neck, and he asked her about it.

"How did you get that scar on your neck?" touching it with his fingers.

"I scratch myself in my sleep. I was dreaming and woke up in terror," she placed her fingers over the scar.

"I didn't know you had those types of problems," expressing doubt in her story.

"There are some things my mother doesn't know about me, and I've been around her all my life," she said with a smirk on her face.

I took her sarcasm as a warning to not further intrude.

"Don't let those dreams get you down," he said, as he walked away.

Two months later Freddie got off early and came home. He saw Gwendolyn standing on one of the main arteries in Oakcliff: she was walking up and down the street, scantily dressed, approaching cars and talking to men passing by. He paid attention. Soon she entered one of the cars. He wasn't a complete fool. He knew what she was doing, though he couldn't believe it. What need would drive her to do such a thing? Didn't he work hard to provide for her? When she got home that evening, he approached her. He had decided what he had to do. She left him no alternative, though he hated to leave her. He thought they had a good relationship; like a lot of men who lose their wives for seemingly no good reasons.

"What were you doing on the street approaching cars off Illinois Avenue?"

She was busted; she had no plausible explanation for her behavior. She thought for a minute, and then broke down and cried.

"I thought I could earn some money to help support the household," still in tears.

"Did you consider what I would think?" feeling betrayed.

"I didn't think it would bother you that much," trying to further deceive him.

"You know what this means. One of us must go," obviously, fed up with the situation.

"I guess I just got lonely being at home every day by myself," she couldn't look him in the eyes.

"You had a job, why didn't you keep it, or get another one," wanting to find some rationale for her behavior.

"I didn't enjoy working," she was coming up with flimsy excuses.

She begged and pleaded for him to give her another chance, but he told her this was one infraction he could not tolerate. A comeback wouldn't be possible in this situation.

"OK. I'll leave."

She packed up her things that afternoon. Freddie didn't know it, but she had an apartment already furnished that she used to take her johns. Secretly, she felt it would be there if Freddie found out. She knew he would never tolerate her prostituting herself while putting up a façade as a faithful wife. So, she had gotten her a special apartment. She sent him the divorce papers in the mail one month later. He signed them, and the divorce became final on May 17, 1975.

Word on the street was she was heavily into cocaine. Five years later she died of congestive heart failure related to cocaine use. He never knew that congestive heart failure was common in long-term cocaine abusers until he studied for the Ph.D. in psychology. Her funeral was the saddest day of his life. He decided to attend a local college and pick up a degree in psychology. Freddie's job gave him a four-year scholarship to study psychology at Michigan State University, and eventually got a Ph.D. in psychology. All he had to do was give them back a year for each year of scholarship. He never will forget Gwendolyn. He made his 1970 GT last through graduate school, repairing it when necessary. When he graduated in 1980, he bought another new Mustang.

It took him almost four years of graduate study to realize that a good relationship shouldn't be based on pathology. Through hearing so much about pathology in school, he realized even in undergraduate school that a fetish was something one could do without.

23

WHAT FRIENDS WILL DO

Carrie first met Helen at a south suburban hospital where they both worked. They quickly became friends and would have lunch most days in the cafeteria. Carrie had been working at the hospital for the past ten years, and had worked her way up to a supervising nurse on the obstetrics and gynecology unit. Helen had recently been hired as secretary for the unit. Helen and Carrie were both young and attractive in their thirties, and well-kept for even thirty.

After many conversations on the unit, and many discussions at lunch, Helen and Carrie decided to get their husbands together and go out on the town. Helen and Carrie had been out before but never altogether with their husbands.

"Let's do something with our husbands this weekend," said Helen, sounding enthusiastic.

"That sounds good to me," replied Carrie, happy to be making friends.

Carrie hadn't gotten over the culture-shock of moving to the big city from a small-southern-country town, and still hadn't made many friends in the city or south suburbs, even though she had been in the area for over ten years. I hadn't introduced her to many of the people I worked with, and none that she could develop a lasting relationship with.

"Why don't we go to the riverboat," thinking it would be a good form of recreation to engage in.

"I have no objections to that," but the riverboat wasn't her first choice as a wholesome activity.

Carrie didn't like the idea of taking a chance with her hard-earned money. She hadn't been to the boat but had heard horror stories about people eventually losing their life savings.

"Maybe we'll have some luck," trying to further persuade Carrie that the riverboat was a good idea.

"I need some luck. Let me tell ya'," Carrie thought she would throw in a bit of humor, she laughed.

"We'll come by your place," said Helen. "You guys can ride with us," offering a further incentive.

It was Friday about two o'clock. It was almost time to get off from work.

"OK," being positive.

"See you tonight about eight o'clock," adding the final touches to their plans.

"We'll be looking forward to it."

We began getting together on various occasions: at times going to nightclubs, at times going to concerts, going bowling, playing billiards, going to the riverboats, going to restaurants, and many other activities. Sean and I were always included in these activities. Sean was Helen's husband.

Once we even went to Nassau, Bahamas. We saw many sights: we explored caves, went out to eat, saw shows, went gambling on Paradise Island, and enjoyed other things. We even went fishing. The land was lush and green, and the waters were crystal blue. People waited on you hand-and-foot. It was a fun paradise

One night, Sean talked me into going to a nightclub alone. Helen and Carrie stayed at the hotel. They didn't even know where we were. Later that night, Helen and Carrie decided to go out. We ended up at the same nightclub. Sean and I walked into a nightclub and saw two beautiful young ladies sitting at a table. They were smiling and inviting us over to sit with them. We just had to go over and talk to them. Things were fine, until a few minutes later Helen and Carrie walked in. I was embarrassed, but Sean didn't seem to care. I was so embarrassed that I got up from the table and walked all the way back to the hotel. It was ten o'clock at night. I had no idea what type of wild animals inhabited the island. I came back to the hotel and went to sleep for the night; I was that embarrassed. Sean, Helen, and Carrie later came back to the hotel. The next day things were back to normal. Not much was said about the previous night between Carrie and me. Soon we were on the beach taking pictures, wading in the water, and drinking Piña Coladas.

That night Carrie and I were kissing passionately, while Helen and Sean were doing the same. Sean yelled out loud enough for all to hear, "Let's switch partners." I didn't think it was such a good idea at first, and Carrie didn't seem to be interested. I knew Sean to be a joker, prankster, and trickster; so, I didn't pay him that much attention, just kept kissing Carrie.

"Don't say that," Helen said, looking at Sean intensely.

"Nothing wrong with it," Sean said, looking in our direction.

"They don't want to do anything like that," Helen rose up from the bed, and also looked in our direction.

Helen was supposedly speaking for me and Carrie. I thought later that they might have had this all planned.

"But it could be fun and exciting," Sean said, spanking Helen on her buttocks.

"Do you guys want to try that?" Helen asked, knocking Sean's hand away from her hips.

"Let's try it," I said, curiosity getting the best of me.

"If you want to," Carrie said, yielding to my judgment.

Helen and Carrie had developed such a friendship that they thought their relationship could survive any test. Carrie and I didn't know at the time that this wasn't the first time for such activity with Sean and Helen.

Sean got up and came over and started kissing Carrie while rubbing her buttocks. Sean told me to go over and try Helen on for size, while pointing in that direction. So, I did. We had never considered doing anything like this before. We had been out on many occasions. I guess it was the idea of being in an anonymous place far from home. At least nothing like this had been verbalized. The next few nights we tried it again. None of us had any complaints and seemed to like the arrangement. Soon we switched partners for the night. We didn't talk about it too much, just kept trying it.

We came back to the states and the activity continued. We would get a hotel room, wherever we went, and switch partners. We couldn't seem to get enough, until it drove all of us to ruin. Some people are not strong enough for certain kinds of relationships.

One night, Carrie woke me up from my desperate sleep, and was standing over me.

"We need to talk," she was gripping my hand as if she was serious.

"What about?" barely opening my eyes.

"This thing with Sean and Carrie, don't let it get the best of you," looking into the distance.

"What do you mean?" finally getting my eyes open.

"It's only temporary. I hope we are just having a little fun," she grinned.

"I know that baby," I rose up to a sitting position in bed.

"We have to get back to what makes our relationship work."

"OK."

"It was fine for a little excursion, but we have to at some point give it up."

I was half sleep and was in too deep to turn around. I couldn't wait to get to work and call Helen in order to establish our next rendezvous point. We had been switching partners for several months. Helen was pressuring me to take our relationship to another level. She was having difficulty convincing me to make that move, but Helen was quite the little persuader.

"Sure baby. I'm sleepy. Let's talk about it tomorrow."

But we never got an opportunity to discuss it.

Soon Helen started meeting me at motels and hotels around the south suburbs and in the city. Carrie didn't seem to be that fascinated with Sean, at least to my knowledge, but Helen was taken with me and I could get excited about her. I could tell by the way she acted when we got together on subsequent occasions. Helen couldn't wait to get intimate with me. Finally, Helen and I spent a weekend in New York City. We had such a good time that Carrie and I have been alienated ever since.

I came back from New York City, packed my bags without saying a word, and moved in with Helen. The first time I saw Carrie after that was when I brought the divorce papers by to present to her.

"What is this bitch doing for you that I wasn't doing?" staring me directly in the eye.

"You wouldn't understand," trying to avoid eye contact.

"Why wouldn't I understand? There's nothing wrong with my understanding!" almost getting hostile and raising her voice.

"You're too set in your ways," I handed her the papers.

"Why hadn't you said something to me about my understanding?" she took the papers out and examined them closely.

"Sometimes people can be so set in their ways that talking to them doesn't help," I sat down on the couch to give her more time to examine the papers.

"I wish you had at least tried to talk to me about my lack of understanding," she was reading through the papers carefully."

Carrie had a quick eye for legal matters. Looking over them didn't take her long.

"It's too late now. The water is already under the bridge. As you can see, you'll get child support, alimony, complete custody; and college tuition should they decide to attend college. The amount is specified. If the amount is not enough, we can negotiate."

"All I can say is don't be late with the child support and the alimony, and I hope you will encourage all three of them to go to college," she signed the papers and handed them back to me.

"Don't worry, I'll send your money."

I worked for a Fortune 500 company as an executive and could well afford to pay her child support and alimony.

"Good-bye, you've got what you wanted, don't linger around like you want some action for old time sake."

"Thank you for signing the papers," I was relieved she didn't give me any hassle.

"I hope you'll be happy with that bitch."

I still thought a lot of Carrie and couldn't find it in my heart to dislike her.

"Don't worry, I'm happy."

"Do me a favor, and at least come by and visit with your children now and then. If shouldn't matter that the divorce papers gave me complete custody," relieved to be finally getting some closure.

"You don't have to ask me to do that," I was outdone that she didn't think I cared enough to visit the children.

"I thought I didn't have to ask you a lot of things, but I was wrong," she inserted a bit of sarcasm.

"Have it your way, you're going to do that anyway."

"I hope you have a happy life."

We had two children and an adopted daughter: two boys eight and ten, and the girl six. I never thought I would leave Carrie for Helen. It began as innocent child's play. It never crossed my mind that I would do such a thing. Carrie couldn't imagine what Helen was doing to lure me away from her and the family.

Helen left her job; I think because she didn't want to be in constant contact with Carrie. Helen and I move into the heart of the city and took an apartment.

Helen and Carrie soon were back being friends again. Helen called her to say she didn't want there to be any hard feelings between them. Helen and I eventually had a son. Carrie acted as if the child was her own. Helen gave him money when it was time to go to college, planed birthday parties, and would take him to museums, sporting events, and any place he wanted to go. Carrie was just built that way.

What is born in iniquity cannot stand the test of time. After ten years, Helen and I couldn't get along any more. Helen had a cousin who was down on her luck and needed a place to stay. Helen being the person she was reached out to her. She was much younger than Helen and much more attractive. Helen would leave Louise and me alone in the apartment while she did errands. It was only natural for a pathological middle-aged male, going through a mid-life crisis, to develop a relationship with her. I left Helen for her cousin. When Helen came home my closet and all my things were gone. I guess she really got the hint when her cousin and all her things were gone as well.

She got my telephone number from a snitch at work and called me, "You could have given me some warning. I had no idea you and Louise were developing a relationship."

"I'm a rolling stone. I can't help it."

"You are a scoundrel, but I still love you. What are you going to do about your son?"

"You can have complete custody, child support, and alimony; and I will pay for his college, should he decide to go.

I was truly testing my limits. I now had four children to send to college. Two of them already in college, and two others to pay child support for. In addition, I had two wives to pay alimony. It would take a great deal of my time simply visiting them in my spare time.

"At least you have some decency."

"Take care of yourself. I will visit my son as often as I can."

"OK."

"I have the divorce papers lying on my desk at the apartment."

"When you bring them by, I'll sign them."

Helen understood that there was no help for me, but I don't think she realized to what degree I was unstable. There was a long history of unstable marriages on both sides of my family. In addition, there was alcoholism, drugs, mental illness, philandering, and some other problems. Neither Carrie nor Helen was aware of the details.

Helen and Carrie were still good friends. Carrie often helped Helen out. Whenever Helen was in the area she would stop by and visit with Carrie.

I let my unstable ways catch up with me. The whole thing never would have come down if I had not listened to Sean that night in Nassau, Bahamas.

The last I heard Sean had gone from bad to worst. He first went to alcohol, then to drugs, and now he is homeless. He lives from flophouse to run-down hotel. I'm not sure why he lost his sense of being productive. At least I am a productive citizen, even though I still have some problems to work out. So, Sean is worse off than I am in many ways. Helen and Carrie are still surviving and doing well. My children all went to college and did well for themselves.

24

GOING BACK HOME IS NEVER THE SAME

I was a student at East Texas Baptist University in Marshall, Texas. I had come to the university from Tyler, Texas in 1966, after graduating high school. It was now April 1969. I was presently a junior and majoring in business and economics. There wasn't a lot to do off campus, and not that much to do on campus. We usually amused ourselves by going to Longview to get some alcohol or went to the movies. You couldn't buy alcohol legally in Marshall at this time. One of our pastimes was to go looking for girls on the Wiley College campus. Otherwise, we spent our time studying at the library, or in our dorm rooms, and rarely got off campus. I didn't have a steady girlfriend, many friends but no steady girlfriend.

I chose the school because of its quiet atmosphere and idyllic environment. In high school I had good grades and a decent ACT score, and so I had a choice of a number of colleges to attend, but chose East Texas Baptist. One reason I chose the university was because I wanted to attend an integrated university, but at the time wanted to be near my parents. But both of them died within the next year.

One of my friends who were worldly-wise and well traveled suggested we go to Dallas for the weekend. He had traveled around the world with the Peace Corp. My travels were limited to Texas, and I had only been to a few cities in Texas. I had been to Dallas on several occasions, but when I did go, I was only traveling through. I never spent a great deal of time in Dallas, and didn't know different parts of the city. All my relatives, who desired city living, chose other cities rather than Dallas, most of them settled in California. I was so happy to get off the campus that I was open to any suggestions for getting away for the weekend. Opportunities for getting away were few, far, and in between; since I didn't have a car of my own. After being on campus for a long period one tends to get cabin fever, and in the mood for some big-city action. My friend, Larry, was raised in Dallas and knew the city well.

Larry was the star player on the basketball team and was majoring in business and accounting. We had some overlap in coursework. We frequently studied together. He was slightly older than I, and had spent some time in the Peace Corp. His experience in the world was a great help to me. He freely gave his advice about how to survive in the world. He was not only worldly and wise but super intelligent. Not much got by him, and few put anything over on him. I didn't like going home for the weekend, because there wasn't much to do their either. Larry owned a 1968 GT Mustang, and he loved to put it on the road. So, we hit the highway.

He told me that he had a former girlfriend who attended Texas Women's University. I inquired about whether she was still loyal to him, and he suggested that once a girl had been with him, he was hard to resist. As intelligent as he was, much of what he said could only be taken in a humorous way. He had a well-developed sense of humor. I told him that I thought a young lady I once knew from Tyler, who was an old girlfriend of mine, also went to Texas Women's University. I hadn't kept up with her but had heard this from some of my friends. Although, I was two years ahead of her, and hadn't seen her since I graduated from high school. The notion came to me that it would be good to have a reunion with her, but there was no certainty she still attended the university. The flame in me still burned for her.

We left the campus on Friday morning after Breakfast. Thinking that this would be one meal we didn't waste, since we were paying for it anyway, and there was no way to get reimbursed for the meal after the time had passed. It would be one meal we didn't have to purchase. Neither of us had any Friday classes. This was deliberate on both our parts: for me it was simply convenient; for Larry, during basketball season, the team usually traveled on Fridays. Dallas was one-hundred-thirty-five miles away. The car was in good condition, being practically new, and we didn't expect to have any problems with the car. We arrived at one o'clock that day. Larry had called his girlfriend prior to our arrival. She didn't get out of class until three o'clock. She told him to get a room at the only Best Western Motel near the campus, and pick her up at Hanna Hall at four o'clock. I should have gotten in touch with Dora but had no idea of how to get in touch with her. I didn't even know if she was still actually attending the university.

We got a room as planned, and came by the campus at four-thirty. It turned out that Larry's friend knew Dora and knew her room number. I called from the lobby, and she said she would be down immediately. I was surprised when I saw her. She immediately came over and kissed and hugged me when she saw me in the lobby. She had no problems picking me out of the crowd standing in the lobby.

"Hello Dora, how're you doing? I can't believe it. It's good to see you."

"I'm doing fine, how're you? It's also good to see you."

"I'm doing well, thank you."

"I heard you were at East Texas Baptist and was surprised you never came back to see me."

"School keeps me fairly busy."

"I'm sure not to busy to keep up with an old close friend."

I explained the situation to her, and that I wanted to spend some time with her this weekend if possible, that we had a room at the Best Western. I also told her that my friend and another girl from her dorm named Cheryl would be joining us. She felt comfortable enough with the idea, and said she was familiar with Cheryl.

"You're in luck," she said. "I don't have any schoolwork or anywhere in particular to be the next couple of days."

"That's great, sorry I didn't give you plenty of advance notice."

"That's OK," she said, "Let me pack a few things I might need. Be back in just a minute."

In the meantime, Larry's girlfriend, Cheryl, was getting off the elevator with a suitcase in her hand. I explained to them that Dora would be a few minutes. She had to get a few things. Cheryl went to check out of the dorm for the weekend.

Dora came back, checked out at the desk, and we headed for the car. On the way there I was basically silent. I kept thinking about how Dora and I had first gotten acquainted.

It was one cloudy-overcast day in March. I was goofing off from class and saw her walking on the sidewalk of another building. She was only in sixth grade, and I was in the eighth grade. She was light skinned, with a pretty face, smooth-firm legs, and a sexy walk. Immediately I was attracted to her. I hadn't noticed her before, and I'm not sure if she hadn't been around, or if I simply hadn't paid her any attention.

257

Later, we had a conversation, and I was hooked on her. She was very mature for her age. She had big hips and a cool dip in her stride that turned me on. She said her walk was because she had broken her leg when she was four years old, and it never set properly. Some people told me that I was attracted to her because she reminded me of my mother, and that I had a Freudian complex. Several years later I would go by to see her on Sundays and sit with her at activities at school. I also walked her to her bus every day. We broke up when I was a senior because I made demands on her for sex, and was unhappy because her father wouldn't let her go out with me—at least that's the story she gave me. Also, I felt that she was being untrue to me, and I had some proof of that fact.

I kept looking at her side ways in uneven glances. She had gained at least thirty pounds. She was already hefty to the tune of one-hundred-forty pounds in high school. Her skin had somehow seemed to darken, and she had a long-dark scar that ran the length of her right cheek. It appeared as if she was bloated with some kind of chemicals. The city life didn't seem to agree with her. Also, one of her front teeth was missing. She had a rather wide keloid scar on her right knee. For a while I wondered if I had done the right thing by coming by to see her.

We arrived at the Best Western about six o'clock. When we got to the room, we sat in the available motel chairs and began talking about old times.

"Why didn't you come back to see me from college?" she asked.

"As I said, I was busy with my school work, and I considered that we had reached an impasse."

"I still cared for you. You never get over your first love, at least I didn't. I was heart broken."

"I didn't think you wanted to hear from me anymore."

"Somehow, I kept hoping you would come back to see me. My thinking was that you would charge in like a white night and save me—when things got rough in high school. Somehow in my mind I expected you to come and rescue me."

"Well, I'm here now, and I'm the same as I always was."

It was time to brush up on old times. We had to get around to it sooner or later.

"What happened to Susan Carter?" she asked. "I thought you two would somehow get together permanently."

"She died in a car accident."

"I didn't know that," she said.

Susan was the girl I dated after Dora and I split.

"Do you ever go back to Tyler to visit?"

"I go back quite frequently. My mother and father still live there. You wouldn't believe the changes that have taken place," she said. "What about you? Do you get back there often?"

"I try to go back as less as possible."

"Why do you feel that way?"

"There is nothing for me to go back for. My mother and father passed away, and most of my relatives have moved."

I moved closer to her and kissed her on the lips with a big wet-mouth-sloppy kiss. She put her arms around me and hugged me tight and gave me a long kiss. We kissed and held each other for at least thirty minutes. Somehow it didn't feel as good to kiss her as it did in high school. But it got both of us in the mood. Larry and Cheryl were looking at TV on the other side of the room.

"Do you want to get under the cover, so we can have some semblance of privacy?" she asked.

"I guess that would be a good idea."

We took off our clothes down to our underwear and got under the covers. Cheryl and Larry pretended to not pay us any attention. We got close in high school, but never actually had sex. She moaned and groaned but it wasn't magical like I thought it would be with her while in high school. When I kissed her in high school it seemed that the earth moved to the tune of a ten on the Richter scale. I would have literally killed to be intimate with her in high school. We had already made plans, but I was disappointed. There was no choice but to spend the rest of the weekend with her, since I had gone through the trouble of conjuring her up. I still halfway expected Heaven and Earth to move when we touched.

When we were finished, she said, "I hope I didn't disappoint you. I know how eager you were for intimacy with me in high school."

"It was good baby; I was just reminiscing."

I didn't want to let her know how I really felt. I felt as if I had wasted my time in high school chasing after her, being a fool for her, and carrying a torch for all these years. My conclusion was that too much water had run under the bridge for our relationship to ever be a success.

Saturday night we all went out to the Steppers Club and had a good time. Larry got too high to drive, and I had to drive back to the hotel. We left at one o'clock and came back to the hotel. We all got under the covers for some more lovemaking.

Out of the blue Larry yelled out, "Let's switch partners,"

I pretended I didn't hear him, because I didn't want to get involved in any such shenanigans. Besides, Larry was high as a kite. Dora and I still had a modicum of respect for each other. I had never been around anyone who proposed switching partners before. But looking at Cheryl and looking at Dora, I can see why he wanted to switch. Dora had been quite a sexy chick in her day, but I'm afraid her day had passed. I never gave Larry a reason as to why I didn't corporate with his idea.

Sunday evening, we took them back to Hanna Hall. Dora had tears in her eyes as we drove away. They were crocodile tears as far as I was concerned. As much as I wanted to see her, I hadn't forgotten how she treated me. We took the long drive back to East Texas Baptist. I kept telling myself this era in my life was over. I never saw Dora again to this day. Word is she's still living in Dallas and has been married and divorced. I maintained a friendship with Larry until we graduated. He passed about twenty years ago. But we never really had much to say about our trip to Dallas. I graduated the next year and moved to New York and took a trainee position as a stockbroker. I am still a stockbroker in New York with a wife and four sons. My wife and I met when I was a junior at East Texas Baptist. She was a junior at Wiley. We got married after graduation. I live in a suburb of Connecticut with two cars, a dog, and a cat.

25

PUT YOUR HAND IN MINE

It was the latter part of spring 1963. The wild flowers were in full bloom into their many colors. You could smell the scent of lilacs and marigolds. The birds were chirping. The paper mill near the school gave off a distinct foul odor. Cotton and corn were knee high in fields just beyond the school. It was another warm-sunny day in East Texas. Spring was exploding before us without a doubt.

This year was the year President John F. Kennedy was assassinated. I was fifteen and in the tenth grade. I was a late bloomer and was just going through many adolescent changes; I had the pimples to prove it. I had been courting this young lady, who was fourteen and in ninth grade, since the beginning of the year. I hadn't noticed her prior to sixth grade, because the high school and junior high had a slightly separate schedule. We were in the same location but took lunch at a separate hour.

I lived in what could be called a rural area in a shotgun shack. We had no telephone, natural gas, or running water; with only a dirt road for three miles to our house. My girlfriend Dorothy lived in the city in a modern-brick house with all the modern conveniences.

Her father and mother were teachers, they taught in a town nearby called Longview; while my mother didn't work—except to help maintain our little-dirt farm, and my father worked as a janitor for an oil refinery on the Gulf Coast. He came home every two weeks and spent the weekend. My parents had lived on this farm since before the Great Depression. They moved here soon after getting married. Until I was in first grade, we didn't even have a road for those three miles—only a trail. I'm not sure why it took so long for the county to build a road, other than the fact that Blacks were generally disfranchised and not quick to complain about their condition. They had little power because they did not vote, because they were not allowed to vote. My parents were older and from the old school. Her parents were younger and more modern in outlook.

Dorothy was about five-two, with caramel skin, smooth-long-scissors-like legs, doll-like face, well-proportioned body, well-developed physique for her age, and a vibrant personality. Even in those years she kept a manicure and pedicure at all times. Her coiffure was also well maintained. She also dressed classy, and was mature beyond her years. She was well trained and cultivated for a fourteen-year old. Needless to say, I was captivated by her.

I was about five-six, a little darker than she, with a few rough edges with respect to cultivation, scrawny, and with clothing straight out of a Sears Roebuck catalogue.

I never thought to ask her what she saw in me, probably because I was afraid to ask. But she saw something in me, since she chose me over all the other suitors. I think she saw a diamond in the rough. There was certainly no comparison between us either socially or economically.

As I was walking her to her bus after school on a Friday evening, she looked at me with those beautiful brown eyes and said, "Sean lets get married."

I didn't know what to say, I wondered if she was serious, or if there was something wrong. I asked her, "What brought this on so suddenly?"

I didn't realize at the time that when people don't have to deal with certain pressures of life, it is easier for them to overlook certain negatives about life.

"When I'm around you I'm so happy, I want to have this feeling for the rest of my life."

"Let's talk about it some more later. Something like that deserves serious consideration."

I felt good enough about her to consider her idea—no matter how immature it seemed. Not realizing at the time that such notions were only a phase that young people who were infatuated went through.

"If you put your hand in mine, we can leave all our troubles behind, keep on walking, and don't look back." She was repeating these words from a song by the Temptations, "Don't Look Back."

This kind of conversation was not unusual for Dorothy, she was normally very deep. But I wondered what troubles she had that she wanted to leave behind at fourteen. Maybe there was something about her I didn't know. Her bus was signaling her to get on board. She kissed me on the cheek and got on the bus just before the driver closed the door. As she kissed me on the cheek, I got a whiff of that Estēe Lauder perfume she was wearing. What a young lady, I thought. I felt I should hold on and never let her go.

I thought about how some of my brothers had difficulty for most of their lives managing their families. I had four brothers. Two of them never had much success with jobs. The other two probably didn't enjoy their work. Only one of them graduated high school. Part of the reason they experienced these situations were because of a lack of education, which led to inability to get a decent job. Quitting school to get married at such a young age could spell even more difficulties for the both of us. This is the reason why I always had planned on going to college. I thought about what she said seriously because I really liked her.

I saw Phil coming out of the school building. He always caught the second bus in his area. He was one of my best friends. I decided to talk it over with Phil.

"Dorothy suggested that we get married."

"Is she pregnant? That's the only reason to get married at such a young age."

"No, we've never even had sex."

"Then why ruin a good thing. At this point your parents have all the bills and responsibilities. If you get married the bills will be yours. Do you know how hard it is to make it today? Doing such a thing could ruin your future."

"I hadn't had a chance to think about it, but I'm glad I had a chance to talk to you"

"My father told me to know when to kiss'em, when to diss'em, when to walk away, and when to run. Sounds like you need to think about running at this point brother," said Phil.

"I believe you're right," I said.

I had never shared with Phil how much I cared for Dorothy.

"I'll talk to you later," he said, and walked away.

I had been driving a car since I was eleven-years old. My brother had left an old 1951 Fleetline Chevrolet, in running condition, parked in the dilapidated shed next to our house, when he moved to the Gulf Coast. Before he moved, he taught me to drive that old standard-shift Chevrolet. When I wanted, I would drive it where we needed to go. Neither my father nor mother had ever learned to drive. That morning I had somehow dallied too long and missed the bus, so I had driven the car to school, even though I didn't have a license. So, I got in my car and drove home. I had a hard time keeping my mind on my driving. I thought about what she said all night long, causing me to toss and turn for most of the night. I could smell her perfume and see her in my dreams.

The next day I met Dorothy coming out of the building, "How's it going today," still thinking about what she said the previous day.

I cared a lot about her and didn't want to simply get scared and walk away from the relationship.

"I had a talk with my parents last night. They suggested that such plans were premature and inappropriate, they said today it was necessary for two people to have an education before getting married."

I knew her parents were too reasonable to ever entertain such a thought, especially not allow us to follow through with it.

"I was thinking the same thing all night long."

"I do love you," she said.

I walked her to her bus, and then got on my bus. We never had any more premature talk about getting married.

The next day Phil told me it was probably some kind of test to see how loyal I was to her and if I truly loved her. That I should just forget about it. I contributed her immature behavior to her youth and soon forgot about it.

School was about to end for the year. I had seen her with one guy in particular for a long time. They would spend quite a bit of time together. I didn't get suspicious until Phil told me that I should watch out for T. J.;

however, it was normal for a young lady to interact with male students in her class. She had the right to associate with her classmate if she wanted. But the situation was getting out of hand. One day I mentioned it to her.

"Why are you and T. J. always in each others company?" I asked.

"We're not courting or anything, just friends and classmates," she replied.

"Every time I look around you guys are either eating lunch together, in the library together, or somehow conversing."

"Nothing serious, don't worry about it."

"I just want to be sure you are still my girl."

"I've been and always will be your girl until you say otherwise."

But T. J. apparently had other ideas.

Dorothy and I went to a baseball game near the end of school. School was out on May 5, 1963. It must have been around May 4th. T. J. was exceptionally good at baseball. He was a second baseman and could really field and hit the ball well. You've never seen anyone run the bases with such speed. He was also good at football, basketball, and track. You might say he was a natural athlete. This situation made the nature of the competition stiff. Once the game was over T. J. came over to where Dorothy and I were sitting. We had never confronted each other before. I'm not sure why he confronted me on this particular day. Maybe he was feeling his oats somehow.

"From now on Dorothy is my girl. Here's where I take over," he said.

"T. J., you have no right to make such a statement. We have always been friends since first grade, and that's what we will remain," Dorothy said.

"I don't know what you see in this squirt, he is no good at anything but his studies, why do you hang around with him?"

All I could do was hang my head kind of low.

"Apparently, I see something in him that doesn't meet your eye."

I never thought Dorothy had anything to do with this charade.

I then got a little angry at his comments.

"I was trying to be friendly by letting you hang around with Dorothy at lunch, in the library, and generally around the campus, but I don't want you hanging around her any more. At first, I wasn't aware of your intentions. But now I see where you're going and where you're coming from. Dorothy is my girl and will always be my girl."

The air was so tense you could cut it with a knife.

"If that's the way you guys want it, I will abide by the rules."

T. J. walked away, and I never had any more problems with T. J. In fact, T.J.'s mother moved to Fort Worth and he went with her that summer. I never heard from him again.

The next year I got my driver's license, and Dorothy's parents were reluctant at first, but started allowing her to go out with me. I spent a lot of time at her place. We also went bowling, to the movies, dancing, to visit friends, and many other outings. We really bonded and got to know each other during this time.

Throughout high school I never had any more problems with those who had affections for Dorothy. She was always known as Sean's girl. We went to all the sporting events and activities together, and I visited with her every Sunday. Dorothy was a little disappointed that I didn't play sports but understood when I told her that I just didn't get started early enough to be good at anything. Her father was a big fan of sports, but she convinced him that my talents lie in other areas. When time came for the junior and senior prom, everyone knew that Dorothy and I would be there together. I never will forget how she cried when Malcolm X was assassinated. The Civil Rights Movement reached its greatest peak during these years.

We courted throughout high school. I went to college not far away from our hometown. Dorothy came to visit on the first Sunday of every month. We both agreed that since I was there to study, once a month was enough visiting, anything more would interfere with my studies.

The next year we went to the same college in East Texas. We had the same major—business and economics. When it was appropriate, we studied together. Usually we went to the library to study every night. Dorothy went to summer school every year, and that made us seniors during the same year. So, we graduated at the same time. I had to work with my brother on the Gulf Coast during the summers to help pay my tuition. Dorothy's way was paid for by her parents.

Martin Luther King, Jr. was assassinated during my junior year. We both felt sad for all the trouble in the world. Riots broke out all across the country in larger cities. Dorothy and I wanted to participate in some of these activities but had no real connection to any of them. We felt that we were doing our part by helping to integrate the university we attended. We were happy just being able to be together.

We decided to commit to each other for life. We both understood that it was our destiny to be together. We got married during our senior year and got an apartment near the campus. It was a fact that two could live cheaper off campus together than trying to live separately on campus. We had a very strong relationship and were able to sustain it through difficult times.

We decided not to have children right away and decided to move to California after graduating college. After moving to California, we both found jobs in the sales industry, and eventually bought a house. Eight years later we had our first son. Twelve years later we had our second son. We still live in San Jose, California.

26

ULTERIOR MOTIVE

I was born and raised in Matteson, Illinois. My parents came to Matteson from Houston, Texas in 1974. They both went to college in East Texas, and both were raised in the South Eastern part of Texas. My mother was not too keen on moving, but my father wanted a different scenario. I think both of them liked the Chicago area once they got here. They have been in Matteson ever since, and wouldn't leave it for the world. My mother was a psychologist until retiring from Tinley Park Mental Health Center in 2010; my father installed telephones for Illinois Bell until he retired in that same year.

We lived in a comfortable two-story-brick house in a south suburban subdivision called Woodgate. A subdivision where the parkways were lined with trees and everyone fussed over their immaculate-manicured lawns. It was a nice-peaceful community with good schools, churches, and stores. My brother and I had a comfortable upbringing; he was two years older than me. My brother was an engineer for Bell Laboratories. We both got everything you could want.

It was now 2000. I was a student at Roosevelt University. I graduated from Woodgate Elementary and moved on to and graduated from Rich South High School. At Roosevelt I had maintained a 3.5 grade point average and belonged to a variety of clubs and organizations. I was voted "whose who" among college and university students for this year. My career was pretty much carved out and defined for me as it had always been. I had gone through several computers since I was a child.

One night I was at the mall having a bite to eat, when a young lady came in the restaurant. The restaurant was exceptionally crowded. The only vacant table was where I was sitting. It was an unusual night for the restaurant. The restaurant was my hangout. I had been to it many times before. Even the manager knew me well. She came over and asked me if she could join me. I said, of course. She had on some sheer-patterned-black pantyhose, and a dress that was split up to midway her thigh. The dress was already a mini. Every strand of her hair was in place. It wasn't a tight dress but was loose-fitting. All I could see was the contrast between the sheer-black pantyhose and her creamy-yellow thighs. I kept thinking how much I would like to get to know her. The second thing I noticed was that it was July, and she had on long dress sleeves the full length of her wrist. For the moment, I thought no more about it, but didn't know what to make of it. I figured she had a reason for her attire.

"My name is Marcus," looking at her with sad eyes.

"Mine is Samantha," smiling.

"Where do you live?" wondering why I hadn't seen her before.

"I live in Lakewood," making eye contact.

"Did you go to Rich South?" trying to place her from somewhere.

"Yes, I did," thinking I had finally got a fix on where I had seen her.

"What year?"

"Between 1993 and 1997," still wondering why we hadn't met before.

"I was there those same years."

"I wasn't too popular. I mostly did what I was required to do and got out of there. I didn't like school very much," she said with some regret.

"I liked it OK but wasn't too popular. I wasn't involved in any extra-curricula activities either. I spent most of my time on my computer."

"Even at that it seems we should have run into each other somewhere."

The waitress came over and we both ordered our food. They were having a special on pork ribs, so we both had pork ribs and a salad. We also both ordered a Rum and Coke and had several more when our glasses were empty.

"Where do you work?"

"Carson, Pirie, Scott. What about you?"

"I'm a student at Roosevelt University, and have been since I graduated from Rich South."

"What're you studying?"

"Computer programming."

I kept noticing those creamy-yellow thighs showing through sheer-black pantyhose. She had a pretty face and was about five-seven and 120 lbs. She had on red lipstick and red fingernail polish. She was very attractive. She had on a pink dress which highlighted her color and her accessories even that much more.

She went into the bathroom and spent at least fifteen minutes. She also seemed slightly nervous and irritated at times. She at times would visibly shake. Yet, she was able to sit there and enjoy her meal. She said she hated to go back to work, but it was her job. I told her I understood the situation, but that when you had a job you had to show up.

"Why don't you wait until I get off?" she asked, "we can go out afterward."

I was attracted to her and that sounded like Heaven to me. I was not attending school during the summer but working at Firestone next to the mall. I worked ten to six—five days a week. It was a Friday night.

"Sure, we can do that," elated that she would make the suggestion.

"I'll meet you back here at eleven o'clock," she started to leave the restaurant.

"OK, I'll see you then," I left the restaurant and went shopping in the mall.

I walked back in the restaurant at eleven, and to my surprise she was sitting there looking appealing and sexy as all hell. She had put on more makeup and re-did her hair.

"Well! What do you want to do?" I asked, trying to not seem anxious.

"Not much we can do at this time of night. I simply wanted to see you again. I like you," revealing her true feelings.

"I like you too."

"Why don't we get a room at a cheap motel? There's a little motel on Lincoln Highway called the Matteson Motel. Neither of us has to be at work tomorrow. It's right down the street."

"I know where it is."

I liked the fact that she understood money was at a premium, since I was a college student, and she was willing to go to a cheap motel. It certainly wasn't necessary to go to an expensive motel for a couple of hours.

I was shocked but figured out later that this was her intent all along. She would have gone to a motel with me on the spot if she hadn't had to be at work in a few minutes. I had heard about one-night and quick stands, but I didn't expect Samantha to be one of them. I didn't see her as the one-night stand type. There was a lot about Samantha that I didn't know. But I wasn't about to turn her down. My father said they used to have a saying where he grew up, *don't kick any woman out of bed*. We left the restaurant and went to our cars in the parking lot of the mall.

"We can take my car. You can pick yours up later."

She was driving a 2000 Mustang. It had a shiny yellow paint job with aluminium wheels. There wasn't a dent on the body anywhere.

"OK."

"Why don't you drive? Can you drive a standard shift?"

"Sure, I can."

I got in her car and drove off but was slow and hesitant about shifting the gears. I hadn't driven a standard shift in so long, that at first, I had trouble shifting the gears, she became slightly agitated. I had learned to drive on a 1990 Volkswagen Beetle, and felt quite competent to drive a standard shift.

"I thought you could drive a standard shift."

"I can. I've never driven this particular model."

The materials from her blouse were shedding all over my shirt. I assumed it said something about the cheapness of the material in her blouse.

We went to the motel, had sex, and went to sleep. I woke up and caught her going through my wallet. I didn't say anything to her about what she was doing. Nothing was missing from my wallet. She didn't take any of the money from my wallet, because she had all the material things she wanted. I turned over, and we had sex again. After that she wanted to go one more time, this time she wanted to go anally, but after looking at my penis said it might be too big. She decided against it. I wasn't in favor of that type of sex anyway. Besides, she said I would need a condom, which I didn't have. I was a bit of a prude, and my father had always indicated that anal sex was nasty. But I was willing to try if that's what Samantha wanted.

I got her number and told her that I would call her. She got my number just in case I didn't call her.

Two days later she called me, and we went to the Holiday Inn. This time she insisted on having anal sex. She wanted me to wear a condom this time, and had told me to bring one. She brought some oil and put it on the condom before I entered her. She seemed to enjoy it. From then on, she insisted on including anal sex as a part of our love making routine. The anal sex wasn't as bad as I thought. She was also a freak for the many positions we could contort our bodies into. She also gave me oral sex, but I declined to do the same for her. During this time, and our previous sexual encounter, I was too involved to notice the tracks on her arms and body. I was only interested in having sex. In spite of her other problems she really seemed to enjoy the sex act for the pleasure it brought her. It seems to have been the one pleasure she got out of life. Freud once said some people are driven by sex alone, and I believe Samantha was one of them. That is not to underestimate her drive for substances.

We didn't make contact until a week later. I called her.

"Hello Marcus. How are you doing?"

"Hello Samantha, you must have been reading my mind, I was about to call you."

"That's what everyone says when they're caught by surprise, after having not called in a long time."

"Seriously, I was going to call you."

I was actually going to call her but had gotten busy with writing an independent study paper for school.

"Were you really about to call me?"

"Yes, I was."

"Can you come by to see me tomorrow?"

"Yes, I'll come by."

"I want you to meet my parents."

"I told you I like you. Don't you believe me?"

"I like you too."

"Come by at eight o'clock tomorrow night. I live right behind Lakewood Bowl on 4462 Spring."

"I can find it."

I came by and met her parents. She was an only child, and her parents were nice. They lived in a modest-brick bungalow. Again, it was a hot July night, and she had on another long-sleeve dress. I wasn't quite sure what to make of it. Her parents had to go out for a while and left us in the house alone. We took advantage of the opportunity and had sex once again. Later we began to talk.

"I told you I like you Marcus. I feel like I have known you for most of my life. It's hard to imagine liking anyone as much as I like you, and I enjoyed being with you the past few nights. I feel as if I could spend the rest of my life with you."

She called me and told me to meet her at the Cracker Barrel for Breakfast. We met and had a good breakfast. She ate like she had the munchies and hadn't eaten in several days. Between bites we managed a conversation.

"What're we going to do Marcus? I think I'm falling for you baby," making serious eye contact.

"I'm falling for you too," a little nervous.

"What's the next step?"

"I don't know."

"Are you ready to take it to the next level?"

"What's the next level?"

"I suppose marriage."

I had never thought about marriage before, although I did feel strongly about Samantha. We both said that we needed to think about it some more before deciding on a plan of action. We departed and said that we would be in contact with each other in a few days.

About a week later she surprised me at home with a call from Milwaukee and told me the whole story. She said she had a problem drinking, with heroin, with crack, and with cocaine. I had never picked up one single-serious clue as to her addiction. Being blindsided by her other deceptive qualities. She said she couldn't see me for a while, because she was in a drug treatment program in Milwaukee, and it wasn't her first time being in such a program. The program would last for six months. Apparently, she had a severe problem. I told her to contact me when she got out. I never heard from her again.

I was beginning to get attached to her, but when I heard about her drug habit, I broke that attachment. I graduated from Roosevelt University in January.

I received a letter from Columbia, South Carolina inviting me up for an interview in February. I went to Columbia, and the interview went well. The next week the company wanted to know how soon it would take me to be in Columbia and ready to work. I told them I could be there in two weeks. The next week I flew to Columbia and was lucky enough to secure an efficiency apartment.

I packed up several suitcases of my things, put what else I could get in my 1998 Chevrolet Malibu, moved to Columbia, South Carolina, and took a job as a computer programmer. Although, I liked Samantha a lot, I didn't want to start life with someone who had a drug habit to overcome and have the odds even more against me. Somehow, I figured all had been said between us.

Be careful when someone is quick to get attached to you for no apparent reason. They just might have an ulterior motive. Also, *be careful what you wish for, you just might get it.* My father used to say, *take it easy greasy, you have a long way to slide.*

27

PERFECT BUT UNACCEPTABLE

We lived on a fifty-acre parcel of land five miles outside a small town called Hallsville in East Texas. It was a farming area, but we had no farm animals or raised any crops. Most people except the big-time farmers had discontinued farming many years ago. Farm animals were too difficult to take care of. My mother did have a small flower garden as well as a vegetable garden. Some people didn't even take the time to grow a vegetable garden, even when there were several children in the family. In some cases, farming was seen as outdated. Our house was basically a modern-brick structure with running water, butane, telephone, and all the modern conveniences. Five years ago, we tore down an old-wooden house that had existed for almost thirty years and built the new structure.

We had an elaborate system of cousins on both sides of the family, and often discussed these cousins in detail. My whole family would frequently visit these cousins; they would frequently visit us and do many recreational things together. We were close on both sides of the family. Every year we had a family reunion where people came from all across the country to commiserate.

My mother was a teacher, and my father worked on the Gulf Coast in the oil industry. My father only came home twice a month and during his summer vacations. My father did this for the latter portion of his life. He retired in 1965 and came home on a permanent basis, after twenty years at the plant. I had two sisters and a brother, all older than myself. Each of my sisters and my brother were away from home and lived in larger cities.

I was sixteen-years old, and it was 1962. My sister's father-in-law asked me if I wanted to go fishing with him. Many people supplemented their diet by fishing. For most people, any meat they could get was considered at a premium, and fish were free for the catching. I mainly went fishing for the sport of it, rarely eating the fish. Some people also hunted wild game to supplement their diet. Mr. Townsend realized that my father was absent a great deal of the time, and he was trying to play a fatherly role. He was the minister at our church. We had occasionally gone on other outings. He would also enlist me to help him out on his farm—with pay of course. We went over the hills and through the meadows until we came to a stream. We had to pass over many rough and rocky places in the road. Occasionally we saw a squirrel, a possum, a snake, or a fox. We had to walk about a mile from where we parked the truck to arrive at the stream. It was rough to travel by truck that close up to the stream.

As soon as we got to the stream, we saw a young lady, and her grandparents standing in an open area, fishing. Most of the stream was in dense forest area. I had never seen this girl before but knew her grandparents. They lived around the corner from me. I found out later that Rhonda lived in Jefferson. She was wearing a cap, jeans, and a shirt—appropriate for fishing in the backwoods, looking more like a boy than a girl, but nevertheless very attractive. Her hair was platted in a single long plat that came together at the back of her head. She had an obviously pretty face and an excellent shape. I knew her grandparents were my cousins but didn't know how these people were related to her. It was obvious she was of some relationship to them.

I immediately started a conversation with her. She was easy to talk to and immediately reciprocated in the conversation.

"What's your name," I asked, anxious to get to know her, but failing to make direct eye contact.

"My name is Rhonda, what's yours?" she looked directly into my eyes with those hazel eyes and tan skin.

"Mine is Maurice," shuffling my feet, beginning to make eye contact.

"Nice to meet you," she said, with great social dept.

It s clear this girl had better social skills than I did: she had better home training, was more worldly-wise, and more sophisticated.

"What relationship are you to the Johnsons?" adjusting the fishing pole along with my stance.

"I'm their favorite granddaughter," she tried to make a joke, and laughed at her own joke.

"I like your sense of humor," I had to laugh myself.

"Thank you," she knew the effect she had on other people.

"Where are you from?" still questioning her.

"I'm from Jefferson. Have you heard of it?" As if to see how much I had been around.

"Sure, I've heard of Jefferson. I've been there a few times," as if I had done my share of getting around.

"I've lived there all my life."

"How long are you going to be with your grandparents?" Wanting to know what her situation was.

"I'll be there for the rest of summer vacation."

Mr. Townsend was signaling me that it was time to head up the creek, if we wanted to get any fishing done.

"See you later," I said, "could I come by and see you sometimes?"

"Sure, you know where we live."

"Yes, I know. I'll call you."

"Please do."

It turned out she was a cousin I had never met. Mr. Townsend and I headed on up the stream. I said good-bye to her, we all went our separate ways. I ended up catching twenty-three wide-mouth perch that day. We were there for several hours. My mother didn't want to clean them but finally gave in. I was proud of my catch and ate until my heart was content.

I didn't see her until several weeks later. Until I saw her again, I kept thinking about her, she ran through my mind day and night. My father was home one weekend, and we went by to visit her grandparents. She spent every summer with her grandparents. I had my driver's license and could go by to see her whenever I wanted. My brother bought me a car on my birthday during my sophomore year in high school. My brother was ten years older than I. I understood later that Rhonda was indeed one of her grandparents' favorite grandchildren. My father told me that this girl was my second cousin, that her father was his first cousin. I'm not sure why he told me that, he must have seen the way I looked at her. My uneven glances were unmistakably those of sincere affection. But I did later tell him how much I liked her. He told me that we were too close cousins for there to be any type of boyfriend/girlfriend relationship. He later said he had always been close to her father, grandfather, and the rest of her family.

I soon started visiting her on a regular basis at her home in Jefferson. I'm sure her parents wondered why a cousin would come so far just to see her. Nothing my father said or anyone else deterred me from having affections for her. Her mother and father knew we were cousins but didn't know we were developing a serious relationship. Rhonda swore to them that we were just friendly cousins: our relationship was of close cousins rather than girlfriend/boyfriend. Rhonda's parents let our relationship last as long as it did because they didn't think it was serious. They seem glad to have her involved in a platonic relationship. Even though I visited her every week end on Saturday evenings, they still thought we were just cousins. We frequently played games, went to the movies, and sporting events. She said her favorite activity was to go riding around the area with me.

Rhonda also had a boyfriend she was seeing on a regular basis. She introduced me to him as a close cousin. We would sometimes double date, but this didn't work out because I couldn't stand to see her intimate with Steve—her boyfriend. Rhonda introduced me to a cousin on her mother's side of the family, but Rhonda couldn't stand to see me kissing her cousin Althea. We figured that wouldn't work and soon discontinued the activity. We dated each other until we graduated high school; we both pretended to see other people but knew our hearts were with each other. Sunday evenings were reserved for Steve. Steve knew I was coming by every week, but even he didn't think seriously about it. We were simply cousins expressing a friendship.

We decided if we got married but didn't have any children it would be OK. We rationalized and convinced ourselves of this. I had asked my father about the pros and cons of marrying a cousin.

"You should never marry a cousin son," my father said, lighting up a cigarette.

"But why not marry a cousin?" I asked, looking at him very intensely.

"Children from such a relationship are prone to many types and varieties of diseases. Too many similar genes coming together in one person," puffing on his cigarette.

I couldn't completely understand what my father meant, but, remembered some of it from my biology class.

"Does that always occur?" wondering about the possibilities.

"Not always, but you don't want to take any chances," trying to encourage and not discourage me.

"More than likely you will get the wrong genetic combinations," trying to demonstrate his scientific knowledge.

"What if you don't bring any children into the relationship?" trying to find some way for the relationship to survive.

I was searching for every possible rationale to help our relationship to survive.

"That's one way to handle it. If there are no children there is no chance for obvious genetic problems," feeling that he had reached some type of compromise.

"I'm seeing Rhonda, and I like her a lot, we've been involved for a year now," revealing my true situation.

"Is that my cousins Charles's and Louise daughter?" Curious about which relative it was.

"Yes, it is," hoping it would be reassuring to my father.

"If you like her that much, I suppose it would be OK. But be sure not to bring any children into the relationship," hoping I wouldn't pursue the relationship, but if I did would do the right thing for everyone.

"OK, Dad," pleased that his dad had helped him to figure out what to do.

We graduated high school and decided to get married, since we couldn't do without each other. We couldn't stand to be apart five minutes without wondering where the other one was. Rhonda's mother and father were surprised and were against it but Rhonda and I persisted. They gave us their blessings, because nothing was too good for their daughter. Rhonda had always had everything she wanted. She broke up with Steve after high school—tired of the pretense involved in that relationship. Steve couldn't believe she was going to marry the guy they used to double date with.

"I thought he was your cousin," said Steve, outdone.

"But I love him," Rhonda said confident that she knew what she wanted.

"That chump of a cousin stole you right from under my nose," feeling that he had been the victim of some type of scam.

"Think whatever you want," knowing it was now in the open.

"I thought you loved me," still trying to make an all-time comeback.

"But this is different. I want to spend the rest of my life with Maurice. We have a closeness that I could never find in another relationship," finally revealing how she truly felt.

"I thought that's what we had," confused about the past few years.

"You will never understand," giving up completely on Steve.

An end finally came to Steve and Rhonda's relationship, after having dated since junior high school.

We got married and moved to Longview, Texas—a few miles away. I got a job at an ammunitions plant. Rhonda got a job as a cashier in a local department store. We got an apartment and were on our way. As a wedding present my parents gave us a down payment on a new car, and her parents bought us an apartment full of furniture. We got many other gifts from other family, well wishers, and significant others.

I would frequently have discussions with Rhonda about the necessity to use birth control pills, and she said she was using them every day without fail.

"Are you using the pill, baby," I asked, about two months after the wedding, remembering what my father had said about children from such a marriage.

"Don't worry baby, I'm on the pill," she said, trying to reassure me.

"Even if we were going to have children, we need to get established first," trying to be sure Rhonda understood my position.

My mother and father have told me about the problems we might have if we decide to have children. They had let me know they understood the situation.

We did well for about a year: Rhonda started having morning sickness and said that she had missed her period. She went to see a doctor who told her she was two months pregnant. She discussed it with her mother, but her mother and father were against an abortion. My father and mother were also against an abortion. In fact, everyone in both families felt that she should give birth to the baby. Both families were highly religious and thought that life began at conception. We even went to see a genetic's counselor, and she assured us there was a good possibility that things would turn out OK with the baby.

We all agreed to keep the baby. Rhonda had a normal pregnancy and didn't miss a day of work until two weeks before giving birth. The baby came on time and never had any major problems. The only problem with the first child was he had severe allergies, and there were allergies on both sides of the family, we later found out. We had a second child twelve years later who had the same problem. We never did face any major problems or faced the severe problems that some of our relatives anticipated.

Both our sons grew up, went to college, and studied law. We still felt that for us to have gotten married as cousins were "perfect but unacceptable." We understood it was not a good thing to do, even if we made it without that many obstacles. We were married for forty years until I died of a heart attack in 2002. My wife died several years later. Both my sons are attorneys in Houston.

28

REUNION OF TWO LOVERS TEMPORARILY

I first saw Dora walking across the campus. It was a small campus located in Hallsville, Texas. The elementary school, junior high school, and high school were all in one location. I was out of class, like always, spinning my wheels, and wasting time. I spent a great deal of my time out of class or daydreaming while in class. Even while in class much of my time was spent as downtime. As far as my teachers were concerned, I had no future along with many of the other students. When I saw Dora, I was love struck. I stood there in a trance watching her. Those big hips, smooth-long legs, and pointed breast were appealing. I would sit in my classroom and watch Dora while she was on her lunch break. I couldn't wait until the elementary lunch hour. Dora was the first girl at my school that I was attracted to. She was only in the sixth grade, but I thought she was beautiful. I was in the eighth grade but had an abundant amount of testosterone. I hadn't noticed her before. The elementary and junior high took their lunch period at different times. At this point I hadn't begun to attend extra-curricula activities. There is a first time for everything under the sun.

From then on, I would walk her to her bus, and sit with her at sporting and other events. I would think about what I would say to her all day but be lost for words when I saw her in the evening after school was dismissed. As we got older, I would go to her house to court her on Sundays. This occurred as soon as I was old enough to drive. Occasionally I would see her around and about the city. I wanted her but was a little nervous about talking to her and was always slow in approaching her. Dora had several other boyfriends in a nearby town. Sometimes they would escort her to events at the school and public events in other cities. When I questioned her about them, she said they were her cousins. She always seemed to give preference to these boys over me. One night after a Spring Musical I caught her kissing one of the boys she said was her cousin. She denied it and said I didn't see what I thought I saw. One of my friends said she was trying to pull the wool over my eyes.

One day in tenth grade after school had dismissed, a guy in my class name Timothy was walking with Dora to her bus.

"What's going on?" I asked, outdone.

Timothy spoke up, "I'm taking over your girl," confident in himself and his abilities.

"Is this true Dora?" dropping my head, almost in tears.

"I have to figure out which one I want," as if she was some type of prima donna.

I kept getting the idea that she was trying to punish me somehow, but I didn't know what I had done to deserve such treatment.

"Let me know when you make up your mind," I was stupid enough to go for it.

I was so taken with her that I would have accepted anything. Timothy had girls in every town within driving distance on a Sunday afternoon. Obviously, he had no interest in Dora. I didn't feel she was his type. Timothy liked his girls a little more upper class. Someone must have put him up to it. Dora wanted her boyfriend to be good at sports, have an excellent personality, intelligent, and smooth talking. I stuttered and was bashful, and I didn't have a chance.

They both walked away. If he or she was expecting me to fight over her, and embarrass myself, they were sadly mistaken. I wasn't about to fight over her. I liked her but didn't feel she was worth fighting over. Besides, I was opposed to violence. Some people saw fighting over your girl as a real test of your loyalty to her. Several people did tell me I should have fought for Dora's honor. But I didn't feel she had any honor. An honorable female wouldn't behave that way. If I had wanted to fight, I could have defended myself without any problem.

Timothy was about my size and I could have handled him. I simply didn't want to fight.

I came back in a few days and asked if she had made up her mind.

"No, I haven't. I'll let you know," she said, obviously leading me on.

"Give her some time," Timothy said, as if he was in control.

Somehow, I thought they were testing me, Dora would have her little fling, and come back to me in a few days.

"Give me a chance, baby," all but losing control.

"I'll give you the same chance a snowball has in hell," trying to be sarcastic, and demonstrate her superior wit in front of Timothy.

I hadn't done anything to deserve this type of behavior, and there was no reason for getting hostile.

"You don't mean that, baby," fighting for some sense of self-esteem.

"It's all over for us," demonstrating that she was tired of dealing with me.

"But I'll take you anyway I can get you," experiencing a loss of dignity.

"It's too late," forcing the dagger deeper and deeper into my flesh.

"Let me come by your house next Sunday. We can discuss it," trying to get one last chance.

"I pity a fool," forcing the dagger into another part of my body for the last time.

My first mistake was to give her time to make up her mind. I should have written her off from the beginning. Now she saw me as just a fool in love with her who would do anything for her attention.

We came back from Timothy's interference and made up. Timothy had had his curiosity satisfied. After that we went through a series of make ups and break ups. Dora wouldn't go out with me for some reason, and I wanted to get her in my car. I felt if I could get her in my car, I could convince her to have sex. Her parents probably felt the same way. I wanted an opportunity to get between those big luscious hips and thighs. Eventually we broke up completely. For some reason she didn't want to have sex with me. I was disappointed. But I didn't trust her, I believed she was having sex with other guys, and wouldn't have sex with me.

She said her father wouldn't let her go out with boys. She was fourteen and in the eighth grade. I guess that sounds reasonable for a young girl's parents. I was sure her parents didn't like me, and that's why they didn't want her to go out with me. Also, her sisters and brothers, as well as her relatives, didn't like me either. I didn't know if this was true or not. I thought this was why she simply didn't want to go out with me. I was in the tenth grade, had a driver's license, and wanted some action. The wise thing to do would have been to find another girl who would be more agreeable. I used to sit at events and watch her legs and thighs in silk-shiny pantyhose.

We quit in the tenth grade, and I started dating someone else, though I didn't forget about her. I kept my eyes on her my junior and senior year, but we never got back together. I dated a succession of different girls but none like Dora.

I graduated and went off to college in May of 1966. I didn't see her again until one day I was walking down a street near the college campus. It was March 1968. I was on my way to pick up some dry cleaning from the cleaners. The home-economics' department at my old high school was attending a state-wide meeting. She and a classmate had come to participate in the meeting. She and her classmate were the most outstanding home-economic students for that year. Dora saw me walking and immediately recognized me. I even recognized her. She waved from the car, but they didn't stop. Later she came by my dorm to say hello. She looked me up in the student directory in the Student Center. The dorm-mother sent someone to my room to tell me I had a visitor. There was no intercom system connected to the rooms or telephones. Such things would be made available after I had long graduated. I came down to the TV room where Dora was sitting and waiting patiently.

"Hello Dora," glad to see her.

She had on her signature shiny-silk pantyhose, revealing most of her legs and part of her thighs.

"Hello Jimmy," she said, she was seemingly also glad to see me.

"What are you doing here?" I sat down on the couch and clutched her hand.

"My home-economics' class is having a state wide meeting," she gripped my hand tight.

"How long will you be here Dora?" I looked directly into her eyes.

"Three days."

"It's good to see you."

"I was waiting for you to come back to see me. I was waiting for you to come charging back on your white horse and rescue me—like a night in shinning armour," she smiled

"I didn't think you wanted to see me," breaking eye contact.

"Well, it's good to see you now," she smiled again.

"Let's go for a walk."

"That sounds good."

We got up and began to walk around the campus.

"What are you doing for dinner this evening?" she asked on our walk around the campus.

"I have nothing planned."

"Why don't we get together?"

"Sure, we can do that."

"What dorm are you in?"

"I'm in 20—room 210."

"I'll pick you up about seven."

"Do you have a car," she seemed to get excited.

"My friend let's me use his car in such situations."

"OK."

"You were at one time afraid to ride with me. You're not still afraid, are you?"

"I told you the truth in high school. Neither my mother nor father wanted me to go out at that age."

"I'll take your word for it."

"Besides, I have no more virginity to lose. My boyfriend took my virginity six months ago. I'm not afraid any more."

I picked her up and took her to the Tasty-Freeze for an old-time hamburger and some ice cream. We ate and left for the campus. On my way back to the campus I got an idea. She had already said she had lost her virginity and had noting else to lose.

I pulled up to the Holiday Inn, got out of the car, and went inside to get a room. I was taking a chance, because I didn't ask her if it was OK. I got the room, came back, and opened the door for her to get out. In high school once I pulled this stunt and lost my hotel reservation. I didn't want to be trying to make out in the back seat of that 1966 Mustang.

"What did you do?" seemingly outdone.

"I got a room," confident she would cooperate.

"That was very presumptuous of you. How did you know I wanted to get a room?" she looked sullen for a minute.

"Oh yeah, I didn't but I was hoping."

"I'll do it to keep you from loosing your money, make up for lost time, and for old-time sake."

My key said room 145. We headed for the room. She had on her old-style shiny pantyhose: the type that use to drive me wild. I kept looking at them, those smooth legs and big thighs. We made love until late in the morning. I couldn't seem to get enough. I really liked this girl. In high school I had no choice but to let her go. I didn't make a habit of chasing a girl who had misused me at an earlier period just to say I finally got over on her, but Dora was special.

I saw her the other two days she was on the campus. Soon it was time for her to leave. We went back to the hotel her last night on the campus. This time she asked me to get the room. I kept in touch with her when she went back home. I called and wrote to her every week. She graduated at the end of that year in May and went to college. I kept in touch as much as I could.

In November 1970 I visited her on her college campus. I had to borrow my brother-in-law's car in order to make the trip to Dallas. She attended college a few miles outside Dallas. She showed me around Dallas. We ate in fancy restaurants, shopped in high-end stores, and visited a number of museums. We also visited her

brother and sister who were married and had families
in Dallas as well as other friends from high school.
Her brother and sister seemed to have relaxed in their
resentment of me. At the movies we saw a good movie
called "Love Story," it was a tear jerker. We got a room
for the weekend, and we made love practically all night
long for several nights. I spent from Friday evening until
Monday evening at the hotel. My schedule at school was
clear on Friday evenings and on Mondays. I thought we
had resumed our pre-college relationship and was on
our way. But it was just my imagination running away
with me.

"Are you ready to be my girl again," I looked at her
with anticipation.

I thought I had completely won her over.

"I can't commit to you Jimmy," she looked away
sadly.

"Why not," feeling that thing were right for such a
move.

"I'm serious about someone," resuming eye contact.

"Then why did you allow me to visit."

"What I'm doing is for old-times."

"What do you mean?"

"I feel like I owe you for what I put you through in
high school, and I always pay my debts."

"OK."

"Enjoy yourself. It will likely be your last time to do
so. Relax and enjoy. Make up for lost time"

I came back to my campus understanding that my relationship with Dora was through. One day she called and said she was getting married. She had met a guy from Kenya and felt she loved him, and he was the love of her life. I attended the wedding, brought them a gift, and wished her and her new husband well, but I will never forget those pointed breast, luscious thighs and hips, and smooth legs in shiny pantyhose. None will ever compare to Dora. But what's good for you can be equally bad for you, and what's good to you can be bad for you as well.

29

SILK STOCKINGS BLUES

I grew up on a fifty-acre-dirt farm in East Texas. I did chores from the time I was six years of age. My youngest brother went to the Army after graduating from high school in 1958, and left the maintenance of the farm to me, when I was eleven-years old. We grew every type of farm produce that would grow in East Texas. We grew several acres each of the various possibilities. During growing season, I had to plow a mule from sunup to sunset. We had peach, pear, apple, and pecan trees. A variety of grapes, plumbs, berries, and walnuts grew wild in the forest. We also had chickens, ducks, guinea fowls, horses, and cattle. We used the food we grew to feed ourselves, and the animals we raised. Later, my father and I would pedal vegetables to the market.

My father didn't do any work on the farm, except during vacations. It was my responsibility to take care of the farm. I had to spend my time taking care of the animals, cultivating the fields, finding firewood, fixing fences, and whatever else was needed. He worked on the Gulf Coast and came home twice a month. It was the best way he knew how to feed his family. My father worked on the Gulf Coast for over twenty years in the oil industry. He retired from that industry.

One weekend my father came home and told me I had done a fine job on the farm for the summer. He was taking me to the Gulf Coast for two weeks as a vacation, and as a reward for my fine work. I was happy to get away from the farm if only for a short while. My mother and sister would have to take care of the farm chores. I wasn't sure how they would feel about this.

He told me to pack and be ready for his ride back to the Gulf Coast on Sunday at five o'clock. It was eight o'clock Saturday morning. I packed a few changes of clothing. I didn't have deodorant or other hygiene items, nor brush for my hair or toothbrush. I didn't start brushing my teeth until later in high school. It was a long time before I started clipping my fingernails and toenails, so I didn't have a set of clippers. I hadn't even heard of mouthwash. I think I did have a comb. I put my few clothes in an old suitcase that would only close on one end. A belt had to be tied around the other end to keep it closed. It was a cardboard suitcase that would fall apart if expose to rain consistently. I wore my only pair of shoes. During that time, I only had one pair of shoes. Gym shoes weren't that popular at this time. It was August 5, 1961, and I was fifteen years of age.

The man who would take us to the coast came promptly at five o'clock. He drove a red 1954 Ford pickup truck. We loaded our things on the back of the truck and headed for the coast. My father had never learned to drive and was always dependent on other people for a ride. I had learned to drive, but the old black and white 1951 Bel-Aire Chevrolet sitting in the dilapidated shed next to the house wasn't running. We arrived on the coast at approximately eleven o'clock. I estimated it to be about a six-hour trip, one that I had made only a few times before.

My father lived in a room attached to a man's house. There was a passageway leading to the rest of the house. The man who rented the room allowed my father to use the kitchen and the bathroom. It was a small room big enough to only turn around in. Once the bed was in there about all you could do is turn around. We slept in the same bed: my dad at the head, and me at the foot. My dad gave me strict orders that the landlord was particular about his house, and to only use the bathroom, don't even use the kitchen.

My father was hoping to go by his friend's house, and let her son know that he wanted him to show me around the city for the two weeks I was to be there. But my father decided it was too late and could wait until morning. My father had to be at work by nine o'clock. Work was only a few blocks away. He said he would get up early and take me by their place at eight o'clock the following morning.

His friend's house was two streets over from where my father lived. We went by there that Monday morning and knocked on the door. A middle-aged woman with a slim-well-kept figure came to the door.

"Hello there Michael," she was talking to my father, greeting him in a familiar tone.

She opened the door and invited us in.

"This is my boy, Billy. I want Willard to show him around for the two weeks he will be here."

Apparently, they had discussed this possibility ahead of time.

"Willard is still sleep. Has Billy had breakfast? Come on in and get some breakfast. Willard doesn't get up until about nine."

Cheryl came out of the kitchen and into where we were sitting.

"This is my daughter, Cheryl," she was looking at me with curiosity.

"How're you guys doing?" asked Cheryl.

She heard her mother offer me breakfast.

"Breakfast will be ready in a few minutes," she said, in a very friendly manner.

My father said, "I have to go. I will see all of you later this evening," as he shut the door behind him and walked toward the street.

"Willard will take good care of him, don't worry about that," said Mrs. Carter, reassuring my father as he left.

I found out later that Mrs. Carter had two children, and her husband was deceased. Willard was seventeen and a senior in high school. Cheryl was fifteen and in the tenth grade. Cheryl was nothing but eye candy. She was five-feet-five, 120 lbs. She had a pretty face and smooth legs, along with a curvaceous body that wouldn't quit. Her hair was in an afro, neat and trimmed, while blown to the max.

Cheryl put before me some ham, eggs, pancakes, and orange juice for breakfast. They must have been expecting me. Cheryl and I sat down to breakfast. Mrs. Carter said she never ate breakfast and had to rush off to work.

"You live in East Texas, don't you?"

"Yes, that's where I'm from."

"I thought that's where my mom said Mr. Crosby was from. What grade are you in?"

"I'm in the tenth grade."

My answers were short, but I was trying to eat. I realized Cheryl was just being friendly and trying to make conversation.

"What subjects are you taking this year?"

"I'm taking American History, Algebra I, Biology, English II, and Shop. What about you?"

"I'm taking English II, Western Civilization, Chemistry I, Algebra-Trigonometry, and Home-Economics."

"Your school is a little more advanced than ours."

I wondered if there was any chance of me getting close to her during the short time I would be on the coast. About that time Willard got up and came in for his breakfast. He came out of the bathroom. He was six-feet tall and about 160 lbs.

Willard came in and said, "Good morning."

Cheryl spoke up, "This is Mr. Crosby's son, Billy."

"Hi Billy, your father wanted me to look after you while you are here, and show you around the city," sounding as if he took his job seriously. "As soon as I have breakfast we'll get started," putting some eggs to his mouth with a fork.

"Go right ahead, I've had mine, and it was delicious."

He showed me the grocery store around the corner; the swimming pool; the community center; the ocean; the movie theater; and a few other places. He wanted me to know where they were, and we could spend time visiting each of them another day. By the time we saw all these things it was five o'clock, and time for my father to get off from work. I told Willard I was tired and was going home to see my father. He said that was probably enough for today.

I came home, and my father's landlord had fixed some fried catfish, macaroni and cheese, corn, and cornbread. We had lemonade with the meal as well. We ate, looked at TV, and went to bed. I was tired from walking, and my father was tired from a hard day's work. I was so tired I didn't get up until ten o'clock the next morning. My father had given me a key the night before, told me to put it in my pocket, and to lock the door before I left.

My father and his landlord had gone to work when I got up, so I headed for Willard's house.

When I got to Willard's house, I knocked on the door, but no one came to the door. I pushed the door and it came open. I walked into the family room, then into the kitchen, but no one seemed to be around. I pushed the door open to one of the bedrooms and saw Cheryl there. She had on Black-silk stockings, and support for the stockings. She also had on a black bra. That's all she had on. She simply stood there looking at me, as if to say come and get it. It yours if you want it. I wanted to go on in, but was afraid to go in. She told me to come on in. I stood there talking to her, a little nervous. I had never seen a more attractive woman, either fully dressed or naked.

"Where's Willard?" I asked.

I was trying to break the ice.

"He had to go over to the school to register for fall classes. He'll be back in a minute. Sit in the family room if you don't want to wait in my room."

I thought I would get in serious trouble if I waited in her room.

"Are you going someplace?" I asked.

"Yes, I have to go downtown for a club meeting. I'll come back in a few hours and fix dinner. You can wait right here for Willard."

I finally took my eyes off her vivacious body, and somehow managed to shut the door. I took a seat in the family room and turned on the TV. But those legs and body kept running through my mind. Soon Willard came home, and we went to the community center and played pool for the rest of the afternoon.

When my father got home, I asked him how well he knew Cheryl, Willard, and Mrs. Carter.

"Why do you ask?"

"I like Cheryl," I said.

"Don't mess with Cheryl. She's too rich for your blood."

"What do you mean?"

"Her mother has big things planed for Cheryl. She plans to send her to one of the best colleges in the country."

"I will attend a good college, also."

Neither my mother nor father had ambitions for any of their children going to college. If I did go to college it would be a miracle. My father knew his children had about as much chance of going to college as a snowball had of making it out of hell. To begin with none of them received the type of education that would support college. Then the task would be to come up with the financing.

"How'll you pay for it?"

"I'll get a loan."

"I still say stay away from Cheryl."

"But why do you say that."

"I tried to steer you in the right direction. Take my advice and leave her alone."

I tried to go to sleep that night, but Cheryl kept running through my mind. Even when I went to sleep Cheryl was in my dreams. I kept pushing in her bedroom door, and she kept saying come in.

"I've been waiting for you since eight o'clock—dressed just like this, hoping you would come. I thought you would like it. I sent Willard out, so he wouldn't be here when you arrived."

"What would your mother and Willard say?"

"It's none of their business. I have condoms if you like."

"Are you sure about this?"

"Don't you want to make love to me?"

"Yes, I do."

"Don't you like my silk stockings and support? They are just for you."

"You know I do."

"You may not get another chance, when everyone is out of the house, and we are all alone. I had a hard time getting rid of Willard."

In my dreams I kept reaching out saying, yes! And she kept stepping further and further into the bedroom, while beckoning me to come on in. I woke up in a cold sweat. I had that same dream over and over during the night.

The next day Willard and I went fishing. As I sat on the rocks feeling the cool ocean breeze and smelling the salty-sea air, I kept thinking about her legs in those black-silk stockings. When I got home, I had another talk with my father.

"I really like Cheryl, Dad."

"Give it up son, that's not for you."

"Again, why do you feel this way?"

"I've tried to be rational with you, but you got to have your way."

"How do you mean that?"

"Cheryl and Willard are my children. Cheryl is your half sister."

For a moment I was in shock.

"I can understand that."

"You wouldn't want to be involved with your sister, would you?"

"If you put it like that, I guess not."

I didn't know what to think. For a while I walked around in a daze. It was Thursday. I was to leave on Friday evening. On Friday I went by Mrs. Carter and told Willard and Cheryl good-bye. It was difficult to look them in the eye. I never did say good-bye to Mrs. Carter because she was at work.

I went back home and resumed my farming duties. It was time to harvest the crops. I never felt the same about my father again. I graduated from high school and was lucky enough to get a loan for college. My father retired and came home in 1962 but couldn't seem to adjust in East Texas. He divided his loyalties between the Gulf Coast and East Texas. I never heard from Willard, Cheryl or Mrs. Carter again.

30

SILK STALKINGS

I grew up in Matteson, Illinois, attended a local elementary, junior high, and high school, and then went to graduate and undergraduate school at Michigan State University where I earned a Ph.D. in psychology. I returned to Matteson, met and married my high school sweetheart, and was now working for a local agency.

It was eight o'clock Friday, March 14, 1980. My friend Mickey and I were in the habit of going to the Black Widow, a popular nightclub in Harvey, Illinois. There was not a cloud in the sky and it was cool-spring weather.

We were both Ph.D. psychologists working for a family service agency in Homewood, Illinois. We both met when we were working on our degree at Michigan State University, East Lansing, Michigan. We were friends at the school but left without knowing anything about where we would eventually make our residence. I had no idea where Mickey was until 1978. We graduate in May of 1974. In 1978 we both found ourselves working at the agency in Homewood. I had recently come aboard with the agency earlier that year. In fact, I was on the committee who interviewed Mickey for the job. Of course, I gave my wholehearted recommendation for his employment. I had no idea he was living in the area. His family had lived in Harvey for most of their lives. I never knew he was originally from Harvey. We had never discussed where he was from. My family had lived in Matteson, Illinois for most of their lives. Matteson, Homewood, and Harvey are small towns in proximity in the south suburbs.

Since we met up again at the agency, we had a habit of going out on Fridays for a little relaxation and recuperation. You know how *the mice will play when the cats away.* We were both married. I had a son and Mickey had a boy and a girl. He lived in Harvey and I lived in Matteson. Going out was our way of relieving stress after a week of listening to people's problems. Within a short period of working at the agency I thought I had heard it all, in reality, I hadn't heard the half of it. In those days, most young people spent at least some time clubbing, it was something everybody did. It was accepted as part of a rite of passage. We would usually have several drinks and be social with the young ladies that frequented the club. If you were lucky maybe you could take someone home for a quick rendezvous. We were simply looking for a little excitement.

On this particular night we had several drinks and were just clowning around. We sat there for about an hour observing the people who came in. We liked to observe people and thought we were astute at it, being psychologists. On this day we struck up a conversation.

"How long do you think we can keep listening to problems without having our own problems?" Mickey asked.

"I hope to last as long as I can, and then take a nice teaching job at a major university, before I give up on it," I said.

"I guest it would be a good idea to try something else within the field."

"Psychology has many areas that could all be possibilities for employment. We don't have to listen to family problems for the rest of our lives."

"I just get tired of listening to the same problems, over and over, day after day."

Suddenly two young ladies strolled in and had a seat in proximity to our table. Mickey touched me on the shoulder.

"Look at that, man," he said.

"Yes, I noticed, they look good," I said.

One had on a long-black dress with most of her breast hanging out, with a split up the side to her hips. When she sat down, she made sure the split revealed her creamy legs and thighs all the way to her hips. She was about a D-cup. She had on some black pumps that were so high, and the heel was so narrow, that I don't see how she could walk without falling. You could tell just by looking that her gold necklace, bracelet, and watch were of the finest quality. Her hair was exquisite, as if she had just left the beauty salon. She was about a 32-22-36. Her black-silk pantyhose was of the finest quality and contrasted her creamy yellow thighs. I thought I was finally going to get a chance to meet a classy young lady. My first thought was how I could beat all the other wolves in the club to her. The men nearby couldn't keep their eyes off her. I didn't want to appear too aggressive, although, when you were on the scene at the club you had to be somewhat aggressive. She was my choice. I would leave the other one to Mickey, and he would have to go along with it. Of course, he always went along with the game. It was just a game to both of us.

The other young lady had on a red-mini dress, with black-silk pantyhose—revealing smooth-flawless legs. She had on some medium-height-red high heels. Her coiffure was also together. She also wore an assortment of gold chains and bracelets. She was about a 32-24-38. She didn't reveal quite as much of her chest, and probably was a B-cup. She was also as classy as they come.

"I'm going after the one in black, take the other one."

It was a hard choice, but I saw what I wanted.

"Okay," Mickey responded.

Mickey was perfectly willing to cooperate with what I wanted him to do. We had played this game practically every Friday night since we found ourselves working at the same agency.

The music was soulful: mostly Jazz and rhythm and blues. Although, it was a bit loud, as the music in clubs normally is. The club was jam packed as usual for a Friday night. The Black Widow was the most popular nightclub in Harvey. I asked her to dance. She took my hand and we strutted and glided out on the dance floor. It was amazing how agile she was in those high-narrow heels.

"You're a good dancer." I said.

"So are you."

"I must confess I take dancing lessons," she said.

"Not many of us can afford dancing lessons. We have too many basic necessities to pay for and can barely afford those."

"It's just something I've always wanted to do."

I began to think that this lady was really cultured.

When we finished, I asked her if Mickey and I could join them at their table. She said yes, and we ordered both of them a drink. Mickey got familiar with Marilyn right away. He was as close in her face as anyone could possibly get, and at times had his mouth right in her ear. The one I was trying to hit on called herself Sarah. Before the night was over, I was all over her. I walked her to her car, kissed her—she almost choked me with her tongue, and we agreed to meet up at the same time next week. Her hands were all over me in the cool-spring air. She seemed to be enjoying herself. She acted as if she couldn't wait.

I couldn't wait myself until the next Friday night. We walked in the club and she and her friend were sitting at a table in the corner. I walked over and grabbed her by the hand and kissed her, as if I had missed her. She rammed her tongue down my throat and put her arms around my neck as if she would choke me. They both had on more revealing and sexy outfits. I couldn't keep my eyes above the level of her breast, she revealed so much.

"I missed you Sarah."

"Oh, really, you haven't known me long enough to miss me that much."

"I really did miss you a lot. I couldn't wait to see you once again."

We had several drinks, danced, and engaged in a long evening of conversation. I couldn't get over those long-sleek-creamy legs and breast. We never discussed our personal lives, whether we had children, a spouse, where we worked, or anything else of that nature. We only discussed remotely related things to our personal lives. We only talked about politics and the state of the economy. Who was going to or not going to get elected? What was the role of Black people in the economy, and the need for Black people to vote? These were the kinds of things we talked about, and she was quite well versed in politics and the nature of the economy.

At the end of the night she invited me up to her apartment, and I gladly accepted the invitation. This was seen as the final act of the play, and the reason why the game is played. Everything else is based on getting to this final point. We had several more drinks and lost total control. We were so eager for each other, and things happened so fast, that we ended up hopping in bed without much conversation. I spent most of the night but left while she was asleep in the middle of the night without saying good-bye. I had to get home to my family.

It was just like me to pick the wrong one. Marilyn was married, and Mickey took her to a motel. They spent the night, and he told his wife that he spent the night at the casino gambling. She never harassed him, even though it was several months later before he saw her again. It didn't bother her that she hadn't heard from Mickey in two months after the conquest. She didn't seem to have the same hang-ups as Sarah and was quiet and never talked very much. That's why you must be able to make the right choices in life.

I didn't see her for another two months. One night, Mickey and I were at the Black Widow and she and Marilyn walked in. They came over to the table where Mickey and I were sitting. She began to speak to me in such a loud manner that the whole club could hear what she was saying. Marilyn was relaxed and cool, even though Mickey had treated her the same way I had Sarah. Mickey was halfway embarrassed; he worried about his image. He was not used to people responding to him this way in public.

"Did you get what you wanted," she asked, "I guess I won't be seeing you anymore."

"What do you mean?"

"You left in the middle of the night without saying good-bye, and I hadn't heard from you since. It's been two months."

I deliberately stayed away from the Black Widow for a while, hoping I wouldn't run into Sarah.

"I've been busy, baby. My job and family life are demanding."

"You didn't tell me you had family."

"You didn't ask."

"You told me everything else."

"Sure, I did baby."

I didn't really understand the scene today. With some women it was understood that when the conquest occurred the relationship was over. It was just considered all in fun. By the same token when some animals mate, it is on to the next one. I didn't expect that she would expect a long-term relationship to come about as a result of the sex act. We were just two animals mating in the wild, and perhaps we would never see each other again. We didn't make each other any guarantees.

"Does that mean our relationship is over?"

"We never had a relationship."

"What did we have?"

She wasn't outdone because I left that night without saying good-bye, or that I didn't contact her in two months, but it was the idea that I could have such an encounter and not care for her. Sarah was captivated with the idea of love; she wasn't in love. She didn't like the fact that I was playing a game and could be cavalier about it. In that way I had underestimated her. I thought she was as much involved in the game as I was, but she was much more serious.

"Don't be facetious. You knew what our situation was all about."

"I thought you cared for me. Why would you take me to bed if you didn't care for me?"

"You're smart enough to know the game."

At least I had the idea that she understood the game.

I was really naive. I was going by the code of the streets. Be a player and don't let anyone play you. Don't get to close to anyone. I had made a mistake in underestimating the nature of the present-day culture. I thought it was all free love.

"I will get you," she slapped me and walked out the club. Security wanted to know if there was a problem. I told them no.

When I got home on the following Monday evening, my wife wanted to know, who was Sarah?

"Do you know someone named Sarah? She called and said you guys were dating and that you had promised to divorce me and marry her."

"Don't worry about it she's just someone I met at a club."

"You better be careful out there in those streets; you know how people are. You're a psychologist for God-sake."

"I'll be careful baby."

"I mean it."

Sarah searched my car and found a copy of my phone bill and called every number, telling them I was having an affair, was an adulterer—a liar and a cheat. She called my mother and father and told them I promised to marry her. She wrote her name in spray paint on my front door. I had reason to believe she kept constant surveillance on my house.

I drove a 1980 Infiniti J 30. Several days later I got up for work and found that the back and front window had been busted, and the car had been badly keyed. I called the police and told them what happened, but I had no proof. No one had actually witnessed her doing it.

She called my job and asked them how it looked for one of their premier-family counselors to be having open-illicit affairs? My supervisor called me in and talked to me about it and suggested that I get my life in order.

I was fortunate that we have regular patrols by the police in our neighborhood. Someone reported a suspicious woman in the neighborhood on June 15 at one o'clock. The police immediately came and caught her in the act of breaking out my family room window. I assumed she didn't have a job if she could spend her time doing criminal damage to property. I found out later the only job she had maintained was in the underground-illegal economy. She was only masquerading as a classy young lady.

She already had a warrant out for her arrest, and under suspicion for having set fire to another man's house. They convicted her for setting the fire and for criminal damage to my house. She ended up spending two years in jail. As a psychologist I should have picked up that this woman had some severe psychiatric problems. But she acted so normal. I never saw her again. I figured out that it was her good looks and not her behavior that led me to assume she was on the normal side. The reason why she could act so normal was that she bordered on being a psychopath.

My grandparents were from Tyler, Texas. They died and left me a hundred acres and a farm house in Tyler. I moved to Texas the next year to take over the land and take a better paying job with a family service agency in the town where my grandparents had lived. The director of the agency was another graduate from Michigan State University.

I had learned my lesson. After that situation, I made a practice to apply my psychology training to life and the people I met in everyday life. I considered myself lucky.

31

THE PERFECT SILK STOCKINGS

I was born and raised in Hallsville, Texas, a farm boy who never had enough of anything. The one exception was that we had plenty of food, since we grew our own food. I wasn't prepared for college but always wanted to go. Classmates laughed at me when I told them I was going to college. It was my conclusion that my elementary, junior high, and high school had provided me with an inadequate education. Basic English, history, mathematics, science, and even socialization was missing out of my experience: and I wasn't the only one lacking in basic training. Since I wasn't prepared for the big times, I decided to start small, and attend Wiley College in Marshall, Texas.

Hallsville is 10 miles north of Marshall, 40 miles north of Shreveport, and 10 miles south of Longview. Hallsville is also 125 miles south of Dallas, and 300 miles northeast of Houston. I frequently visited all of these places. I lived in a remote area of Hallsville, about midway between Hallsville and Marshall. We lived on a dirt road that ran west off a long-winding, curvaceous, hill-ridden, two-lane highway. Prior to getting the highway constructed in the first grade there was nothing but a trail to our house. The trail led for three miles off the highway. The trail could only be negotiated with a horse or wagon. There were tree limbs, mud, dew and other obstacles along this trail.

We didn't have running water or telephone by the time I was a senior in high school. I would have stayed home and commuted to Wiley if we only had a place to take a shower. My parents' style of life was somewhat primitive. Any choice of colleges would involve staying on campus.

My parents weren't interested in education for their children, and never tried to encourage me toward an education. My parents seem to think that education for a Black man was a waste of time, primarily because in their day, even if a Black man had an education it would be difficult to find a comparable job. Neither my mother nor father had much of a chance to get an education. They thought it was best to just get a job and not waste time. My parents were sixty-five-years old when I graduated from high school. I decided on my own that an education was much better than ignorance. I remember having a brief conversation with my father about furthering my education.

"Dad, I think I want to go to college," I said, looking away across the field.

"How're you going to pay for it?" he fiddled in his pockets and looked directly at me.

"I'll get a loan," acting a little unsure of myself.

"Go ahead, if you think you can pay for it," letting me know, I was almost grown, and it was my decision.

"That's what I want to do," having already made my decision.

"Your mom and I are getting old. Maybe you should just get a job," still trying to show me the pros and cons.

I knew better than to attempt a discussion of college with my mother, because she had no idea what a good education would mean to an individual.

I can only speculate. I have no idea what my parents' ideas were about getting an education. All I know is what I was able to observe in their behavior.

I considered getting a job and helping my parents out for a long time, but then considered that I needed to be concerned about my own quality of life. It was possible for me to get stuck out on the farm, and I wanted to prevent that if at all possible. My brother also suggested that I get a job at a factory. He suggested that I wasn't prepared for college. He wanted me to move to Houston and get a job at a plant or factory, but I had other plans.

I graduated in 1980 and decided to go ahead with my plans. Many of my relatives, friends, and significant others attended my high school graduation. They all brought gifts and wished me well. The college was close to Hallsville, and I figured I could stay on campus and keep my car. I could have stayed at home and went to Wiley, but my parents didn't even have adequate facilities; because they had no running water, telephone, or natural gas. We lived in an isolated rural area. My brother-in-law was an auto-mechanic, and I figure he could keep my car running. He had always done just that. I didn't have a steady girlfriend in high school and had no fear of losing any one special close to me. I didn't have anyone to leave behind. I dated in high school but had maintained no inseparable relationships. I didn't want to leave Hallsville and go to a strange city because I doubted my own level of maturity: I wasn't sure I could handle it.

A few years earlier, my brother had given me a 1959 Chevrolet Impala, Coupe. It was still in good condition. It was black with moon hubcaps, white racing stripes down the side, and black and white with red interior encased in bubble plastic. It was in good working order. If I handled it right the car would meet my transportation needs. I couldn't conceive of going to some strange place and trying to make a go of it. I preferred to stay where I had things in some kind of order. If I went out of town to school, I would have a lot of travel expense for holidays and vacations.

It was 1982. I had spent two years on the campus while living in the dormitory. I had done well in school my first two years, and my car was still running well. I visited my folks frequently and stayed in touch with my sister and brother-in-law in Marshall, as well as the rest of my family. My brother-in-law was indispensable in keeping my car running. In fact, he kept it in perfect running order.

I was happy on the campus. My major was pre-pharmacy. I pledged Alpha Phi Alpha and had a good social life. I would frequently go to the casino in Shreveport to gamble, trying to make some money to help pay my school bills, sometimes I was lucky and sometimes I wasn't. The casino was partially responsible for helping me to get through school. Frequently on weekends I traveled to Dallas or Houston to a show or a sports activity, occasionally to pick up a little action. In a squeeze I would simply go to Longview for a little recreation.

One fine day in January 1983, I was sitting in my Inorganic Chemistry class when a pretty girl caught my eye. It was unusual for someone that beautiful to be at that level in chemistry—but there she was. Girls didn't frequently major in chemistry during this time. She walked in and sat down next to me. There were about fifteen students in the class. At first, I didn't want to look at her, in fact I was trying hard not to look, but out of the corner of my eye, I could see the top of her stockings just below the hem of her skirt. It was very cute and attractive, as well as inviting, and I couldn't help but stare. I got turned on right there in class. She wore flesh colored stockings almost the color of her legs. The top of her stockings had several two-inch concentric rings. Her legs and thighs were smooth and perfectly formed.

Her legs were about the same size, passed her knees, all the way up her thigh. Her knees were not knobby but uniform.

The instructor asked a difficult question, just to see what level we were on, and she was the only one to raise her hand. She answered it in a very intelligent way. The instructor said that was correct. The instructor seemed impressed with her. She was beautiful and smart.

I couldn't wait to get a chance to ask her out. The chance came later on that week when I saw her walking across campus. I hadn't seen her prior to that day in class. I thought about her all week. In fact, I was thinking about her immediately before I ran into her on the sidewalk. I walked up to her very boldly as I was passing her on the sidewalk.

"How're you doing?" I asked, obviously, pleased to see her.

"Good, how're you," she smiled in a most friendly manner.

"You're in my Inorganic Chemistry class," thinking about those adorable legs.

"Yeah, I remember seeing you," she said, trying not to seem overjoyed.

"What's your major?

"My major is chemistry. What about you?"

"Mine is pre-pharmacy."

"That's a good major," she said.

"Where're you from?"

"I'm from Memphis, Tennessee. Where're you from?"

"I'm from a small town near here called Hallsville."

"I hadn't seen you around campus," she said, "have you been attending here long?"

"This is my third year on the campus," I said in a proud manner.

"This is my third year as well," she also seemed proud.

"I wonder why I hadn't seen you before, especially with both of us taking chemistry classes. At least I should've seen you in the chemistry club."

It was also unusual to not run into her on such a small campus at one time or another. Most of the students loved basketball and football and attended every game. I should have seen her at one of these venues.

"We can do something about that," she said in a bold way.

"By the way, what's your name?"

"Sharon, what's yours?"

"James is my name."

"It's good to know you."

I had dated a number of girls on the campus but nothing serious, and none that I liked as much as I liked her. I had always been slow to get attached to girls—especially.

"Why don't we start doing something about it by having a coke at the Student Center this evening?" anxious to start a relationship with her.

"That sounds good. I'll meet you there at eight o'clock," she seemed pleased to be getting together with me.

"I forgot to ask if you lived on campus."

"Yes, I live in Washington Hall—room 320."

We met at the Student Center, had a Coke, and from then on were an item. We were as thick as thieves. You never saw her without seeing me. Two months later our relationship was in full bloom. One evening we had a conversation about the casino.

"Have you been to the casino in Shreveport?" she asked, as if she was interested in going.

"Yes, I have."

"Most of the students say it's fun and exciting and the slots are loose."

"I won a few hundred dollars on my last trip."

"Would you take me on Friday night?"

We went to the casino, and both won over $2,000.00. It was more than enough to get some needed repairs on my car and pay my tuition for my senior year. I decided to suggest getting a room for the night. We had a good relationship up to that point.

"Let's get a room, baby. We can stay longer at the casino and leave in the morning," obviously with an ulterior motive.

"I guess that would be OK," seemingly unaware of my intentions.

"Are you ready to take our relationship to the next level?" but she was completely aware of my intentions.

"I think so," seemingly unsure, but definite about what I wanted to accomplish.

We walked into the casino hotel and registered as Mr. and Mrs. Johnson. After we got to the room she fell in my arms. We kissed for about ten minutes before looking at our surroundings. She had never kissed me that passionately before. I looked at her and noticed those smooth legs, and the concentric rings on the top of her stockings that came almost even with the hem of her black skirt. I was instantly turned on.

We engaged in foreplay for another ten minutes, and we were standing there just looking at each other. We both began to undress.

I said, "Don't take off your stockings."

"Why don't you want me to take off my stockings?" she asked.

"When I make love to you, I want to be able to see your legs in those stockings. I have a stocking fetish."

"You're weird!" she said.

But she pulled off her skirt and blouse, and removed her panties, leaving nothing but her stockings and their support. I was so turned on that I had sex for at least eight separate times. The last time was as good as the first. This time she slapped me as hard as she could with both hands and clawed me in my back many times. During one act of coitus she almost bit my tongue. We had sex like it was going out of style, and it was our last time to have sex in quite a while. She woke up in the middle of the night and asked if she was dreaming. We both left there completely satisfied. The next evening, I saw her in the Student Center. She was grinning from ear to ear.

We had many more trips to the casino. It became our major form of recreation. Sometimes we won and sometimes we lost, but we continued to go. We kept that up until we both graduated in May of 1984.

Sharon and I both graduated Magna Cum Laude. Both our families were there to wish us well. I had a scholarship to study Pharmacy at Xavier University in New Orleans. And Sharon had a scholarship to do graduate work in chemistry at the University of Illinois, Urbana campus.

We didn't make each other any promises, but said if things went well, we could consider getting married at the end of our studies. We wrote to each other and visited over the holidays—while we were in school.

We visited each other on many occasions. Sometimes I would visit her, and sometimes she would visit me. In March 1986 I visited her, and she got pregnant. We decided to get married after we graduated in May. We had the wedding in Memphis, she and her mother wanted it that way. Many of my relatives came to my graduation, my parents were ill. Again, many of my relatives came to the wedding. I felt as though I had married the girl of my dreams and was set for life.

32

UPSCALE STALKER IN
SILK STOCKINGS

I grew up in a project in Roxbury, an inner-city area of Boston, Massachusetts. I got tired of never having enough of anything. I had spent most of my time as a youth reading in the library or my room. I made every attempt to stay away from drugs and gangs. I had a 3.8 grade point average in high school and made 33 on the ACT. I then decided to go on to Boston University. I never liked math or the more-hard sciences and decided to major in social work. I made it through undergraduate school and continued on to graduate school. I left with an MSW in social work.

I had always heard that Chicago was the place to be. So, I sent out several resumes, eventually landing a job with the Department of Children and Family Services. I married my childhood sweetheart and headed for Chicago. My wife and I were young and restless. All we had in terms of material things were the clothes on our backs and a few other clothes. So, we packed our trunk, said good-bye to everyone, and got on the road.

It was 1988. I owned a 1987 Malibu Chevrolet. My wife had graduated from a local nursing school. Both of us wanted to get out of Boston. We both thought that Chicago would be a much better place to live. However, my only visit to Chicago was when I interviewed for the job.

The trusty Malibu made it to Chicago with only minimal problems: the usual problems of gas, oil and water. We didn't know anyone in Chicago, so we got a hotel room while looking for an apartment. We stayed at the Holiday Inn in the South Suburb of Matteson for about a week, and soon found an apartment. We were able to find a furnished apartment at a reasonable price and took it without hesitation.

My wife was able to get a job at a local hospital and drove to work every day. Part of my job required me to drive around the city and make contact with people in their homes. So, I bought a 1988 Cavalier. I needed dependable transportation, and it never gave me any mechanical problems. I worked for about two years providing services to neglected and abused children before meeting Susan.

Part of my job had to do with going to court with parents when their cases were being adjudicated. This was the most threatening part of the job. You never knew when a judge would have a bad day and give you a Contempt of Court charge. It was enjoyable though in making contact with all the young female attorneys.

This is how I met a young attorney that I never will forget.

I was sitting in my car waiting for the time for my case to come before the judge. Suddenly, I saw the most beautiful-classic creature. She had on a navy-blue dress with white polka dots. Her coiffure was immaculate. Her long-smooth legs looked gorgeous in those silk stockings. She was shaped exquisitely. On top of all that she had a Barbie-doll face. Immediately, I got out of my car and came over to meet her, as she walked toward the court building,

"Hello there, how're you doing?" I asked, being sure my clothes were fitting properly, after sitting in my car waiting.

"Fine, how're you doing?" she replied, looking directly at my eyes.

I figured she was an attorney. Only an attorney carried herself in such a manner as she.

"What time is your court case today?" I asked, without even verifying if she was actually an attorney.

"I'm late for work. I should have been here at nine o'clock this morning. I have a number of court cases today," as she hurried her step

"What's your name?" trying to keep up with her hurried steps.

"Susan," she said, with confidence.

"I hope to see you around the court," not knowing if I was overstepping my bounds.

"I'm here everyday, I'm sure I'll see you again," she smiled and seemed very friendly, as well as inviting, as she headed in the direction of one of the court rooms.

I wondered around like a love-sick calf that was lost from its mother for two weeks. Finally, I had a case where she was the attorney.

"Has Mrs. Patterson made reasonable efforts toward getting her children back? Has she attended parenting classes? Has she fixed up her home? Has her attitude changed?" the judge asked.

"Yes," I spoke up with confidence and enthusiasm.

I shared information with the court to demonstrate that such efforts had been made.

"We'll give her six months. If she continues to progress, we'll consider at that time if she should have her children back," said the judge, as he hit his gavel on the desk.

I always felt that the court was a little too abrupt and matter-of-fact in adjudicating their cases, but the nature of the situation called for the judge to be cold and a little punitive.

I waited for Susan outside the courtroom until she walked out.

"How're you doing today? I've missed seeing you," I said, obviously glad to see her.

"I was hoping to see you around also," she was without knowing it feeding my ego.

She had on a silk-white blouse with a black skirt that came slightly above her knee. Some white silk stockings. Her pointed breast acted as if they had a life of their own. Again, her hair was immaculate. I was beginning to get in too deep with this girl. I knew I shouldn't but wanted to take her out and get closer to her.

"I'd like to take you out sometimes, if I'm not being too presumptuous," I said, still not clear of what direction she wanted to go.

"No, that's OK. We can go out and do something sometimes," confirming to me that I was on safe grounds.

I felt I was breaking through the ice.

"Where do you live?" I asked.

"Homewood."

"I live in Matteson."

"We're close to each other. It shouldn't be too hard to get together."

I never asked her if she was married, and she never asked me if I was married. At the time it didn't seem to matter. We were just two people trying to get together. She had such a pretty face, and such an adorable body. I wanted to be with her.

"When do you have some free time in your schedule?" after being sure I was on the right track.

"I'm free tonight," seeming a little over anxious.

You can always tell a person who doesn't have much of a social life. When you push them for some of their time they'll say, how about tonight, after bothering to take out a little black book and carefully reviewing their schedule.

"Good, meet me at the Holiday Inn at eight. I'll meet you in the lounge," confident that she wanted the same thing as I did.

"I'll be there at eight," she seemed enthused.

"Bye, see you tonight," happy to feel that I was getting closer to her.

"Bye-bye," she said, she smiled and winked at me as we parted.

I couldn't wait until tonight. It was Friday about one o'clock. I kept thinking about her pointed breast, her pretty face, and the perfect curves on her buttocks.

I walked into the longue at the Holliday Inn in Matteson at eight. She was sitting at the bar with a drink in her hand. My father always told me that if you tell a female to meet you, chances are she's going to get there before you. I felt that Susan's behavior was a partial verification of his theory.

"Hi, baby." I said, overjoyed to see her.

"How's it going," she replied while smiling.

"I'm glad you could make it," while trying to get the bartender's attention.

"Same here," crossing her legs, showing me part of what I was about to take pleasure in.

"Where're you from?"

"Southern California. What about you?"

"Boston," I said proudly.

"What made you be interested in me?" she seemed to wonder about my sincerity toward her.

"You're a very pretty girl. I would think a lot of men would be interested in you," trying to make her feel good about our relationship.

"Not as many as you think."

"Why did you decide to go out with me?" I was questioning her motives.

"I like your straight forwardness and your self-confidence. I felt you were finally someone I could really like?"

"I'm glad you like me because I like you," putting all my cards on the table.

"I'm glad you decided to have a drink in a place where we could get a room before the night was over," letting me know what she had in mind for the night.

I was glad to here her talk that way, but I had no expectations of being able to get a room. We talked for several hours and she finally wanted to get down to business. I didn't think a classy lady would want to hop in the sack so soon.

"Are you ready to get a room yet?" she asked, griping my hand tight.

"Sure, we can do that," not as confident as usual.

"Well what are we waiting for?" she leaped off the barstool and kissed me on the cheek.

We got the room key and headed up to room 202.

In the hallway she was kissing and touching me all over. She was acting as if she was desperate and couldn't wait. I couldn't believe such a lady would be so deprived. Finally, we got to the room. I managed to stop kissing her long enough to get the door opened.

"Let me freshen up. I'll be back in a minute. Get comfortable," she seemed to be in a hurry.

I got undressed and got in bed. It didn't take her long to come out of the bathroom. She stripped down to her birthday suit. After coming out of the bathroom, she got in bed with me, immediately getting on top of me. We had sex time after time until it was late in the morning.

"I have to get home, baby. I can't stay all night," I said, looking away from her as if to suggest guilt.

"Yes, I know you have a wife. I checked up on you. I also know where she works and where you live," she avoided eye contact as if she didn't feel comfortable with the situation.

I thought no more about it. We got dressed and said good-bye.

It became a regular thing for us to have drinks on Friday nights, and get a room. We didn't do much else in terms of activities. One of these Friday nights she confronted me.

"I think I love you, Jeff. What can we do about this situation?" looking serious.

"You know I'm Married. I've known my wife since first grade, and I owe her something, even though I care a great deal for you as well," tears almost coming to my eyes.

I came home the following Monday evening and my wife had gotten a call from Susan.

"Who is Susan?" obviously, aware that something was going on between us.

"An attorney I work with," practically acknowledging my wrongdoings

"She called here today, and said you want to marry her, if I will give you a divorce," a sad look on her face.

"Don't pay her any mind, baby," not wanting to admit my weakness.

"How deep are you two involved," sure that something was going on between us.

"We met and had a few drinks, but nothing else," still trying to somehow deny the relationship.

"You had better get her under control," seemingly very upset.

I called Susan and told her to meet me for what I considered to be the last time.

"Why did you call my wife, you are messing with my life."

"I thought you loved me," she was livid, and threw her arms around me.

"Don't call my wife any more. As a matter of fact, it is over between us," I pushed her away.

"You don't want to do that. I'm an attorney I can make life difficult for you," speaking as an authority.

"Why would you be that vindictive?" acting in unbelief.

"I won't see you again, and don't call me or my wife any more," I turned away from her.

I walked out the door hoping she would get the message.

She called me and asked me to meet her just one more time at our old meeting place, the Holiday Inn. She said she had some information that I should be aware of. We met and she wanted to get a room. After we got to the room she begged for a little sex for old-time sake. I felt sorry for her. She seemed to have some sort of addiction with sex. We had sex and were sitting around talking. The police knocked on the door and said that they had been informed that someone was selling drugs from that room. They searched and later apologized and left. I assumed that this was another scheme on the part of Susan to carry out her vendetta against me. I didn't want to dignify the situation by asking her if she was responsible. We left the hotel, and it was a few weeks before I heard anything from her. She never did give me any information like she promised.

I had a first-floor apartment. About two weeks later she either broke or had someone break my back window and wrote SUSAN on the door to my apartment. Someone also put sugar in the tank of my Cavalier. On many occasions she would call and hang up without saying anything. Late at night someone would knock on the door to my apartment, but when I came to the door they would be gone. She seemed to have a deep love-hate thing going on.

I called her and told her this had to stop, and that I still cared for her, but we couldn't continue in this way. She said she loved me and admitted that she had been stalking me. That her mother had given her some good advice, she had renewed her relationship with the Catholic church, she had met someone new who had advised her that such activities was a useless pursuit, and that she was an attorney who had too much to lose. She apologized and said she would never bother me again.

After all she did, I still longed for that girl, but decided to give it up as well. I frequently saw her in court, walking around with that perfect body, and in those silk stockings. I still wanted her, but she was too much girl for me. Several months later we became the best of friends, and would occasionally have a drink at the Holiday Inn, but we never got a room again. We used each other as sounding boards only.

33

SUPPORTING A VILLAGE

There were ten children in our family, and we were poor as church mice. The only saving grace was that we raised our own food; otherwise, we would have been hungry much of the time. We all grew up cultivating our little-dirt farm. Most of the older children soon left the farm. They got tired of the trials and tribulations and navigating that three-mile trail that came to our front door. My mother and father were the products of farm families, and their parents were the product of farm families, as most of the parents in the village and their parents were. At an earlier time in the village most had survived on subsistence farming. The difference between my parents and the other parents were that most of the other parents wanted no parts of the farm life, while my mother and father had been conditioned to farming, and it was all they felt comfortable with. They were still trying to carry out their farming legacy. I think the old saying goes, *why buy a milk cow when you can get the milk for free.*

We lived in the rural area of a small town called Hallsville on a dirt road in East Texas. The dirt road was three-miles long, and ran west off a long-winding, curvaceous, hill-ridden, two–lane, blacktopped highway. It was not uncommon to have mostly dirt roads going to the homes of Blacks in the South during the 1960s— particularly in some areas. The blacktopped highway ran north and south in the direction of Marshall to the south—approximately 45,000, ten miles away, and Hallsville to the north, approximately 1,500, twenty miles away. Longview was 20 miles to the north, a city of approximately 100,000; Dallas was 125 miles to the north, a city of approximately 1,000,000; and Houston was 300 miles to the south, slightly larger but approximately 1,000,000; Shreveport to the south, a city of approximately 200,000, was 30 miles away.

Prior to my entering the first grade we only had a three-mile trail that led to the blacktopped highway. We had to fight the tree limbs, the creeks, the mud, the dew, just to get to the blacktopped highway. The trail was narrow and not wide enough for a car. Trees hugged the trail, and there were deep ditches along the way. After a rain you never knew what you might find along the trail in proximity to the creek. When it rained the creeks in the area would overflow. All the families contributed to the maintenance on this trail. We got no help from the county. I remember helping to cut weeds and remove fallen limbs from the trail before the road was built, before I was seven years old. The trail ended at our front door, except for the fact that there was a lesser used trail that continued past our house to eventually connect with another dirt road that went north and south. The dirt road connected with a road that led to Hallsville proper.

Before the road was constructed there were of course no cars, only wagons and horses for transportation. We were a self-contained community who took care of its own needs. We didn't have to go outside the community to take care of our needs. There were people who cared for animals, people fixed fences, built houses, built barns, birth babies, gave advice, etc. Individuals mostly took care of their own needs, but when they couldn't they found readily available sources of help. It was most effective to be self-reliant. Most of the people had come from a farming background. It was my idea that most people didn't like farming and was trying to move to another level. The small subsistence farming life has always been known for the necessary amount of back-breaking labor.

Inventions became diffused at a slow rate, especially in my family. We got electricity when I entered the first grade—soon after the road was built; butane when I was a freshman in high school; a telephone after I was in college; and a pump put in the well sometimes later, which allowed for running water. My mother was especially resistant to trying anything new; a mule and a plow were the only consistent things in her life. Most modern inventions took place after she was born, but she paid no attention to them. She knew the kind of life she wanted to lead and was set in her ways.

We owned a small-dirt farm where we grew: watermelons, peas, corn, cantaloupes, cushaws, sweet potatoes, Irish potatoes, okra, tomatoes, peanuts, a vegetable garden; at an earlier period, we even grew some cotton. We raised pigs, chickens, ducks, guinea fowls, and cattle. We also had peaches, pears, and apples in the orchard. Plumbs, buries, grapes, pecans, and walnuts grew in the forest nearby.

The dirt road came through the heart of the village. Most of our fields were situated along both sides of the dirt road for about a mile and a half as you approached our house. This was our land, and there was nothing but vacant fields on it. We lived at the very end of that three-mile dirt road. During the growing season someone could easily go into our fields and pick whatever they wanted without us knowing it. I never gave any thought to the idea that people in the community were helping themselves to what we grew as they chose, until one hot summer day, as I was looking out for crows in the watermelon patch.

People in the village had their choice of whatever we grew or raised on our little farm. All they had to do was allow a chicken, duck, or stray pig to wander into the woods near our house. The forest was so thick that it could hide a multitude of sins. We had ducks who roamed freely between our house and the stream flowing through our property—about a mile away, and people were aware of this. We all know that ducks love water, and this stream was the closest source of water. They had become semi-wild but used our homestead as a home base. In extreme situations they could raid our chicken coupe or barnyard at night. Once we got in the bed there was no getting up to check on a noise. We were too afraid of what might lurk in the dark. We weren't about to confront a vicious fox or wolf who might be searching for a meal. People could also pick whatever they wanted from our fields. We were growing food for the entire village.

As I approached the field, I saw a group of boys in our field eating watermelons. They hid as I approached, but finally came out from hiding. I guess they figured I was no threat to what they were trying to accomplish. I knew what they were doing. After that I began to figure they did this as a matter of routine.

"What're you guys doing in our watermelon patch?" I asked.

"We're just looking around," Louis said.

Louis was the oldest of the group and I suppose the spokesman for them.

"You picked a strange place to just look around. Couldn't you look around someplace else?"

"Can you prove we were doing anything other than just looking around?"

"No, I can't, but if I had an X-Ray machine, I could probably see the watermelon in your stomach."

At fifteen I never considered whether this was realistic or not.

"You're dreaming. No X-Ray machine is going to show watermelon in your stomach."

"If it was possible, I bet that's what it would show."

"You don't really mind if we have a few watermelons, do you?"

I didn't mind if they had a few but didn't think it was right for them to go onto other people property and take what belongs to them without asking.

"That's not for me to say. My folks would have to say what they think about it. I don't mind myself."

"Letting us get a few melons is just being neighborly."

He was trying to positively condition my attitude toward his mischievous behavior, but I wasn't going for it.

"If that's what you want to call it."

"Sure, it is. See you around. Don't tell anyone we were in your watermelon patch."

"Ok."

"If you dream about telling anyone, you better wake up and apologize."

It seems he was moving toward threatening me. I didn't want to give them the idea that I might tell their folks. If I did, they might figure out some way to try and persuade me not to tell. I noticed one of them was carrying a .22 caliber rifle, and I wanted to seem like anything but a threat.

When I got home, I talked to my mother.

"I caught those Allen boys in our watermelon patch. They were filling their guts from our hard work." I said.

"I figured they might be doing that from time to time," she said.

"What can we do about it?"

"We could tell their parents, but their parents probably encouraged them to get some and bring some home."

Besides, it was generally accepted, everybody in the community raided our fields.

"It must be something we can do."

"As long as we can't watch the field 24 hours a day, there is not much we can do."

"I'll watch out for them when I can."

"You do that."

None of the people in the community raised a chicken or grew a garden to put food in their own bellies. They acted like farming was a lowly occupation that was beneath them. This was unusual for people who lived in a rural area. My mother wasn't concerned about them raiding our fields or our barnyard; she was mainly concerned with keeping me busy and carrying on a farming tradition. She had her own limited philosophy and approach to doing things that came from her background.

I would frequently see cars come up the road to our house at night, during growing season, turn around in front of our house, head back down the road, stop along the road where our fields were located, and turn their lights out. I should have known then what they were doing. Neither my mother or father ever became concerned about the possibility of such pilfering going on, but they should have known what was going on.

No wonder few people in the community bought farm produce from us, or for that matter raised anything of their own. They were getting all they wanted for free—mostly at night. They waited on us to put the blood, sweat, and tears into it, and all they had to do were pick what they wanted. In this way we were raising food for the whole village.

Occasionally a pig would come up missing, chickens would come up missing, and a cow would get lost. As I look back on it, I can see what was happening to these animals. People in the community were simply taking what they wanted, without having to put work into it.

When my brother, John, came home from the Gulf Coast I was eleven, he started teaching me how to drive a car. Before the road was built, we only had a wagon and a horse for transportation. It's the only thing that would navigate that trail. Soon he left and went back to the Gulf Coast after several years. He left a 1951 Fleetline Chevrolet sitting in a dilapidated shed next to the house.

I could get in it and go where I wanted. In this way I refined my driving skills.

A few years later, John, sold the car to my oldest brother. He then bought me a more functional 1959 Impala Chevrolet, Coupe. It was black with white racing stripes down the side, red and white seat covers with bubble plastic to keep the seat covers clean, moon hubcaps and dummy-fog lights. By this time, I already had my driver's license.

About this time my father retired from working in an oil refinery on the Gulf Coast. My father had worked for twenty years on the Gulf Coast. He only came home twice a month and spent his summer vacations fixing up on the farm. He wanted to pedal our farm produce to people in nearby towns, so he bought a pickup truck for this purpose. It was a green 1958 Chevrolet pickup. So, we went from having no transportation in our earlier years to having two sources. Even then I wanted to sell our produce to stores; I figured you could make up for loses in retail by selling in volume. At the very least I figured we could place a roadside stand on a main artery. This would probably increase profits and save ware and tare on the truck.

There were no buses, taxis, or trains; and we lived 20 miles from a decent size city in either direction. People in the community would hire me out as a taxi to transport them to the city. My folks were a little backward when it came to such matters. They would hire me out to drive twenty miles for a two- dollar fee. I'm sure if they hired anyone else to transport them, they paid more than this. I virtually ran my car into the ground on these dirt roads for two dollars a trip. That was just enough to pay for gas; it was not enough to keep a car repaired. I think they knew they were taking advantage of me and didn't care one way or the other.

I ended up ruining my car on those dirt roads, and when it was time for college my car was in disrepair. If I had taken better care of it, I would have had transportation for college.

We were the big joke of the community, but taken somewhat seriously, because they knew we were helping to support and provide for the village.

I tolerated the farming life for as long as I could, and then decided to attend college. My background was somewhat deficient, but I made it. After moving to Chicago, I entered law school in September of 1972, and graduated in May of 1976. I moved to Boston, Massachusetts and became a Public Defender. I had come a long way, and soon my humble beginnings were only a faded memory. My connections with the farming life are only a few insignificant dreams from time to time. Sometimes I think about my background and wonder how I got over.

34

THE WOMANIZER

I was born and raised in Harvey, Illinois. My parents owned a medium-sized-brick bungalow in a modest area of the city. We had lived there all of our lives. My father worked for the railroad, my mother was a schoolteacher, and they were more than happy with their jobs. I have every reason to believe my parents were happy living in Harvey. I grew up in a psychologically and socially healthy household, my parents were good people. I had one brother, and we got along well. At least I felt our situation was healthy and happy.

In the eighth grade I first started liking girls but had no steady girlfriends. Sometimes I would engage in child's play with some of the neighborhood girls; they would come by when my parents weren't home. Frequently, we engaged in sex play. I attended the local public high school and did well. One of the most popular boys in school: I played football, ran track, and had a 3.4 grade point average. In addition, I was a member of the Student Council, the Drama Club, and the Chess Club. I had several girlfriends in high school, but again not a steady girlfriend—one was never enough. I had a girl in each of several suburban towns.

After graduating high school, I went to college. I supported myself by working at a steel mill while going to college during the day. I stayed at home and attended a local college. My parents couldn't afford to send both my brother and I away to school. What money they had went toward his education. I even had extra money to help my younger brother. He drew the long straw. I bought my own car and had any number of girlfriends. Occasionally, I would visit a prostitute just for the fun of it, even though I had a number of girlfriends. My friends encouraged me to visit these prostitutes; they all did it. In school I received a B.S. degree, then a Masters, degree. My degrees were in the humanities area. I continued to date a variety of women. School was a playboy's haven, and I was in contact with lots of cute young girls. Both the girls and the boys were open for play. I graduated from undergraduate school in four years even though I had a full-time job. I also worked at night while getting my graduate degree.

When I graduated, I went to work in the human services area. Women were drawn to me. There were a lot of lonely women working in the field, I had my choice, and I got my share. I was like candy to them. Many of them would proposition me before I did them. If I did get desperate, I could always seek out a prostitute. But there was usually no need for a prostitute, there was always an abundant supply of women hanging around nightclubs in the area, and further away in the city. One girl was never enough for me. I had to have any number of girls at any one time.

I met Ester at the Emporium nightclub in Harvey one night in November 1980. It was a cold-rainy night. She was attractive. Her breast hung out of her designer gown, and she had long-smooth, scissor-like legs. She also had a pretty face. This girl appeared to be a classy young lady. She pretended there was no where to sit and came over to my table. I found out later that she had it all planned.

"What's your name?" I asked, curious about her boldness.

"Ester," she said, smiling.

"Do you come here often?" I took a sip from my drink.

"This is my favorite nightclub. I'm here every Friday night," for the first time she made eye contact.

"That's good to know."

The night was about to end.

"Why don't we get a room?" she asked, she looked directly into my eyes.

She surprised me again with her boldness. The night ended with us going to a small motel in Harvey.

"OK."

I wasn't about to turn such a lady down. We used to always say, *don't kick any lady out of bed.*

Before sex she said, "It's not necessary to use a condom."

"Are you sure?"

After we had sex, she said, "I want to have your baby," she spoke in an aggressive way.

I didn't bother to ask her the whys and wherefores. I thought at first, she was on the pill, or just knew what she was doing.

"But you don't know me," seemingly outdone by her behavior.

"I know all I need to know," she seemed sure of herself.

I couldn't understand why she wanted to have my baby. Except, I was what some people would call handsome: curly hair, light skin, and six-feet tall. It was apparent why she didn't want me to use a condom. I didn't know what to say. My ego got the best of me: I was proud of myself. One year later I saw her, and she told me I had a son. I was befuddled. It wasn't until the child entered college that she sued me for child support. At the time I took Ester to the motel she was thirty-two years of age. She was apparently trying to beat her biological clock, and I was not aware of her intentions. It was convenient for her to use me for this purpose. After all those years, I did help her send the child to trade school and kept contact with him.

One warm night in May I came to the Emporium. I met a young lady named Sarah. Sarah had all the qualities I desired in a woman, she had everything. She was a financial officer at a local bank. I could have rushed her for the sex but decided to wait. I had learned that some things were better if you waited for them. She was sitting at the bar, and I came over to her.

"Can I buy you a drink?" I asked, obviously interested.

"Sure, that's fine," she said, pulling out a cigarette.

I had already found one negative. I didn't like women who smoked. Drinking I could put up with, but smoking was annoying. Later I was instrumental in getting her to quit smoking.

"Where're you from?" anxious to establish a relationship.

"Originally from Ohio, but I presently live in Homewood," she seemed anxious to share, "what about you."

"I was born and raised in Harvey. Never been more than 300 miles away in either direction," sounding a little dissatisfied with my own past itinerary.

"Do you come here often?" she asked.

"I come here every now and then," I said.

I kept thinking I had seen her before or was it just that she had a familiar face. She had a face that one might often want to see.

"Did you go to school in the area?" she asked.

"Yes, I went to Roosevelt University. What about you?" I asked.

"I went to Lewis University," she said.

I didn't try for the sex that night but got her phone number and began calling her on a regular basis. Soon

I was going by her place on a regular basis, and we established a good relationship that lasted for the rest of our lives.

I met a beautiful young lady, and we decided to get married. Sarah and I weren't doing so well at the time. Laura came from a fine local family. She didn't know that I wasn't satisfied with one woman. We thought we could make it together. So, we got married, bought a home, and soon had a child on the way. I continued my philandering ways. My wife probably knew I was seeing other women but never had much to say about it. She kept hoping that I would change. While married I would go to nightclubs and other places and pick up women, pick them up at work, or off the street. Where I got them from it didn't matter, I just had to have them. I wasn't satisfied unless I was chasing women. Something about my socialization process and my background that told me it was the thing to do.

I met a therapist who had done a lot of mental health counselling. He told me, after discussing my background with him, that I had an acute Oedipus complex. It was a case where men search for a woman to replace their mother. They search for a woman to replace their mother, but obviously would never find a woman to replace her. So, the search got more intense as they got older, going from woman to woman. It could sometimes be a never-ending search.

I went to a nightclub in Harvey called the Razorback on a warm-spring night in April. I had a seat at a table and ordered a drink. I was in the company of my therapist friend. A young lady caught my eye. Susan was sitting a few tables from me. I sent her a drink—she accepted, and I asked her to dance. We danced, and I asked her if I could join her at her table. She was a young attractive girl. She had on a mini-dress, that showed her smooth legs and thighs, had a pretty face, a small waist, and about a D-cup. We danced for most of the night, and she went home with her girlfriend. However, I did get her number.

She was attractive, and I liked her. In fact, I was smitten by her. She was exactly the type I liked: kind of classy and charming. I called her the next day to see if I could come by her place. I didn't ask if she had a boyfriend. After checking her schedule, she told me to come by that night, as if she couldn't wait.

I came by about eight o'clock on a hot night in May. We had a drink. She told me she had a boyfriend, but he was a doctor, and was usually to busy to come around. He simply paid the bills and took care of her. Susan was a nurse. She had met her doctor friend at the Razorback. As the night progressed, we convinced each other that it would be OK to have sex. We both were anxious to climb in the sack with each other. I didn't know her boyfriend had a key to the apartment. We were in the throws of making love when the bedroom door opened.

It was her boyfriend. For a doctor he had a lot of nerves, but he was paying for the apartment.

"What are you doing, bitch," he asked, with his hand in his pocket.

I thought for sure he had his hand on a gun. I grabbed for my pants and shirt attempting to put them on.

"Oh, baby I'm sorry." Susan said.

"You're a whore and a slut," the doctor said.

"Don't say that baby," pretending to be upset.

"You are absolutely no good and can't be trusted. You're not worth a plug nickel."

"It won't happen again."

She was going along with the game. It had happened before, and he continued to put up with it.

"Put on your clothes stud and get out of here. You've done all the damage you're going to do tonight"

Apparently, her boyfriend was an older man who enjoyed seeing her in compromising positions, and he liked being able to call her a whore and a slut. He got off on that. He continued to take care of her but wanted to be able to degrade her when he wanted. I put on my clothes and left. He didn't say anything else to me, didn't pull a gun, and didn't attempt to attack me.

Susan and I kept seeing each other. If her boyfriend did catch us, he would berate Susan: calling her a whore, a slut, and just no damn good. Every time he caught us together, he went through the same ritual. But he never said a cross word to me even though he caught me with her any number of times

My wife was getting wise to me and was beginning to have an affair of her own. I don't know when it started. Maybe it started long ago. She began to stay out late and hardly came home. She shifted the duties of taking care of our son to my niece.

I had begun to go to a party house in another state. A place where you could go and get all the sex you could handle. All you had to do was pay a small admission fee and obey the house rules. Men would come there with their wife or a girlfriend and switch partners. If you didn't have a partner you could simply have sex with the other guy's partner while he watched. I took Susan on several occasions. She seemed to like it. We didn't talk a great deal, just selected someone based on their appearance, and enjoyed a night of uninhibited sex with the one you had chosen.

My wife and I finally got a divorce. My wife's boyfriend had a wife. This woman somehow got my wife's telephone bill, called everyone on it, and told them my wife was having an affair with her husband. This was embarrassing to my wife and to me. We decided to get a divorce.

I kept going to the party house. It was more convenient than being married. After I lost my wife I went into a deep depression. My minister told me I should get therapy. I was involved in therapy for two years. Finally,

I decided what my friend told me several years ago was correct. I did indeed have an Oedipus complex.

Sarah and I maintained a good relationship all through my marriage. It finally came to me that I loved Sarah, and she was the best woman for me. She should have been my first choice of a wife. I decided to leave all the other women alone and marry Sarah. Since my second marriage I haven't seriously looked at another woman. I had learned a valuable lesson. If I had been wiser, I would have kept the first wife. I was glad I finally got counselling and thankful to my friend for helping me to recognize I needed counselling.

My counselor had motivated me to desire a greater understanding of psychology. So, I went back to school, at this late date, obtained a Psy.D. in Clinical Psychology and became a full-time counselor. I was able to give to others what had been given to me.

Sarah and I had three children: two boys and a girl. We were happy with our children, our jobs, and our bungalow in Homewood.

35

A BLESSING IN DISGUISE

I was born in a small-rural-farm town called Hallsville, Texas. I've heard some local radio announcers refer to the area as the ARK-LA-TEX; because of its proximity to Arkansas, Louisiana, and Texas. Tall pines and oaks abounded the area, and magnolias and azaleas grew plentifully in spring. There were also plenty of good hunting, catfish and bass fishing. The town of Hallsville itself only had a café, a Dairy Queen, several gas stations, a bank, several general stores, a drug store, and a post office. These were mostly all one-story, unpainted, wood buildings. There was only one red light in the town. The town was inundated with cattle farms and horse ranches.

We managed a small-dirt farm, and grew whatever the land would bare: corn, cotton, squash, cushaw, tomato, okra, sweet potato, Irish potato, and a vegetable garden. Most of the land would only grow the hardiest of weeds, but we continued to grow what we could, it had been used by my ancestors since slavery—and probably by others before that. We farmed a fifty-acre parcel of land. We also raised cows, hogs, horses, chickens, ducks, and guineas. Some of the land was for cultivating, and the rest was used for pasture. If you fertilized the land it could be more productive than ordinary.

I had inherited the management of the farm at eleven years of age from my last brother who moved to the Gulf Coast. I was the only one left at home to manage the farm. I had to plow, during growing season, from sunup to sunset. The only ones left at home were my mother, my sister, and I. My father was a janitor in an oil refinery on the Gulf Coast, three-hundred miles away, and came home every two weeks—as he had done since I was born. He spent his summer vacations working around the farm fixing fences, hog pens, buying supplies, and other things. He didn't seem to care much about the farm—that was strictly my mother's baby. My dad had another complete and separate life on the Gulf Coast and couldn't seem to wait to get back there. I can recall on several occasions him trying to get my mother to move to the Gulf Coast. She refused to move. I believe that he was only giving her lip service in asking her to move. He wasn't about to ruin his good thing on the coast. As long as she had a roof over her head, some ragged clothes to wear, and food to eat, she was satisfied. She didn't feel that she could make it in the city. All she ever knew was a rural, isolated, and farming way of life. My mother was short staffed but was still going to manage the farm—come hell or high water. The farm was her legacy.

At this point I was sixteen-years old. I was a sophomore at the local high school. My brother had given me a car for my birthday, so I did have transportation. He felt sorry for me being back in those woods without any form of transportation. Neither my father nor mother could drive. My sister didn't learn to drive until after she got married. They had built a graded-dirt road when I was six and had attempted to blacktop it. The blacktop had washed away because of lack of continuous application. It was usually dusty in summer and muddy in winter.

When the road was built, we got electricity, and not until ninth grade, did we get butane. We used no other source of energy. We still didn't have plumbing or a telephone. It wasn't until I was in college, did we get a telephone, and not until I had worked for many years, did we get any type of plumbing. My mother was old-fashioned and chose to live much as she had lived all her life. She had lived an isolated existence for most of her life. If civilization hadn't creped upon her suddenly, she would have gone without a road, without electricity, without butane, and without a telephone. She was just that set in her ways.

I had to plow, cut wood for the fireplace, cut weeds, fix fences, heard animals, serve as a taxi (some people didn't have a car, and they would enlist my services to take them where they wanted to go), and do whatever else my mother required. As I said, the management of the farm was mainly left to me. In spite of these chores

I went to school on most days. Neither my mother nor father cared much about me or the rest of their children getting an education. All they cared about was that the chores on the farm were done. I tried to be studious and intellectual, and wanted to spend my time reading, but my mother wasn't going to have it. Once she caught me reading before school and made me get up and plow before going to school each day—for several weeks. Anytime she caught me reading she would demand that I engage in some other worthwhile activity. I figured she thought as many others did, that there was no value in book knowledge for a Black man. My mother had been conditioned to this type of thought by her father, grandfather, and great-grandfather.

When she caught me reading, she asked, "What're you doing reading this morning? Did you do your chores?"

"Yes ma'am, I did."

"Are you lying to me?"

"No, I'm not."

"You don't need to be reading this time of the morning, do your chores."

I guess she figured if I had time to read, I had time to plow. I always felt that it was her way of getting me to drop out of school without directly telling me to do so. She didn't see an education as having any place in her children's futures. She intended to apply so much pressure that I would drop out on my own accord.

My mother had a habit of turning the cows loose in the fields and allowing them to graze in the hills all day, once harvesting was complete in the community. This was usually in the fall just after school had started. I guess she figured the cows could eat what was left of the crops in the fields. I suppose this habit went back to her father, grandfather, and great-grandfather. The same way many of her other habits were formed. I'm not sure she knew why she did it. She stated that her reason for doing it was that the grass had dried up, and there wasn't enough grass in the pasture to feed the cows. So, she turned them loose to find what they could in the hills and fields. I felt it was a complete waste of my time, and it was probably just a way to keep me busy. I felt I had better things to do with my time, like preparing for my future.

Once I asked her why she turned the cows loose in the hills during the fall season and had me look for them every-single day.

"Mama, why is it necessary to turn the cows loose, every day, and have me waste my evenings looking for them? They could be anywhere."

"Because the cows are hungry and need food in their bellies. There's not enough grass in the pasture for them to eat."

"Then why don't you buy them some hay and feed them?" I insisted.

"We can't afford hay."

"It's a waste of my time to be looking for them every day. Why don't you just let them stay out until they come home, and not have me looking for them every day?"

"I have to milk two of them every evening."

That was the end of our conversation, it was getting somewhat circular. The practice still didn't make sense to me. Other people did the same thing but allowed their cows to roam the hills for most of the winter.

The only problem was that sometimes the cows wouldn't come back and would keep going for many miles. When this happened, my mother would get alarmed, and stop everything to send me looking for them. She feared someone was going to pick them up. Folks had a reputation in the community for picking up stray cows. They would simply back up their truck, load the cattle on, and carry them to the auction. Some people did it for a living. Cattle rustling was still a felony in Texas.

There were a number of farmers that lived passed our house, beyond the hills. There was a trail that led beyond our house, to their farms, but no road. They grew a lot of corn, and the corn remaining made great food for the cows once the farmers had made their harvest. The cows didn't come home on this particular Thursday evening after school. My mother noticed because she would milk two of them every evening when they came home. She wanted me to go looking for them on Friday, but I convinced her that I needed to go to school on Friday. I told her I had a special examination, because I wanted to be in school every day I could possibly be. She told me I would have to look for them on the weekend.

After school on Friday she told me to immediately go looking for them. So, I got on my black mare and went looking for them. I saw many cow tracks in the neighbor's cornfield just beyond our house, but couldn't see hide or hair of the cows themselves. I looked until dark and came home. When I got home my mother was angry, she told me to look for them early Saturday morning, and not to come home until I found them. My mother could be rather harsh in her perspective and came from the old school. As I said, she only cared about the running of the farm.

Saturday morning, I went looking for them once again. I took her literally when she said don't come home without them. This time I took a backpack with a blanket, matches, some cheese, crackers, sandwiches, nuts, can of spam, several cupcakes, and some frozen bottles of water. I didn't know how long it would take. I was prepared to be gone a few days.

I was a good tracker. I tracked the cows to a field about six miles away from where I had searched on Friday evening. I was so tired I couldn't go any further. This time I didn't ride my horse. The horse was kind of nervous, and I didn't want to be bothered with its panicky behaviors. I made camp near one of the fields. I figured my mother wouldn't want to see me come back without the cows. That night it was about fifty degrees; I guess I was lucky for that time of the year. It was my first time being away from home in the open elements, and I was somewhat afraid. Wolves were howling at the moon all night long. I made a fire and gathered wood for the night, so I would have enough to last all night. I didn't know exactly how cold it would get. I had to get up and put wood on the fire all night long in order to keep warm. The night air chilled my bones. The blanket was barely enough cover, while lying on the cold-damp grass. I had learned how to make camp in the Boy Scouts.

A white farmer saw my camp early the next morning and must have wondered what I was doing on his property. He came over to where I was in his new 1962, blue, shiny pickup truck. I was at first scared he would cite me for trespassing on private property, which could possibly be a felony in Texas. He had an M-16 in the window of his truck. He had on blue jeans, a red-plaid shirt, cowboy boots, and a traditional western hat.

"What's going on young man?" he asked.

"I'm camped out for the night; I was tired of walking." I said.

"Where're you going?"

"I'm looking for some cows. They left on Thursday, and I tracked them to this field."

"I saw some strange cows up around the Noonday Road this morning. I bet they were the ones you're looking for. Was there a solid black cow, a red bull with long horns, and several red and white Herefords?

"Yes, those are the ones."

"How come you camped out rather than return home?"

"My mother told me not to come home until I brought the cows back with me."

He looked perplexed but didn't say anything.

"It hadn't been that long ago since I saw them. I'll help you find them. Get in my truck. I bet I know exactly where they are."

I gathered my things, got in the truck, and rode for about two miles. There was a cornfield next to the road that had been recently harvested. The cows will feast on a recently harvested field for the loose corn the equipment leaves. I immediately spotted the cows. They had come at least eight miles in three days. They must have been able to smell that corn. The smell of corn was like freshly-baked bread from a bakery on a city block.

White farmers in the area usually weren't so friendly, but he said he recently moved from Boston and bought his farm about a year ago.

The cows acted as if they had been bad children and jumped to my command. I was able to drive them all the way home without a great deal of trouble. They initially resisted but eventually gave up all fight and came on home. They acted as if they were lost and needed someone to show them the way home. I made it home at approximately six o'clock that evening. My mother wanted to know what took so long. I didn't bother to explain.

It turned out that the farmer's wife was a freelance writer for the *Shreveport Times* and several national publications. The farmer told his wife about me, and she bought my life story for $25,000.00. Her husband had wanted to know where I lived. The wife explained that she wanted to write a book and several articles about my life. She came by my place on many occasions to gather the details of my story. By the end of the year the book and articles were finished. My mother never knew the farmer's wife was writing the material, and I'm sure she never read it. The farmer's wife would take me on an outing to get the details of my story. She chose to not let my mother know what we were doing. My mother still couldn't see anything wrong with her behavior. I never told her about the money I received from the story. I bought myself a new car—through my brother, some new clothes, and was able to pay for four years of college a few years later. I saved what I had left especially for college. I was lucky. At the time I didn't quite know how I was going to pay for college. Though, I figured it was the only way for me to handle my education. This whole situation must have been some sort of divine intervention.

My mother finally decided to sell the animals and quit farming, after my father read the story, he advised her to finally give it up. My father convinced her that it was something about the situation that she wasn't clear on. She hated to give up the farm because it was all she knew. It's what her father, her grandfather, and great-grandfather had done; and she intended to pass it on to her children. But decided the thing to do was to give it up under the circumstances. From that point on my time was my own. I decided I would read and get prepared for college. I read everything I could get my hands on within the next two years. It was a little late, but not too late, since I knew I had definite plans for college.

I believe my mother was getting senile in her old age, while still trying to live in the past. My mother's ignorance was indeed "A Blessing in Disguise."

ABOUT THE AUTHOR

JAY THOMAS WILLIS is a graduate of the University of Houston, Houston, Texas, where he earned a Masters' degree in social work; he is also a graduate of the Masters' degree counselling program at Texas Southern University, Houston, Texas. He attended undergraduate school at Stephen F. Austin State University, Nacogdoches, Texas, where he earned a B.S. degree in sociology and social and rehabilitative services.

He worked as a Clinical Social Worker for seventeen years, providing direct clinical services as well as supervision. He has been a consultant to a nursing home and a boys' group home; taught college courses in sociology, family, and social work in community college and university settings; and has worked as a family therapist for several agencies in the Chicago area. In addition, he was a consultant to a number of home-health care agencies in the south suburbs and Chicago. Mr. Willis is a past CHAMPUS peer reviewer for the American Psychological Association and the American Psychiatric Association. He also spent a number of years in private practice as a Licensed Clinical Social Worker in the State of Illinois.

Mr. Willis has traveled and lectured extensively on the condition of the African American community.

He has written twenty-nine books, and written many journal articles on the subject of the African American community. He has written several magazine articles. He has also written Op-Ed Commentaries for the *Chicago Defender*, *Final Call*, *East Side Daily News* of Cleveland, and *Dallas Examiner*. He currently lives in Richton Park, Illinois with his wife and son.

Printed in the United States
By Bookmasters